RELIEF | A QUARTERLY CHRISTIAN EXPRESSION

VOLUME TWO | ISSUE ONE

RELIEF | A QUARTERLY CHRISTIAN EXPRESSION

EDITOR-IN-CHIEF
Kimberly Culbertson

ASSISTANT EDITOR
Heather von Doehren

FICTION EDITOR
Alan Ackmann

CREATIVE NONFICTION EDITOR
Lisa Ohlen Harris

POETRY EDITOR
Brad Fruhauff

TECHNICAL EDITOR
Coach Culbertson

EDITORIAL ASSISTANT
Margaret Krueger

COPY EDITOR
Margaret Krueger

ADVISORY BOARD
Mick Silva
J. Mark Bertrand

CNF CONSULTANT
Karen Miedrick Luo

Relief: A Quarterly Christian Expression is published quarterly by ccPublishing, NFP, a 501(c)3 organization dedicated to advancing Christian literary writing. Mail can be sent to 60 W. Terra Cotta, Suite B, Unit 156, Crystal Lake, IL 60014-3548. Submissions are not accepted by mail.

SUBSCRIPTIONS
Subscriptions are $48 per year and can be purchased directly from the publisher by visiting http://www.reliefjournal.com. Single issues are also available.

COPYRIGHT
All works Copyright 2008 by the individual author credited. Anything not credited is Copyright 2008 by ccPublishing, NFP. No part of this publication may be reproduced, stored in a retrieval system, or transmitted by any means without prior written permission of ccPublishing, NFP.

SUBMISSIONS
Submissions are open year round via our Online Submissison System. Please visit our website at **http://www.reliefjournal.com** for instructions. Sorry, but we are unable to read or return submissions received by mail.

THANK YOU

We thank the following people who, by subscribing before the first issue or by donating, have financially supported *Relief*.

WE OWE EXTRAORDINARY GRATITUDE TO OUR DONORS:

HEROES:
HEATHER ACKMANN
ROBERT AND LAURA BAKER
THE MASTER'S ARTIST @ HTTP://WWW.THEMASTERSARTIST.COM

FRIEND:
CHARMAINE MORRIS

AND TO THE REST OF OUR FOUNDERS, WHO HAVE HELPED US TO MAKE THIS JOURNAL A REALITY:

VASTHI ACOSTA
ADRIENNE ANDERSON
KARI L. BECKEN
JILL BERGKAMP
STEVE BOGNER
SUSAN BOYER
SUSAN H. BRITTON
SHAWN COHEN
JONATHAN D. COON
CHAD COX
JEANNE DAMOFF
DIANNA DENNIS
BEN DOLSON
STEVE ELLIOTT
CHRISTOPHER FISHER
DEEANNE GIST
DEBORAH GYAPONG
SYLVIA HARPER
APRIL HARRISON
MATTHEW HENRY
GINA HOLMES
LEANNA JOHNSON
JILL KANDEL
MICHAEL KEHOE
BILL AND PEGGIE KRUEGER
ALLISON LEAL
DAVID LONG
JEROMY MATKIN
ANDREW MEISENHEIMER
CHRISTOPHER MIKESELL
CHARMAINE MORRIS
MARGARET M. MOSELEY
SARAH NAVARRO
NANCY NORDENSON
KAREN T. NORRELL
RANDY PERKINS
SHANNA PHILIPSON
CALEB ROBERTS
SUZAN ROBERTSON
CHRISTINA ROBERTSON
LISA SAMSON
LANDON SANDY
AOTEAROA EDITORIAL SERVICES
MICHAEL SNYDER
CATHERINE STAHL
DOROTHEE SWANSON
AMBER TILSON
SHERRI TOBIAS
PHIL WADE
DAVID WEBB
CHRISTINA WEEKS
REBEKAH WILKINS-PEPITON
MARYANNE WILIMEK
MANKATO
AND THOSE WHO PREFER TO REMAIN ANONYMOUS

If you would also like to help keep the journal going, please visit our website, www.reliefjournal.com and click on Support The Cause.

TABLE OF CONTENTS

FROM THE EDITOR'S DESK KIMBERLY CULBERTSON	6
COACH'S CORNER COACH CULBERTSON	8

EDITOR'S CHOICE

BIOLOGY FICTION BY HELEN W. MALLON	10
DOOMS OF LOVE CREATIVE NONFICTION BY LINDA MACKILLOP	20
THERE AND HERE POETRY BY MARIO SUSKO	36

FICTION

ARBOR JOHN KEATS	44
THE DEATH OF NEW AURORA DAVID BOROFKA	64
DEBORAH MEG SEFTON	81
OCTOBER'S ORCHID JOYCE MAGNIN MOCCERO	87
THE INSTITUTE OF TRANSCENDENCE KIRSTEN EVE BEACHY	101
ELI BISON BECOMES AN ANGEL JEREMY BURGESS	147

CREATIVE NONFICTION

LOOK UP J. STEPHEN RHODES	96
THE LAST GOOD DAY JEFF E. BROOKS-HARRIS	113
THE SIGNIFICANCE OF PLACE ALLISON SMYTHE	124
LITTLE PROOFS ROSS KENNERLY	139

POETRY

THE OTHER SIDE MARIO SUSKO	38
WHAT I WANT TO SAY MARIO SUSKO	39
THE COLOR OF BLOOD MARIO SUSKO	42
SLUMMING WITH LAZARUS FREDERICK LORD	58
COMMUTING THROUGH THE RAPTURE FREDERICK LORD	59
SUBVERSIVE MARYANN CORBETT	60
MID EVIL MARYANN CORBETT	61
READING THE FIRE CODE MARYANN CORBETT	63
AGREEMENT JENN BLAIR	77
NOTE JENN BLAIR	78
CATHOLIC WORKER RICK MULLIN	79
MAN NAILED TO CROSS IN PHILIPPINES CHRIS FLOWERS	80
INTIMACY KATIE MANNING	85
SUMMER BURIAL HANNAH E. FRIES	86

IT ALL COMES DOWN TO LAUNDRY MICHAEL MARTIN	93
CARDINAL'S EVE SALLY ROSEN KINDRED	94
MISCARRIAGES BRIAN G. PHIPPS	99
WINTER SOLSTICE BRIAN G. PHIPPS	100
BEYOND MAUREEN DOYLE MCQUERRY	109
CONVERSATION MAUREEN DOYLE MCQUERRY	110
EROSION BARRY L. DUNLAP	112
FORGETTING GRACE MEREDITH STEWART	119
JOHN CHAPTER TWELVE KATHERINE NICOLE LEE	121
WHISPER NEW ORLEANS JUSTIN WHITMEL EARLEY	122
SOMETIMES IN SHANGHAI. JUSTIN WHITMEL EARLEY	123
PSALM 19 HANNAH FAITH NOTESS	133
A WRECK HANNAH FAITH NOTESS	134
THE DISASTER TOURIST HANNAH FAITH NOTESS	136
SINGLE-POINT PERSPECTIVE HANNAH FAITH NOTESS	138

COVER ART

"BE_ORIGINAL," A PAINTING BY JOSHUA BARKEY, GRACES OUR COVER IN SURREAL ELEGANCE. THE WORDS IN THE BACKGROUND, IN CASE YOU CAN'T READ THEM, ARE AS FOLLOWS: BE ORIGINAL—BUY OUR PRODUCT—EVERYBODY'S DOING IT—YOU ARE IN CONTROL.

SEE MORE OF JOSHUA'S WORK AT WWW.BARKINGREED.COM.

PLUS!

YOU'LL ENJOY "HINKY JINKS," A PREVIEW FROM THE SECOND VOLUME OF *COACH'S MIDNIGHT DINER*, THE GENRE ANTHOLOGY COMING IN OCTOBER 2008 FROM CCPUBLISHING.

FROM THE EDITOR'S DESK KIMBERLY CULBERTSON
EDITOR-IN-CHIEF

For about a month during sixth grade, I experienced a recurring nightmare. It began innocently enough—a dream about playing at a pool during a family vacation. I climbed from the pool and walked up a staircase that was increasingly dark and overgrown with moss. I glanced up to see—forgive my sixth grade mentality—a hooded figure that seemed part demon, part reaper. I realized I must be dreaming, but I was sure he was there to steal my soul. I tried to kick and cry out, but my body was paralyzed by sleep. I fought to move until I finally woke up screaming.

Every time I fell asleep the figure invaded my dreams. I began to keep myself busy at night with books and music, opting to sleep during the day instead. I remember sleeping on the floor of the living room in a window's square of sunlight—I felt intrinsically that the light would help. Eventually, though, the figure arrived anytime I slept, day or night. I told no one because nightmares seemed so childish. So after about a month of trying to run, I stared down the figure and told him—I'm sure this will sound clichéd—that Jesus already owned my soul so he couldn't have it anyway. And I woke up, safe. I've sometimes wondered if that was the real day I "got saved."

After that night, I found the rosary I had received for my first communion and draped it over my bed. As long as the rosary was hanging from the bedpost, the figure didn't make it into my dreams. Later my brother stole the rosary to mess with me, not knowing what the "big deal" was, so I drew a cross on paper and placed it in my pillowcase, where it stayed until I went to college. Whether the dream resulted from an intellectual fear or from a real spiritual attack, the cross became a symbol of protection and safety for me in a very personal way. As I grew up spiritually, I realized that the paper drawing didn't matter so much as what it pointed to, what it meant to me—that I was beginning to look to Christ for my protection.

FROM THE EDITOR'S DESK

In the Old Testament, God often asked his followers to build altars marking the intersection between man and God. These structures were symbols that celebrated His miracles, marked that He had appeared to them, and commemorated promises He made. Bill Hybels, Senior Pastor for Willow Creek Community Church in South Barrington, Illinois, has taught that these altars were requested by God, but that they were not *for* God. The altars were necessary for the Jewish people to remember those interactions with Him each time they passed the monuments, to remember how they were blessed, awed, or graced by His presence. God designed our reasoning; He asked us to build altars partly because He knows the pyschology of symbolism.

Our second volume of *Relief* begins with a fantastic issue filled with bits and pieces of symbolism and imagery, some religious and some not, some cultural and some personal. This issue is rich with imagery that points to something more, for the characters and for the reader. The cross, of course, is a symbol with meaning beyond my own adolescent experience. Authors in this issue ponder the sign of the cross, a cross on wheels, and a staged crucifixion. We'll also consider the religious imagery of breath, angels, the rapture, and a hand that's already been cut off. Some of the images in this issue are not well known Christian symbols, but a great story can turn a very commonplace image into something spiritually and emotionally significant. In this issue flashlights, a smeared painting of an orchid, laundry, a sketched portrait of a face, and landscape—be it beach, city, country, or college campus—all take on deeper meaning, becoming altars of characters' interactions with the divine. Some of the symbols in this issue, however, point toward something less divine, a betrayal or a turning away. Clothing labels, a stainless steel kitchen, an accident, and a karaoke funeral offer heartbreaking glimpses of destruction.

In each issue, we have chosen to showcase a piece from each genre by honoring the author with the "Editor's Choice Award." In this issue, we offer our congratulations to Helen W. Mallon for her story "Biology," Linda Anne MacKillop for her essay "Dooms of Love," and Mario Susko for his poem "There and Here." Each of these pieces is rich in imagery and symbolism.

Here at *Relief*, this first issue of Volume Two is an altar of sorts, a monument to the ways that God has blessed us, to a new year standing on a stronger foundation. When we began this adventure, we hoped we'd make it to a second year. Today we're looking toward an exciting horizon, thankful for what we've learned, for the people God has provided that make this project possible, and for being allowed to participate in God's vision for this journal. Enjoy these works, and as you read them, may you find symbols of God's provision and intersection in your own life.

interviews, readings, workshops, lectures, panels, signings, plays, discussions, exhibits, conversations

3 days

Elizabeth **Berg**
Michael **Chabon**
Gail **Godwin**
Mary **Gordon**
Edward P. **Jones**
Mary **Karr**
Yann **Martel**
Kathleen **Norris**
Katherine **Paterson**
Luci **Shaw**
Krista **Tippett**
Franz **Wright**
and many others

festival of faith & writing

April 17-19, 2008

www.calvin.edu/festival

CALVIN
College

RELIEF | A QUARTERLY CHRISTIAN EXPRESSION
CONGRATULATES THE WINNERS OF ITS
EDITOR'S CHOICE AWARDS

<u>FICTION</u>
HELEN W. MALLON
BIOLOGY

<u>CREATIVE NONFICTION</u>
LINDA ANNE MACKILLOP
DOOMS OF LOVE

<u>POETRY</u>
MARIO SUSKO
THERE AND HERE

BIOLOGY HELEN W. MALLON

My older brother Charlie was a holy fool. He was also a plastic surgeon. He would have said that everything that happened had to do with enlightenment, but I say it's about stupidity. Choose your poison. Charlie did. His almost-ex-wife, or rather, his widow, Angela, tells me she knows in her heart that Charlie meant well. Okay, then, so did our Mom and Dad, but that didn't stop Charlie from making that ludicrous accusation, which he never recanted until the day he died.

This is about something that could be seen and felt. To me, it seems fitting that in the end, I was the only one who actually touched the thing, that is, without the added protection of surgical gloves. All of us had a different reaction to it. I'm not sure what Charlie's pastor would have thought. He's a little hard to place, one of those hip, overeducated guys with earrings and a misleading vocabulary that makes him sound like a street musician. I do know that Charlie told him nothing about the Hand. I wonder why?

Charlie's life was one sweeping epiphany after another. In high school, he showed me a book on past life regression he'd smuggled into the house. He had the chutzpah to bring the book in, zipped under his jacket, while he nodded respectfully to the circle of ladies gathered in our living room for Wednesday night Bible study. I came to learn when Charlie was in a trance state because of the silence that emanated like a gas from the slot beneath his closed door while I was dutifully playing Yahtzee with our parents. Mom and Dad, respectively a homemaker and a professor of history at a small evangelical college, left him alone. Maybe they thought he was masturbating during those sessions. At least that's what I thought, and I envied him for striking out on his own, so to speak, in the middle of a long Saturday afternoon. But I also loved the quiet surface of our daily household. Charlie told me he had discovered a few of the people he used to be. I don't know how he managed to keep track of them all. He claimed that centuries before he was burnt at the stake for propagating the Word of God, he had been the original Doubting Thomas—the apostle who claimed after the resurrection that he would only believe if he inserted his finger into the wound on the Savior's side. I had enough trouble with the mathematical ambiguities of the Christian Trinity, with its legalistic Father, forgiving Son, and bodiless Spirit, to consider extrapolating myself across myriad lifetimes. I listened when my parents told me I had the gifting to be an accountant, but I clung to my furtive independence. I declared my atheism to the darkened ceiling in my bedroom as I lay momentarily sated, nights on end, with the afterglow of unclad, imaginary women still ripe in my head.

During Charlie's college days, spent as far away from home as he could get and still benefit from state-funded tuition, my brother dove into journal keeping and repressed memory retrieval. He was guided by a graduate student "therapist" who told him that his deep-seated belief that he was called to be average was a sign of childhood trauma—right up until his death, our parents acted pretty stiff around Charlie despite his "forgiveness." His idealism gave way to the sex appeal of the Almighty Dollar and his future estranged wife, Angela, when he went to medical school, but he still took fortune cookies a little too seriously.

LAST APRIL, CHARLIE CALLED ME up from his hospital, a mile or two across town from my office. I'd already put him off several times because of the tax crunch, so I took the call. "Eric. I've had the most amazing experience." His voice was pitched high with excitement. "This week I had to amputate a hand. Off a middle-aged guy, a lawn-care specialist. He was brought to the ER after a run-in with a piece of equipment, and reattachment wasn't indicated. You should have seen the Hand lying there in a tray. It was beautiful."

"*Okay*," I ventured. Long ago, I had honed the art of listening to my brother without actually supporting his enthusiasms.

"He had major circulatory problems," Charlie explained. "But at least the guy says he'll quit smoking." My brother had never cut off anything that intricate before, and he said he might never get a chance to do it again. "Here's the thing," he added, "the patient wanted to give the hand to *me*. I asked, you mean to *science*? He insisted, no: he'd seen a TV special on the black market trade in organs and cadavers, and he didn't trust the system. He said I should use it for my personal research. I told him I don't do research. I tried to explain that you can't hand over your own hand to just *anybody*."

"What'd he say to that?" I ignored Line Two, which was flashing on my phone as if possessed by the spirit of tax panic.

"He didn't believe me. He thought I was being bureaucratic. The guy insisted that since I was involved in saving his life, I'd surely find a use for his hand. What could I do, Eric? I was taking his livelihood away from him. I couldn't bludgeon him with the truth."

"What *did* you do?"

"I got a resident to wash out a big mayonnaise jar, then had her fill it with formaldehyde."

"And?"

"I brought it home."

"*Home?* Does Angie know?"

"The jar's inside the box of Christmas lights in the garage. It's only July. You think I should tell her?"

"*Yes*, you should tell her. What if she just—found it one day?"

Charlie blew out a long breath. "You're right. But Eric. You've got to see this thing," he told me. "It's . . . ethereal. Almost plaintive. The fingers touch at the tips, like a benediction. The calluses sort of tell the man's life story."

"*Maybe*," I said firmly. "Show Angie first."

It turned out, he told me later, Charlie brought the jar into the living room and set it on the Nakashima shelf, a piece of carved wooden artistry for which he'd paid a cool four thousand. Angela stared at the Hand for two minutes without blinking, then asked him to move it out of sight. He pulled a couple of hardback books from the built-in shelves on either side of the fireplace and put the jar behind them. That weekend, their two young boys got the babysitter to climb up to fetch a thick edition of *The Tales of Hans Christian Andersen*. With the volume in hand, she pulled the jar nose-close out of curiosity. She screamed and dropped the book, narrowly missing the andirons as she fell. Charlie and his wife had to rush home from the symphony, and after he ascertained that the sitter was not seriously injured, my brother paid the woman double and drove her home. Before he returned, Angela wrapped the unopened jar in the Sunday Styles section of the New York Times, tied the bundle up in a plastic shopping bag and dropped it in the trashcan in the garage for pickup on Monday. All she told him was, "It's gone."

Angela is a tentative Catholic. When they got married, Charlie wasn't anything, even though we were raised Presbyterian. The *right* kind of Presbyterian, according to our parents; catapulted straight from the heart of the Reformation, salvation by faith alone apart from works, *Soli Deo Gloria*. If we admitted to veneration, John Calvin would be our family's patron saint.

The Sunday after the babysitter incident I happened to be in Charlie's garage, trying to ascertain whether *his* safety goggles might happen to be safer than the ones I'd just bought for lawn mowing season. He was in the middle of cleaning up blown-in leaves and hectoring me about intelligent risk-taking being what distinguishes us from lower life forms, such as our parents, when he spotted the bundle inside the Rubbermaid Brute.

"Angela!" he yelled, three times. He held up the jar as she came into the garage. I caught a glimpse of a yellow palm and I sat down fast—on the tire of Charlie's Vespa, as it turned out later when I examined my pants. I stared at my shoelaces. The end of each lace was precisely the same length.

"I'm trying to inch my way back to the church, and you're not helping," Angela said. "Remember Sister Bellance?"

"Eric doesn't want to hear about Sister Bellance," Charlie insisted.

"Maybe not, but you need to know that that damn thing reminds me of her, Charlie!" Angela stood beside me. I got up to be polite, even though I felt woozy in the presence of the Hand. I stared at the laces on Angie's sneakers. They were crooked and not very clean. "Sister Bellance was my fourth grade teacher and she was a harpy." Angela grabbed my arm. It was a not unpleasant sensation. "Sister cracked a blackboard with the head of a student," she said. Poor Jimmy Molino froze up in front of the class, unable to spell the word "penitence" on the blackboard, so Sister Bellance had shoved him into yesterday. "The woman gave me nightmares, but not because of Jimmy. It was her pilgrimage to Rome."

Charlie interrupted, holding the jar like an external heart against his chest. "She told the kiddies how every Pope from Sixtus V to Leo XIII had been eviscerated at death. Their livers, spleens and pancreata are even today venerated as relics inside the Palazzo Del Quirinale." Charlie enacted a protestant's crude parody of genuflection, catching the jar at knee-level when he dropped it. I leapt into the sunny driveway. "Ha! Then she rubbed it in," Charlie added. He set the jar on a shelf of canned goods. He held his hands as if he were massaging a protuberant stomach after a good feed, and assumed a throaty contralto. "Bowels, class. Guts," he said. "Remember, your body is a temple."

Angela's laugh was a strained octave higher than her usual hoarse-casual one. "Don't forget *this* dream. *Charles.*" She gave his shoulder a punch. "I was in a long line of people in this fancy palace. Ahead of us rows of livers lay on golden shelves like flat Jello-molds. Like they were breathing. If one slithered off, you had to genuflect, then pick it up. You had to hold it until some authority came and took it from you. You couldn't escape. Sister was there, watching."

"Sweetie, that's awful," Charlie said sympathetically. "It's a good thing we don't *both* suffer from religious baggage." He started to give her an extremely empathetic kiss, and as I discreetly turned away to leave, with the goggle question undecided, I thought I heard a slap.

A MONTH OR SO LATER, CHARLIE CALLED AGAIN. "I have a problem."

"Yeah?" I retorted.

It seems he had secreted the Hand in the cabinet underneath his nightstand, then locked the door. "I told Angela she was safe," he insisted. "But she pressed me to tell her where it was. She claimed she'd already sensed it in there. Like a baleful curse." He paused. "I promised to get rid of it."

"After how many weeks of celibacy?" I asked.

"Three," he admitted.

"And did you . . . ?"

Charlie sighed. "I didn't know she was planning to donate my old sweaters to the July fete for the hospital. They looked perfectly good to me. I thought they were in that plastic box until next fall. I was *going* to hide the Hand in a permanent location, once I found some crevice Angie never looks in. Can I stay with you and Margarite for a while?"

"I'll check," I said.

My wife cleared her Tai Kwan Do mats out of our basement and I took out additional accident coverage on our homeowner's. Charlie and the lawn-care specialist's hand stayed for a couple of weeks until he rented a condo in the city with a month-to-month while Angie worked on finding a marriage counselor.

Around this time, Charlie began going to church. He hadn't set foot in a house of worship in decades. Liberti Church meets in the cafeteria of a struggling private school in an up-and-coming neighborhood near several big museums. "You'd like the service," he told us when he took me and Margarite out to dinner. "It's not the same old thing. The whole aesthetic is different. The music is really great, kind of a sacred garage band."

"You're afflicted with mid-life adolescence," I told him. "What does the cafeteria look like?"

Charlie considered. "It looks like a slaughterhouse," he said

"No, thanks," I said. Margarite just smiled, poking at her salmon.

ONE SUNDAY CHARLIE PHONED ME to say he had discovered spiritual renewal. "I finally understand what Mom and Dad were talking about with all the Jesus stuff," he said. "Christianity is about one beggar telling another where to find food."

"Does this mean you've realized our parents didn't molest you?" I asked. This had always irked me. They may have been terminally boring, but did Charlie have to create a dark underbelly?

"Uh-unh," Charlie answered. "God forgives them just the way I do. Will you come to church with me next week?"

"Nope," I told him. "No way."

"Then come see me in the afternoon. I'm lonely."

"I bet you are," I retorted.

The next Sunday after lunch Margarite went outside to practice breaking slabs of wood with her feet, but she stopped kicking to give me a kiss.

"Be careful," she said, which is usually my line. I wasn't sure if she was referring to the traffic on the Expressway or to my older brother, but I didn't ask for clarification.

Charlie's Center City condo was so empty, I was aware of the dolorous beating of a fly against the large living room window from across the room. My brother greeted me with a shaved head. He looked like Ben Kingsley or a Tibetan monk. "It was either take the radical approach or start a combover in five years," he said. "Life is all about inner freedom. I'm divesting myself. I must be the only plastic surgeon in the country who doesn't have a leather sofa." Charlie didn't have any sofa at all, or even a TV. We sat on loose-jointed Ikea chairs and between us on a small white table sat the mayonnaise jar with the Hand in it.

I couldn't *not* stare. Fingers pointing up, tips slightly touching, it floated in its zero gravity. "Would you mind moving that?" I asked. "It makes me uncomfortable."

"You don't think it's beautiful?" Charlie's eyes at that moment reminded me of fried eggs.

I was all of a sudden suspicious. "What are they teaching you at these religious services?" I demanded.

"'If your hand offends you, cut it off!'" he cackled, quoting the Sermon on the Mount.

I wasn't laughing. "I mean it," I said. "The *church* sounds a little off."

"Who are you to talk about *off*?" Charlie shot back. "You're an atheist."

"I may be totally empty of anything resembling faith, but I know whacko when I see it."

"They're not whacko." Charlie leaned forward, dead serious.

I looked at the Hand. Its palm faced me like an alabaster moon, with a slightly dark Sea of Tranquility in the center. "I'm not convinced," I said.

"There's only one way to find out," Charlie told me.

"What do you *get* from that thing, anyway?" I suddenly wanted to shove his shiny, bald, head off his shoulders. "If you didn't cart it around with you everywhere, Angela wouldn't have kicked you out."

Charlie sagged. "You're right. But it seemed cruel to say no to the guy. He was determined to make something positive out of tragedy. After I took the Hand home, it began speaking to me."

I darted a quick look at Charlie's front door, which was locked, and considered the blurry line between religion and derangement. "Not literally," he hastened. "I studied it. You can still see the fingerprints. No one in the history of mankind has had exactly those fingerprints. See?" He held the jar up to my face. The Hand bobbed majestically in response to Charlie's motion.

It looked dead, slightly yellow. It seemed to be made of something other than flesh, not vegetable or clay, not plastic. It was luminous and angelic, marred by a few reddish shadows or blotches on the skin. My lunch went queasy on me. I couldn't discern any fingerprints. A scattering of fine black hair covered the back, and the nails needed a trim.

He put the jar down. The Hand rotated a slow half-turn on its wrist stump, as if it were sending a signal. "The longer I looked at it, the quieter I got inside. It made me want to pay attention. Then it hit me—the Hand was a gift from the universe. It represents something."

"What?"

"Beats me. But it led me to church."

"By the hand? You mean you carry it around with you? On the street?" I tried to prepare mentally for Charlie's Miranda-rights phone call from a police station.

"No, no! I *think* about it. And one Sunday I was wandering along after several days of tummy tucks and butt lifts, worried about how the lawn-care guy was adjusting to life without his hand, and I heard this cool music wafting over an iron fence. It sounded like someone shredding at Woodstock."

"And?"

"And I went in. The pastor started talking about how God beckons us in love, never forcing the issue. He quoted Sartre . . . 'The man who wants to be loved does not desire the enslavement of the beloved . . . if the beloved is transformed into an automaton, the lover finds himself alone.'"

I looked around Charlie's new condo. I couldn't see Angela anywhere. "*You're* alone," I pointed out.

Charlie smiled at the Hand. "Not quite," he said.

I WENT TO CHURCH WITH MY BROTHER the next Sunday to make sure he wasn't being brainwashed. The musicians were neo-freaks, all young and scruffy, and I suppose the music was good, but if I believed in God, I'd prefer a well-clipped choir. Charlie introduced me to the pastor, whom I took at first to be one of those rehabilitated drug addicts.

"Dude," he said, and shook hands lefty. The really strange thing was the way the guy grabbed my right hand, as if he reached across some sort of divide, coming at me from the wrong direction. I thought he was going to bring *my* hand to his lips and kiss it. He must have seen my bafflement, because he pushed up the sleeve of his Astro Boy jersey and showed me his nicely engineered, lightly tanned, fake right hand.

"I shake with the fake when I don't have to be the spiritual honcho," he told me. "Sometimes I get a charge out of scaring people."

I stared at Charlie, who was grinning as if he'd tricked me into meeting the actual Jesus in the flesh. He shook his head. "Nope," he murmured. "I haven't said a thing."

The pastor gave Charlie a puzzled squint, then turned to me. "I used to be a biker," he explained. *Oh, great*, I thought. *Here it comes. The pitch.*

"Yeah, right," I said. "Then you found Jesus and got cut off from your former ways."

"Not exactly," he said. "Then I got hit by a moving van on the expressway. Just one of those things."

"Ah," I said. For someone who has staked his life's work on mythology, he was refreshingly casual.

Later, over cheese steaks, Charlie asked me if I'd come back to church with him. I said I'd think about it. I said it to humor him, mostly.

* * *

WOULD I HAVE DONE IT EVENTUALLY? I'd like to say yes, but in the eight months that have passed since that conversation, I only got back there once, for Charlie's funeral. After the accident, tangible help was what mattered. I did the only thing I could think of. I reassured a tranquilized Angela that I'd do the clean-out of his apartment.

At Charlie's service they really should have gone acoustic, for the sake of dignity. In his collection of offhand remarks that turned out to have been the eulogy, the pastor said that Charlie "died well." If it hadn't been for Angela huddled next to Margarite and clutching her hand, I'd have stood and shouted down that sanctimonious double-talk. You can't have it both ways. I say it was an asinine death.

At the reception afterwards, Angie came up to me with an arm around each of her boys. "Eric," she asked, "Don't you think that all things work out for the best?" She drew them closer. The younger one narrowed his eyes as if challenging me to be fool enough to agree with her. "Don't you think that's true?" Any answer I gave would have choked me. I gave her a pat on the shoulder and a kiss on the forehead. The thing is, none of this should have happened. At the very least, Charlie shouldn't have struck out on his own, roaming the city at all hours to find the homeless, to give them blankets and absorb their tales of woe.

Not that I tried to stop him. At the time, I considered his behavior an improvement over the obsession with the Hand. Around the time that Margarite refused to help me confiscate the damn thing, Charlie's pastor asked him to help out at the church. His religion took a healthier turn after he went in for good works; although, when I mentioned the Hand, I had a feeling, from his sly and deferential shrug, that he had kept it around. Still, he and Angela were planning to reconcile when the bus ran over him near City Hall. He had a backpack full of gloves to give out on that frigid night, and the bag lady who tried to revive Charlie was a prophet: He was a good man, but sweet Jesus, no common sense. You don't wear black to roam the streets at night, not when you're on and off the sidewalk looking for people asleep on steam vents. That bus driver didn't even know the bump under his wheels was human until it was too late.

The clean-out job was more complicated than I'd thought, considering Charlie's Francis-of-Assisi policy of not owning anything, and it didn't help that I was seeing double, still drained from grief and shock.

The place was sparsely furnished—not even a fire extinguisher, for god's sake—but the closets were jammed with flotsam that he'd trash-picked for the church's thrift store, the profits of which benefit a re-entry program for homeless people.

I spent a couple of hours in the apartment, sorting things into sticky heaps for the thrift shop folks. All I thought about was doing a good job, wanting to help Angela out, wanting to make a clean sweep of Charlie's religious zeal. I scoured the place, even moving the refrigerator in case something had fallen back there. When I found a single, lonely sock under his slab of a bed, I sniffed it and held it to my face, taking in Charlie's homely foot-smell before I put it in my pocket. It's criminal what some people throw away, not to mention the germs the stuff contained. I found unwashed, working blenders, TV sets, shoes slightly worn at the heels, microfiber bags with a latte stain or two. Since it was getting dark, I turned on the overheard light. For a few minutes, I stood in the middle of all those raunchy, harshly lit piles. Taken as the sum total of my brother's life, they were a depressing sight.

"Great," I fumed. I'd missed the cabinet over the refrigerator. I carried over a plastic chair, eager to load everything into trash bags. One layer of my mind already knew, I suppose, and yet all I thought was, *I'm ready for a shower and a brew, at least Angie won't have to see any of this crap.* I had to tug the door open. The jar with the Hand was front and center, and there was nothing else in the cabinet. The leg of the plastic chair made a *tic tic tic* sound on the floor, and I realized I was trembling. *I can't leave it*, I thought, *they'd come after Angie with questions.* I took the jar down, and the fool thing was heavier than I expected. I set it on the kitchen counter. Were the fingers more splayed than before?

"God," I snarled, and looked at my watch. "Damn. It." The maintenance guy was coming for Charlie's apartment key in seventeen minutes. A precise, airless feeling of anger like metal bands tightened around my chest, and I lifted the jar and give it a small thump on the Corian. "Oh, shit." I smelled the leak before I could see the crack, which was a hairline fracture circling just above the base of that cheap jar, exuding the formaldehyde smell of laboratories and arrested death, and already seeping onto the countertop. I threw on my raincoat, and, leaving the door of the apartment open, I ran down the silent, carpeted hallway to the elevator with the jar cradled like a foundling child against my belly. Wet trickled under my shirt cuff. It being Saturday afternoon, the elevator was not empty. Two well-dressed young women stared at me, two talkative women with shiny hair who went silent as soon as I stepped in and who drew together at the rear of the elevator, their mouths implacable as minus signs. I stared at each green, lit-up number as we descended all twelve floors at the pace of glacial melt. One of the women gave a nervous laugh. There was an obscene-looking streak down one of my pant legs. I kept my arms crossed under the jar. The smell. The smell.

"Ladies." At the lobby, I nodded to the young women as they jumped out; I was almost ready to thank some higher power that the jar had thus far remained intact. I hit B for basement and commenced to respirate again.

The elevator stopped. Past the laundry room, there was an exit door to the trash area. It was chilly out there. The concrete alley held a blue Dumpster and another for recycling, lit by harsh floodlights, against a cinderblock wall. The jar was one-third empty now, and the wet had left a streak on the concrete. The Hand listed slightly, the tips of the fingers touching the glass, as if feeling for my warmth outside the jar.

I opened the dumpster. *Investigators*, I thought. *Angela*. I closed the lid and set down the jar. For a long moment, I stood under the floodlights with that unnatural thing at my feet. I had locked myself out of the building. A siren wailed nearby. Charlie was gone, but the Hand wasn't. Not yet. I had to give biology a shot against that ghastly formaldehyde. The recycling container was almost overflowing. Never before in my life had I opened a trash receptacle to take something *out*. The greasy tuna fish can was sharp to the touch. Kneeling in the grit, I worked on a broken corner of the concrete pavement, finally a prying up a section roughly the size of a legal notepad. I dug, holding my breath, as if not inhaling might protect me from the dust I'd churned up. It was city dirt, packed with hairy clumps and snarled strands from a broken trash bag. I arched my head away to breathe, but the acrid dirt smell mingled with the chemical odor. If rats laid eggs like turtles, I'd have found rat eggs under that slab. I did find a small cut on my thumb. I held my right hand away, waving air over the germs. I prayed that no one would show up with a bag of trash until the burial was complete.

When the hole was ready, I couldn't turn the lid. It was fused shut, and the crack in the glass hadn't expanded, so the bottom wasn't going to shear off. It was just as well. With the trembling in my arms I might have sliced myself if the Hand got stuck. I put the jar in the hole, but it protruded. I half stood, suddenly dizzy, and smashed the jar on the pavement. I heard my own primitive, strangled cry of reaction, which startled me so much I almost yelled again. Shook glass shards off my shoes. The Hand glimmered pale on the concrete, the color of the moon, wet fingers bent no more and no less than they were before the impact. Despite my haste, I knelt down. It had to be cleaner than the dirt I'd been in. It was even chillier than I expected, the flesh hard, not pliable on the bone. As I turned it palm down over the hole, almost biting through my lip, there was the gristle of the wrist stump.

DOOMS OF LOVE LINDA MACKILLOP

my father moved through dooms of love
through sames of am through haves of give,
singing each morning out of each night
my father moved through depths of height
   —ee cummings

THE MILE AFTER MILE OF DULL FARMLAND lulls even me, the driver, into a dreamy state. As the oak trees on the edge of the highway speed past, I remember how Dad once loved my mother. How sometimes warm with vodka, lights turned low, they danced to classical music in the living room. How one day they began to hate and fight like drunk cats and dogs over lost jobs and unpaid bills until finally they divorced. Once they had been married for eighteen years. Now they have been divorced for longer.

My father moved away from us when I began college and he never made it home again. The last time I saw him, he pulled out of my driveway in his car with all of his worldly possessions stashed on the seats and floorboards, embarrassing me because he looked so much like the homeless man that he had become. My tall, handsome father vanished, and in his place lived a scruffy stranger with an unruly gray beard, jeans—Dad *never* wore jeans—and a sagging sweater. Among his belongings and suitcases, his ever-present boxes of "files" and "papers" sat ordered as if tomorrow life would begin again. The last time I saw him was in his car.

DOOMS OF LOVE

A MEMORY. WHEN I WAS THIRTEEN and spending the night with my best friend, Lindsay, she had a nightmare about her own father. She bolted upright, tearing off my side of the orange flowered quilt we shared in her double bed. Several months earlier, her dad had committed suicide. Against the backdrop of wrens singing and seagulls soaring over Duxbury Bay, within feet of his private salt marsh and lush woods, he walked into the garage of their Cape Cod style home, turned on his car engine, closed the door, and ended his life.

In her dream someone was knocking on her kitchen door. When she answered it her father was there, dressed in his favorite tennis outfit, but suddenly he disappeared. She heard a knock on the back door and ran to answer it. Again he was there briefly and then gone without a word. There was a knock on the front door and she ran to answer it and, again, found him standing there. This time, though, he spoke to her.

"I'm not really dead," he said. And then he was gone. I sat speechless and awkward, too young and inexperienced to comfort a friend battling an adult-sized war.

MY OWN FATHER HAD SENT ME that message, too. "I'm not really dead," was the unspoken message for the last two decades of his life, as he wandered into my days after a two-year absence then disappeared again for another two years. "I'm not really dead," he was saying when he briefly came close to me and then sped away, whirling with madness, grief, and regrets, turning from us, turning to face us, leaving everyone in a blurry background, unsure if he wanted in our lives or out. "I'm not really dead," he was saying when he refused to acknowledge major events, holidays, or the birth of his grandchildren. "I'm not really dead."

But now he is.

The idea of trying to plan a funeral for Dad frustrates me as I drive. He had been dead to me for so many years, and now I had to get into a panic, pack up my family, and drive to Florida for a funeral? Isn't it just *over* now? For someone who had done things so illegally and unconventionally up until now, it seemed too conventional to have a funeral. Could we simply tack "The End" onto the end of his life and move on to breakfast? He hadn't gone through the normal reaction when his own father died—the feelings of sadness and grief, wanting to be with family for comfort, wanting to honor his father. Instead he took off with his father's credit cards, causing us to arm wrestle over their return. How do we honor this man without honor? I want to hide behind the years and block out his memory; instead I cry. We were family, and we needed to do something about Dad.

Once Dad moved away, everything changed. He dressed differently, talked differently. Anger and defeat lived across his face and in his voice. Visits and calls became rare. His address became a post office box where we could reach him in emergencies. My brothers and I would cynically joke, "Where *is* this post office box anyway? Out on some beach with seaweed and sand blowing past?"

I drive along remembering his last two decades of life on the run from tax collectors, car repossessors, bankers, and his children. I think of his lonely nights in truck stop restaurants, reading the paper, still following the sports page as if on Saturday he'll take his sons to a game one more time and eat hot dogs and drink sodas, reading the program with its starting lineup, looking down at the paper in his hand and up to the players on the sidelines, trying to catch sight of his favorites.

I remember the ending years of his life and grief moves in, heavy and dark, as we drive through the Carolinas into Georgia. There is a rundown gas station on the side of the road with a little coffee shop and a dirt parking lot. A hand-painted wooden sign says, HAM, EGGS, COFFEE $2.99. I see men sitting at the lunch counter, and I am remembering. Him. He will never find his way out of late night diners and lonely black highways to his home with its firelight and quiet music and children yelling, "Goodnight, Daddy," running upstairs gleefully in flannel pajamas with fuzzy doggie slippers, chased by a scary monster who roars into the night.

As I drive by the diner, I notice a bearded man with a straggly sweater take a slow sip of his coffee, watching me pass by.

scorning the pomp of must and shall
my father moved through dooms of feel;
his anger was as right as rain
his pity was as green as grain
   —ee cummings

"YOU MADE IT AT LAST!" My sister, Jennifer, greets us at the door with her two excited children behind. Nothing like a funeral to create a party atmosphere. In the last year of his life, Dad "landed" here to be around family, although he never reconnected with me or my older brother. We unload coolers and endless duffel bags and the kids run to the in-ground pool and dive in.

After a twelve hour drive the first thing I want to see is Dad's room, which will pull me back time after time over the next several days. Jennifer and her husband finished off their garage into two separate rooms—an office and a small bedroom that barely fits a twin sized bed and a nightstand, an extra chair and table and small closet—and invited my homeless father to live with them. I slip in and realize I haven't been in one of his rooms in nearly twenty years. His shoes are perfectly lined up beside his bed, a habit from his army days. A sweater is folded crisply on his chair. His bed is made without a wrinkle. If I lifted the bedspread, the sheets would be tucked evenly and invisibly into the mattress. His books and notes to himself sit in ordered and neat stacks, a to-do list—*check car battery, mail packages, exercise, money order*—as if he'll be walking in later in the day to continue his schedule. Death is such an interruption. You can't even mail your packages. I look around his room, at his creased pants and meticulous dresser top, thinking that all his life his belongings have made me sad, as if I always knew that everything would end this way.

Jennifer and I go out to the grocery store to stock up for the next few days. Before we get into her car I pause at Dad's fading blue Chevrolet Caprice sitting beneath the trees.

"How did he register his car if he didn't have a legal driver's license?" I wonder out loud. We all knew this truth about Dad. He hadn't filed an income tax form or owned a driver's license from the same state where he registered his car in decades.

"And how could he insure it?"

My sister explains, "He had about three driver's licenses and he never insured his car. Every time he showed a license, it seemed to be from a different state. I was wondering how his car stayed registered. One night a new sticker appeared on his license plate. I asked him how he got that sticker."

She pulls out of the driveway, telling me that Dad took *her* license plate off her car when she wasn't home one day, then went to the library and photocopied it. He cut out the registration sticker, colored it, and covered it with vinyl, and put it on *his* license plate.

"Pretty creative, wasn't it?" She's laughing, and I'm not seeing the hilarity of the situation. If he could be creative about license plates and cars, couldn't he have found a way to creatively solve the problem of broken relationships, twisted thinking, or unpaid debts? I guess those problems can't be resolved on the library photocopy machine.

WHEN I WAS IN KINDERGARTEN, *and before I realized Dad wasn't rich or highly educated, before I knew that depression haunted him, and that we only lived in a working class town in a small, non-descript house, I thought he was someone important. He used to take us to work with him at the old Woolworth store he managed.*

My father's Woolworth store in Glens Falls, New York, was near my school. He would take me to work until the school day began. After he unlocked the store, he sat me at the lunch counter. The waitresses supervised me until it was time for our short walk to the parochial school. I sat next to the regular breakfast crowd with their coffee, cigarettes, and morning chatter. My favorite snack consisted of plain donuts on plain white dishes and a glass of cold, white milk. As I twirled around, I'd try not to slide off the slippery vinyl seat. I still remember what tasted so great about those donuts. The outside of the donut was always fried to a crisp, and a little stale, while the inside was chewy. Today, I still look for stale donuts, feeling a little gypped if someone sells me a fresh one that hasn't sat *for a day or two, picking up that crunchy exterior that I want to swallow with a memory that never goes bad.*

My father often went to work on Sundays when the store was closed to do some catching up, and often he took us with him. Sundays had a completely different feel. The lunch counter was closed and the grill scrubbed clean. The dry milkshake maker gleamed with no ice cream in sight. To run free in a locked store with no security guards or employees watching over you was a child's dream. My brothers and I ran free through the toy section, riding tricycles down the empty aisles, or plastic dinosaurs with handlebars, skidding dangerously around curves, giggling wildly. While we were screeching and sliding and squealing around the store, holding clothes up to see if we liked them, spinning on the stools at the un-manned lunch counter, passers-by dressed in overcoats, mufflers and gloves stood at the smudged plate glass windows with faces cupped by their hands, blocking the sun so they could see what we were doing. Bob would point them out to me, "Uh, oh . . . Should we go get Dad?"

"No. The store's closed. They can't come in," I determined for the spectators.

"That guy's trying the door! What if it's not locked?" Jon asked, panic building in his voice. For a minute we all had visions of unwanted customers coming in, buying things we didn't want to sell them, standing in line at cash registers we were too short to operate.

Eventually the crowd outside would look puzzled and finally walk away. Some acted in a huff, like they'd never shop at that Woolworth again. I don't know if they thought we were breaking and entering and riding and playing; or if they were wondering if the store wasn't really closed. There was a slightly privileged feeling of being allowed to run wild in the store while others could only look in from behind the glass, longingly eyeing the five and dime. Those are simple days if you can feel privileged, not because your dad is a CEO or a doctor, but because he runs an ordinary, inexpensive, mediocre department store. I remember being proud of him then.

On Saturdays in the 1960s Dad would make his weekly drive to the town dump. "Anyone want to come for the ride?" he asked.

We jumped in the car for the short, two mile trip down a forest-filled road. He drove along in his usual silence. I'd chatter about what kind of house I was going to build when I got older, and maybe I needed to take voice lessons, and should our dog go to obedience school? He'd answer Mmm hmm. Mmm hmmm. At the dump, he drove to the far corner. Seagulls squawked overhead and dove into the piles of rubbish for their dinner. Dad backed the car up right to the edge of the pit and stopped. At times I felt like screaming *We're gonna fall in!* as I imagined the car slipping off the side into the trench of filth and sinking underneath it all until we were buried and unable to climb up, even our voices smothered by the layers of refuse.

"Oh, nonsense," he'd say, putting the parking brake on, jumping out and opening the back of the station wagon. After throwing the trash bags over the side, an attendant on a *bulldozer dumped piles of sand and dirt over the garbage and then plowed all the rubbish under to keep it from rotting and smelling. My parents said strange things about the dump like, "It's such a clean dump. It doesn't even smell bad."*

At intervals the dump workers burned different sections of the refuse to keep it from overflowing into the picturesque town. Great billows of smoke swirled to the sky, and I'd want to hold my breath until we drove at least out of the parking lot and out of range of the fumes. Occasionally after covering an area with dirt, they'd plant grass over a section, letting that area lie dormant for a while. You'd never know that underneath the wavy blades of fescue lived rotting refuse and unwanted belongings, garbage and useless things. Dad would get back in the car and we'd drive down the twisting road where the shadows were alive and making shapes, to our home on a wooded street with a Labrador retriever wagging her black tail in the yard.

WE HAVE ONE DAY BEFORE THE FUNERAL and need to throw together a service. I sit in the tiled family room chair while Jennifer putters in the adjoining kitchen.

"Did Dad ever go to church with you, Jennifer?" I ask, flipping through a hymn book, trying to choose songs. I knew over the past decades there had been brief spurts where he sought answers from psychologists and pastors, usually for about one session before he threw up his hands in frustration.

"No, he wouldn't go. But sometimes I'd see him reading my Bible." She's wiping down the kitchen counter and emptying ashtrays, her hair pulled back in a thick, auburn wavy ponytail draping halfway down her back. I wonder what passages he read.

For a brief period during my senior year of high school, Dad was serious about church. He had moved us all to Florida from our idyllic New England town because he was running away from debt and another lost job. He had lost our beautiful home in Massachusetts and all of his money. After uprooting us all to Florida, he lost *that* job too, which followed many attempts at starting businesses—real estate ventures, purchasing a hair styling salon, buying and selling land, doing a middle of the night paper route and even picking up extra dollars by working a Saturday shift at 7-Eleven.

In my memory, he was always working but always changing jobs. He seemed to want to work, to be willing to work, but he kept failing. Was that inattentiveness or irresponsibility, or did he simply make terrible decisions? I'll probably never know.

One day, several months after my high school graduation, he got into his car and decided he didn't want to live anymore. All of his problems seemed to become something insurmountable in his mind. There seemed to be no place to run anymore. Finally, his neglected business caught up with him.

He let the family know by giving us a series of phone calls throughout a very tense morning. He told my mother death was calling him. She begged him to come home.

We can work this out. Where are you? We worried that he'd drive his car into a tree, or overdose on pills. Did he have a gun?

"There's nothing left to deal with. I don't have any choices anymore," he said.

Finally, his father flew down to Florida. Dad called late in the afternoon and when we told him his father was flying in, he agreed to come back. He arrived at our ranch-style house and ducked into his back bedroom to avoid facing his family. For the afternoon we tiptoed around like someone was napping, or sick in bed with the flu.

I picked up my grandfather at the airport, spotting his tall frame, slumped and weary-looking coming from the plane. When he saw me at the gate he picked up his walk to a jog, "Have you heard from him?"

"He's home," I told him.

"Oh, thank God!" raising eyes and hands to the ceiling.

My grandfather walked into the house and my father finally emerged from his bedroom. It's uncomfortable watching two six-foot tall men weep.

MY SISTER SITS DOWN IN THE FAMILY ROOM. I ask her, "Do you know if there were any hymns he liked? We need to pick something for the funeral."

"He never mentioned any."

"Then we'll have to choose some that we like. How about 'Amazing Grace,'" I ask, wondering if it's appropriate to sing a song about turning your life around at the funeral of a man who continued on in the same devastating direction.

"I really like 'It is Well with My Soul,'" she says.

When peace like a river attendeth my way, when sorrows like sea billows roll . . .

"That's my second favorite," I tell her.

Whatever my lot, Thou hast taught me to say it is well, it is well with my soul.

"So how much is this funeral going to cost?" my brother Bob asks, coming in the room and slumping on the couch with his feet on the glass top coffee table.

"Oh, I forgot to show you guys this. I found it in his room after he died," Jennifer goes into the kitchen and pulls out a thick envelope from the kitchen drawer. "Two thousand dollars in cash from his dresser drawer. Exactly how much it'll cost to have him cremated."

"Whoa. It's like he called the funeral home and asked how much it would cost to die," I say with amazement.

"That dirty son of a gun actually took responsibility for something for once in his life," Bob mutters. My father burned him over and over in the past decade by "borrowing" money and never returning it, taking out a loan with Bob as the co-signer and defaulting. Their relationship ended when Bob called the police one afternoon to turn in my father who had been driving an uninsured van registered in my brother's name. When Bob asked him to change the name on the registration, insure the van or give him the keys, my father refused all three options.

My father and brother stood in the driveway of Bob's house when the police arrived. The officer came up behind my father, who was whispering to my brother, "Please don't do this, son. Please don't do this," begging him to call off the law.

They glared at each other as my father slipped Bob the van keys.

"Everything's O.K. now, Officer. You can go," Bob said, keeping his eyes on my father. After the cruiser drove away they broke out in a screaming, swearing match. Bob pocketed the keys and his guilt and sent my father walking away down the street wheel-less and homeless, since my father had been living out of that van for months.

Now Dad could add "broken relationship" to his list of broken things. He couldn't seem to fix anything in need of repair. Not a car, an appliance, or a relationship.

Sometimes I wish he could've been more like my husband in that area. Give my husband a sputtering small engine, an iron that doesn't get hot, a lamp with a worn out cord or a door that won't shut properly, and first he'll figure out how it works. His engineering mind takes things apart, figuratively and physically, until he knows what to solder or replace or tweak a little. He approaches broken things confident that there will be a solution, a repair.

My father was different, though. He walked away from broken things. If something died in our house growing up, either it had to be thrown out, or someone else needed to be called in to repair it. When his money was gone and he couldn't afford repairs, broken things piled up—house repairs and broken radios. The dryer sat silent in the laundry room for months, or up to a year, while we took the wash out to the clothes line. Only two burners worked on the stove, and we'd adapt by cooking meals for six people on the remaining burners. The stove problem wouldn't be solved until we moved into a new house—a drastic solution to a minor problem.

There came a time when my father left broken relationships abandoned, too, like unwanted appliances in the yard rusting under trees, hoping someone else would meander by and figure out this problem. He never tried to see how they were put together, or how they worked, what made them tick. If he did, maybe, just maybe, he could've pinpointed the malfunctioning part and replaced it, letting their engines hum along, good as new. Maybe he could've seen how he hurt my brothers, or me, or anyone, and tweaked the relationship a little, solving the problem.

"Is your minister going to do the service, Jennifer?" I ask her, doodling on the paper.

"He's out of town. There's some fill-in guy from the funeral home."

The idea of a fill-in guy makes me nervous. "Well, does your church have a vocalist or a pianist?"

"No one is available," she says, meticulously folding the morning newspaper.

I can't imagine how no one is available to play piano or sing, but we choose songs from a list provided by the funeral home. They'll play tapes in the background and we'll sing along. A karaoke funeral.

"No one has ever done it that way before," the funeral director tells us.

IT'S THE NIGHT BEFORE THE FUNERAL. We all go to Chili's for dinner. The children stay with my mother at her house. We eat fajitas and chips and salsa. My brother Bob says very little.

After dinner we walk out into the sultry Florida night. There is a restaurant next door and Jon tells us that's where my father was headed the night he died. Every night at eleven o'clock he'd sneak out to break his low-fat, cardiac-care diet by eating a greasy hamburger and fries at Steak and Cheese. From what the hospital told us, we surmise he died out in front of that restaurant on the main highway through Orange City, a stone's throw from his last meal.

Jon says he isn't going over there, but Bob and I walk over and slip inside. Someone wants to seat us but we say we're not staying. We look around the fifties style restaurant. There's an old-fashioned lunch counter with metal seats and a vinyl cover. The floor consists of black and white tiles and the waiters wear uniforms from a *Happy Days* episode. I can see him here. He'd sit right at that counter, hunched over his burger and fries, pretending he was in a 1950s episode of his own life where there was a job, a mortgage, and a few little kids who thought the world of him. My brother and I don't say anything, but we both see the past and hear him making small talk with the counter help who still pile scoops of ice cream into the old, metal milkshake maker on the counter, spinning and whirling together chocolate and vanilla, and the past and the present.

"Let's get out of here," Bob says.

MY SISTER AND I DRIVE HER LIGHT BLUE IMPULSE to the funeral home where we'll hold the service in their small chapel. I feel jittery that a stranger can say anything in the least bit comforting to the loved ones. The fact that a *stranger* is doing the ceremony is pitiful evidence enough that something is a bit askew here.

There's a man in a gray somber suit and tie directing traffic in the parking lot. He's showing us exactly where to position the car so he can efficiently "squeeze" all the vehicles into his small lot. I imagine what his expression will be in an hour or so when he realizes there was plenty of room for all the cars attending *this* funeral.

Before the service we wait for the funeral director and the fill-in minister. Even among ourselves, my siblings and I have very little to say.

* * *

MY FATHER SHOWED UP UNEXPECTEDLY at my home in Massachusetts. "What are you doing here, Dad?" I let him in the backdoor on a wintry day and he entered with the wind and flurries. He was wearing a dark gray overcoat and rubber boots with a wild, angry look across his face. It had been a year or so since I had seen him. He acted as if we were picking up a conversation we left off on last week

"I went to see a psychologist today. The idiot charged me $85 an hour and didn't even help me! I'm feeling worse than I've ever felt!" He pounded his fist on my kitchen counter and it scared me, like I was still thirteen and it was his house, not mine. His voice was loud and filled with rage. He bounced off my kitchen walls and cabinets like a caged animal. When I tried to stand near him to console him, he flew away and stood on the opposite end of the room, avoiding my face, my touch.

"Dad, you have to go more than one time. He stirred everything up and now you need to work it through. Can I make you a cup of tea? Let me take your coat."

"No, I don't want a cup of tea."

He was always in constant motion in my home, never sitting anywhere except the very edge of my couch for five minutes, unbuttoning his coat so he wouldn't roast, but never taking it off. He seemed afraid to stay. We might say something to upset him, or find out something he was trying to hide. He'd pretend he had important meetings or business lunches. I knew the truth though: he'd leave, drive into Friendly's and order a cup of coffee, adding two creams and two sugars, pulling out the newspaper. At my house he'd stay for fifteen minutes, usually to ask some pointed question that bothered him. Why did Lindsay's father commit suicide? You mean he had all that money and because he lost his family he didn't want to live? I think my problem is that all these years I've had attention deficit. Will you read this book so you can understand me better?

"No. I can't take my coat off. I can't stay. I don't think I can go through with this counseling thing. It's not going to help me. It's too painful." He was in agony, crushing his head in his hands.

"It will help you, but you need to go back and face everything before it'll get better. You have a lot of garbage that needs to be uncovered."

"I feel like . . . I'm . . . going . . . crazy!" His face was contorted with pain. In fifteen minutes he was gone, leaving only a little track of caked and dirty snow in the shape of his boot at my backdoor. His footprints always headed out the door in my home. He'd never go back to the psychologist, and I wouldn't hear from him for another year or so.

THE FUNERAL DIRECTOR AND THE FILL-IN GUY come into the room. They shake our hands and the fill-in guy repeats our names warmly as if he is going to commit them to memory. They stand side-by-side at the head of the table. Why do I feel they are accusing us of something? My sister slips the funeral director the list of songs for the service. "Amazing

Grace" and "It is Well." It's an amazing grace that all is well. He rushes out of the room to set up the karaoke tapes.

"What I like to do at these services," the minister begins, "is to have you speak, since I didn't have the pleasure of knowing Bob." He smiles a saccharin smile at us and I do not like this not one little bit. My siblings are silent.

I wonder how anyone can sort out my father in thirty minutes. There is no extended family here. No aunts or uncles or cousins who had known him when he was young. No childhood friends or military friends came to pay their respects. Here we sit with a short half-hour and the burden set firmly on our shoulders to somehow do justice to this man's life. The fill-in guy is having difficulty picking up the magnitude of the family dynamics as he sees our four faces staring dumbly and numbly at him, four "loved ones" who have done a pretty poor job in planning a funeral service. What he doesn't ask, and what we don't offer, is that we are honoring our father as much as possible, considering the material we have to work with—a man who couldn't file a simple income tax form without government officials descending on him saying, "We've finally determined his location. Let's take him alive."

The fill-in gives a brief history of how he "performs" funerals and why he needs to leave immediately after the service. I try to form a quick summary in my mind of "who Bob was," and I begin to drift away into a myriad of scenes where I am old and young and Dad is playful or forlorn. We've been all those people together.

"I probably won't be able to talk without being emotional," I tell the minister, "so maybe you could say what I wanted to say?" He nods. I explain that Dad was estranged from us for a long time, but he really had been shown grace from God in his last few weeks of life. I say that my father was like the thief on the cross at Jesus' crucifixion. One thief cursed and ridiculed Christ while the other one silenced the mocking one, knowing they were the guilty parties hanging up there, not Jesus. If you pinned my father down, he knew his guilt, too, but he couldn't do anything about it. He had always been able to say he was sorry, but he never changed. Despite the fact that he broke every rule of parenting, I could always let it go with him because he wanted to be forgiven. But one day he stopped saying he was sorry to people, and I think that's when he got so sick. He'd apologize for an offense that he'd repeat the following week, so why bother saying you're sorry anymore? Eventually his offenses snowballed into one large, insurmountable object, piled so high, and reaching toward heaven like the dump with its old refrigerators and couches and unwanted television sets. Old crimes and arguments and careless words, all stacked up and rusting, spending time exposed then rolled under with a bulldozer, still existing out of sight with a long, underground life.

How do I explain all that to the fill-in guy who has somewhere else he needs to be? He is running through a series of facial expressions that attempt to show deep concern.

I talk for five to ten minutes about our family history and my siblings remain silent. I'm not sure how much he is absorbing. He finishes with us and we go to take our places in the small chapel inside the funeral home.

I HAD BEEN LIVING IN VIRGINIA for seven months when I got a phone call from my husband's previous employer in Massachusetts.

"Linda, we've had a phone call from a man who says he's your father, and he's trying to locate you. He wants us to give him your new phone number so he can call you. We just feel a little funny about giving out your number to someone who had no idea you moved."

"Oh . . ." I chuckled at the pitiful absurdity of it all. "That really would be my father. He doesn't like to keep in touch. You can go ahead and give him the number."

Within several minutes he called, surprising me with how distraught he was feeling. I think he assumed everyone else would stay put while he drifted. Apparently we were all supposed to be patiently waiting for him to return.

"How could I have let this happen? This has really shaken me up. I went to your house and I was feeling so cutesy. It was Valentine's Day and I had brought you flowers. I rang the doorbell and this stranger answered, so I said, 'Is Linda home?' I thought she was a friend of yours watching the kids or something. She said that she lived there and that you had moved. I'm sure she thought I was a loony for not knowing my daughter had moved. I guess your neighbors weren't very welcoming to her. No one came over and introduced themselves." The image of my dad bringing me flowers that no one would accept still had the power to break my heart for him.

"This has really bothered me that I couldn't find you. I'm struggling with some terrible depression that I can't get a hold of. I . . . I was thinking that maybe if I could just call you sometime . . . then maybe I could get on top of this thing."

"Dad, you can call me anytime."

After we hung up, I wondered what he did with the flowers he brought to my old house.

THERE ARE SEVERAL BOUQUETS OF FLOWERS. About twenty or twenty-five people are sitting in the pews, all spread around, a couple of ladies here, a man alone over there. I look around feeling surprised that *this many* people have come. The fill-in welcomes everyone, thanking them for coming, and tells everyone to open their hymn books to Amazing Grace. The funeral director starts a background tape that is a slow dirge and everyone in the group is singing at a different speed, with different and conflicting words. We begin to laugh in the middle of the song, and the laughter grows more uncomfortable as we all look at each other realizing *we are laughing at a funeral!* I yell to the funeral director who is out of sight, "Could you just please turn that off?"

We sing a cappella.

When the singing is done, the minister begins to speak. I expect him to share all that we had explained to him in the backroom—the stories we had asked him to relay to the group. Instead he says, "Oh, we just had the most wonderful conversation in the back before this service. I learned all about Bob and, oh, I just wish all of you could have been there. Oh, there were just too many things to share, but we talked about grace and forgiveness and all sorts of things." And that was it.

Now I know why he's just a fill-in guy. He relayed none of the stories I asked him to share. I stare at him in disgust, thinking this funeral is actually so appropriate for Dad.

The funeral is over and I avoid the fill-in guy. I'm grateful to be done with the whole service. We are standing at the door, "Bob's children," as people leave with hugs and condolences. My sister is almost giddy. "It was perfect. Dad would have loved it." I moan and mourn inside, staring off through the open door out into the barren parking lot, flooded with Florida sun, feeling let down because it was such a pitiful service, which said to me that my father was pitiful. But underneath all the garbage, I still insist there was more to him.

BACK AT MY SISTER'S HOME, my two brothers and I slip once again into Dad's room to talk and look through his boxes once more. I find a list, written in Dad's familiar, lovely cursive. Finally, some reward for my search:

> *Begin work on improving my relationships with Linda and all the kids.*
> 1. *I want her and all the kids to love me again.*
> 2. *I want to be able to communicate with her/them easily and the grandkids.*
> 3. *I want to have a good relationship with her kids.*
> 4. *I want to try and build a better rapport between us.*
> 5. *I want to try and have a closer relationship with all the kids.*
> 6. *I'd like them to feel better about me.*
> 7. *I'd like to be able to be more of a father to them.*
> 8. *I'd like to do things to help them improve their lives materially.*
> 9. *I'd like to feel that we're closer as a family than we have been and make it happen.*

I read the words and gasp while my brother impatiently grabs the paper out of my hand. "Geez, Linda. Why are you torturing yourself?" he asks.

Because I need to know what he thought, in his own words. I take the paper back and put it in my purse. I'll keep it forever. It's my inheritance.

I DREAM ABOUT HIM THAT NIGHT, eerily and vividly. The view outside the window is rolling hills. He has a business that he works out of our home. In our yard, three dogs are tied up with chain leashes and two of their leashes get caught together. One is being pulled down the hill by the other dog with the chain around his foot. There is no way to escape. They are tied together permanently. When one runs, the other runs. When one falls the other falls. They stay connected.

Dad is working on some equipment—like farm equipment—in the living room but it is broken. Finally I hear him say with patient defeat, "Well, I guess it's over. This equipment is dead and there's nothing left I can do to keep the business going." He is preparing to close up shop. Something has happened and his business will never run in the black again. I hear him wondering what else he'll do for a livelihood. I look out the window at the green, lush landscape, wondering too how you make a living in this rural area. In the dream I feel hopeful that something always can be bought or sold, a service performed, or a repair made. He's creative enough to find something to do.

I go to the living room where he is packing up his equipment, defeated. I stand before him, looking up into his face, noticing how much taller he is than me. He's wearing a green plaid shirt buttoned all the way to the top and I like the pattern on him. "Dad, it's OK the business didn't work. It takes courage to start a business, and it especially takes courage to start another one after one has failed. You've done good." His expression is familiar. He wants to turn away and dismiss my encouragement as "nonsense," but his face stops between dismissal and a hope of finding truth in my words. Was that a hint of comfort in his face?

I wake at 4:30 in the morning going over the dream. Some rare dreams have that feeling that you've really spoken to the person—like it was more than a dream. I know there was truth in those thoughts and images. We were tied together, too, like those dogs on their chains; and when he fell, I fell. When he hurt, I hurt. I'm the true product of a broken home and hurting parents, always dreaming in my most longing of dreams that I could've made all of his hurts go away.

As the memory lingers, I wonder if it is ever too late to offer words of comfort to a person who has left his tormented life. If a person is dead, where do words of encouragement go?

his sorrow was as true as bread;
no liar looked him in the head.
if every friend became his foe
he'd laugh and build a world with snow
    —ee cummings

THE NEXT DAY WE PACK UP THE VAN and all the boys. Hugs are passed around and my family pulls away from Jennifer's house and from Dad's Chevy in the driveway, down the main street where Dad died in his car in front of his favorite restaurant in this rundown little town so far from where we once were a family. I plug in a book on tape to occupy my children. I had borrowed a Star Trek tape from the library—we hear "*Eech Nei Grova*" coming from the speakers.

"What in heck are we listening to?" my husband asks. "Did you get a German version of Star Trek?"

The tape continues, "Translated: put on the phasers." My husband picks up the box that held the tape and reads the side—*Star Trek: How to Speak Conversational Klingon*. We laugh uproariously for miles and miles, past the diner with men in straggly sweaters, sipping coffee. Past the towns that descended from nowhere and the funeral home where my father's ashes will be. We pretend we're going to learn conversational Klingon. The boys have to listen to the tape until we nearly get to Jacksonville. I find myself comforted that after death, life and laughter eventually return to the living.

I watch my boys in the rearview mirror as they nudge each other for more room on the seat, or dreamily stare out the window. He is in them. My father is in them. They wear the shape of Dad's nose and his build. We'll go home after this week, as we would've before the funeral, and they will be my family. We will laugh for years together and I will teach them to clean up their messes.

At least I don't worry about my father anymore. I don't worry if he's cold somewhere, or grieving, or missing his family, or nursing regrets, or wishing he could come home. I don't worry that he's hurting or sleeping in his van, or that he's feeling ashamed or thinking that we're ashamed of him.

A part of losing someone is how you miss them forever, how they've become etched in your mind and memory, and how your mind and memory are changed. People ask me simple questions about my growing up years, my life, my children or my family, and I'm struck silent because the answer is so complicated. I want to share a Woolworth story that was only a blink in time and how men look when they cry and how that makes people feel. Sounds and voices ring in the background of my mind—an apologetic father and a screaming match, a lonely funeral with six bouquets of flowers and an empty parking lot, a drawer with a short stack of greeting cards and a yellow piece of paper with unaccomplished wishes and goals for a relationship with your kids. I answer in short sentences. *No, my family wasn't close.* Or I answer in clichés. *I come from a broken and dysfunctional family.* But those words don't say it all. They can't possibly say it all. In a far and distant place I hear him calling me through time, with valentine roses, saying, "I love you, dear."

* * *

DOOMS OF LOVE

*My father moved through grief of days
taking us lonely in his ways,
darkening black the evening skies
saying hello to all our goodbyes*
　　—linda anne mackillop

THERE AND HERE MARIO SUSKO

if there are days, years when the mind
turns itself off, wanders out of time,
in order to survive, one's only hope
is that it will be somehow called back.

maybe that's why i sleep with the light
on and from time to time tie my mind
to a bedpost, or put it under the pillow,
my hand resting on it all night long.

however, i don't have a phone; whenever
i picked it up, a voice would say: Sorry,
Wrong number, though i knew it wanted
to check whether i was still there.

and i don't answer my mail; in fact, there
isn't any mail to answer now, unless i
wish to pick a cemetery plot; displaced
from home, i'm already marked: prospect.

You think too much, mother would say,
And that is poisoning your mind, so i look
unabsorbed here; i put all theres and thens
in boxes and buried them at different places.

but, i do act as though i am not, as people
say, all there, and sometimes i am truly not,
especially when i believe my mind has gone
to find a then of now and a here of there.

THERE AND HERE

it presumes hindsight madness, if exposed,
should foreshadow foresight sanity, but i think
it tries to see whether someone who's run
out of life could still be all there and here.

THE OTHER SIDE MARIO SUSKO

You'll get through this, she said.
I was looking at the wall, trying
to figure out what could be behind it—
another wall, a city, an open space,
another woman who would also tell me,
having caught me staring at the wall,
that I would be able to go through.
I don't mean the wall, she said,
her face straining to keep a calm look.
This situation; well, not this, really.
Oh, you know what I mean, don't you?

I didn't. I mean, I did not know.
Or maybe I did. Should have known.

The sun pricked my skin, but I managed
to discern my image in the wall, as if
it appeared slowly in a blurred mirror.
A small bird descended, its wings still
for a moment, and pecked at something.
A tremendous pain shot through my eye.
Blood started to course down the wall
as though someone wanted to restore
the primary color to the old faded bricks.
The bird hopped a few yards to the left
and I lost vision in my right eye.

Stumbling forward I finally touched
my grainy face, realizing all of a sudden
I was through, feeling the windless air.
You are a real illusionist, I heard her
yell behind me. What do you see there?

WHAT I WANT TO SAY MARIO SUSKO

if it were plausible to gauge
the top and the bottom leveling
limit and thus escape death
in between, I would not be
alone now, without my wife
who could not see that, and
my dog who couldn't know that,
stranded on this vast island
that looks like unconquered land,
yet swarms with forlorn souls
that search for a veritable answer
to the question: what am I
looking for here if the leveling
of limitless opportunities is
to pinpoint the limits of
opportunity, and though I keep
telling myself: I am looking
for a wife, my wife, and I am
looking for a dog, my dog,
the war is still on, and it
is not my war, yet it seems
I am not able to get out of wars,
a remnant of the old slogan:
we shall live as if peace will
last forever and a war break
out tomorrow, its logic implying
reciprocal causality and thus
mutual exclusion, which is not
that far from what we resort to
these days: we can talk, but we
have really nothing to say

to each other, so the only thing
we shall end up with is to agree
to disagree, and that often leads
to this: both sides may be right,
and wrong, so we'll have a truce
and then let each side play on
according to its own conception
of reality, which is certainly
what a child in the park entertains,
coming to me in the fenced-off
area, saying: my dad is not around,
and I refrain from gauging the sense
of his words, so you can now play
with me, you'll be a skeleton and
I'll be a pirate because I have
the sword, swishing before my eyes
with a blade, a battery-powered
fluorescent blue rod which I know
belongs to another movie, so I ask,
pointing at the plastic structure
with turrets, walkways, and chambers
whose windows have been blown out:
can that be my space ship, and
the child yells: you play my game
and in my game you get killed
at the end, so I look at his mother
as if pleading for her help
to sort out, if nothing else,
chimeric realities, but she does
not move, keeps standing outside
the theater, staring at me as if I
were an enemy unworthy of being
played with and done in, her german
shepherd on the leash, immobile,
ears up, waiting for a command
that had my uncle, whose name I
inherited, pass water in his pants
at the transport train platform,

though I was almost at the point
of asking her whether, once playing
is finally done, she could be
my wife, even her dog my dog,
but now I suddenly turn away,
realizing I am right in the middle
between the two of them, and I run
out of the playground, away from
the swings, slides, and sand boxes
with unexploded mines, and keep
on running, again, telling myself
this time I could, I have to, get
to the end of the island, the earth
itself, simply step off, drop
into the airless silence to take
a deep breath and shout at the top
of my voice: I was there, I played
all those games, and what I want to say
is:

THE COLOR OF BLOOD MARIO SUSKO

Whenever the sunset horizon was flushed
with the color of blood, mother would
cross herself and say under her breath:
God help us, there's going to be a war.

That late afternoon when I first laid
My eyes on you, she mused aloud one night
while I held a receiver in my hand, watching
the lightning set the sky ablaze, Two streaks
Of blood were on your cheeks, your screaming
Was like a battle-cry, and for a moment I
Resented the sight of you because of the pain
You caused me coming into this world, but I
Knew you'd not grow up to be a war dog.

While I was wheeled on a clanking stretcher
that wobbled down the corridor, fighting
the blood that oozed down my throat, I caught
a glimpse of a woman on the examination table,
holding her belly like leavened bread dough,
her hands the color of her red blouse, the nurse's
trying frantically to move them and scissor
the soaked fabric: Where's the entry wound,
and the doctor's rasping voice: The baby first,
trailing behind me as a double door burst
open for the lifeless light to receive me.

On the horizon, ten years later, another night
of exile seeps down the sky's crimson glow
as I stand at the window and watch the sun

THE COLOR OF BLOOD

get swallowed by the open sea, my fingers
tracing the scar's ridge along the lower jaw
to make sure the shrapnel is no longer there,
the pain now only in my memory, so I can go
to bed, close my eyes, and have the color
of blood fade for a while from consciousness.

ARBOR JOHN KEATS

A FEW WEEKS BEFORE MY MOTHER DIED OUT FRONT, she said that I would be going through a lot of changes. That's what getting older meant, especially for a girl. I remembered her while I watched my father yank drawers open and slam them closed in the hot kitchen, screaming so loud I saw spit fly out of his mouth. I was almost glad to see him show some emotion. He had been too blank since the snow, flat and sort of empty. I even felt wrong being around him. I got goose bumps sometimes, and was ashamed of myself. I peeked at him from the hall like he was an intruder I was about to surprise. I wondered if one of the things that changed when you grew up was that you got crazy over things like batteries and really calm when your wife shot herself.

He saw me. His face weakened so fast, like I stole something from him. Shame came again. But his voice was alive with anger.

"Some kind of hero we've taken in, Juney. A soldier who collects flashlights he's not capable of operating. Where is he, anyway, your uncle?"

I shook my head and took two steps forward. He was usually upstairs. I had been sitting at my desk all morning, scribbling in a notebook, listening for the cracking noises his weight made on the floorboards. He could have been in bed. He was in bed a lot. I would sit on the stairs and peek at him through the railing. He knew I was watching. Sometimes he would almost answer my questions. Sometimes he said nothing. I liked the smell of wood up there. He said he didn't sleep very much. My father didn't believe him. I was leaning an open palm on the closed attic door. I asked if I should go up.

"No. He makes me nervous, June. Your mother..." He was standing over three flashlights on the kitchen counter with the tops screwed off. Two batteries dropped onto the floor. "Vera would say he always did. She never thought I gave him a break. She credited me with trying, but said there were too many obstacles. She said my life had—and she loved to say this—my life had 'conditioned me for ignorance.' Then she would tell me not to get too down, because everyone's did. No one stayed open enough. But she didn't know him like he is now."

I knew that this new uncle Toby still wasn't my uncle. He was African American. My mother's parents took in foster kids for a few years, and Toby was the only one who kept in touch after he left. He might have been quieter than the old Toby, but, like I said, everything had been quiet for a long time. He had a green serpent with spikes and wings tattooed onto his neck. The tail ran down into his shirt. I lost my breath a little every time I saw it. My father was more different, I thought, and maybe that's what made Toby seem more the same. He still patted my head like I mattered, and had big eyes that looked the way I think I felt when I was younger and wanted to know everything. My father used to call them orphan eyes when he wanted to make my mother mad. I don't know. Sometimes they looked too big, and he didn't ever seem to blink anymore.

My father bent down to pick up the batteries. He had changed into a skeleton in baggy sweatpants and a baby blue T-shirt. I didn't notice as much when he sat and watched me eat the meals he made, leaning on the table with an elbow, his legs pointed at the door as if he were ready to be called somewhere, while he picked at bread crusts with his smooth fingernails and stirred wet noodles around watery broth. He hadn't been back to the police department since December. We had a lot of visitors at first, in the winter. There always seemed to be at least one squad car in the driveway, which made me sad and mad, or confused. I just kept thinking: you're all too late. Then I felt like laughing. My father started to yell at them, in a sleepy, irritated way. He blamed them for letting my mother become a cop, and he yelled when they said they didn't really know her until she was one, or when they went quiet, or changed the subject. So they left us alone, and we never went out.

He was a good cook. He learned when he was a boy, because Nana Waters was sick when he was very young and couldn't reach the stove from her wheelchair. He was an only child like me, and like my mother, when orphans weren't around. He cooked for us most of the time when she was alive. I think we would have missed her more if she'd made the food. So I didn't look like a skeleton. Toby didn't either. He devoured everything.

"I didn't forget you, June. Sit down."

The late morning sunlight seemed weird, like a lie. I felt tricked, until I was in my chair, like night had come and the light was really artificial. I thought I had lost time waiting for boards to creak. I didn't care that much. Part of me wished I could skip the daytime. Maybe the flashlights threw me off. I don't know. But my father served me turkey and Swiss cheese in wheat pita bread, with a glass of low fat milk, on a scratched wooden tray I'd used since I was little. A scuffed pocket flashlight rolled against the blue plate. I squinted at the patio door and the swaying vertical blinds that looked like strips of hot skin in the sun. When he pulled out the chair beside me, my mother's, and sat down, I stopped chewing. His seat had always been at the other end of the table. He said he could see the whole room from there. He said cops thought like that, especially about their families, and my mother would say, most of the time: I'm a cop, too. Then she would stare hard at the ticking pendulum on the wall clock, like my father was doing now.

"Do you know they're everywhere, Juney, those lights? I find them in closets, in the garage, out in the yard. And most of them have the batteries in wrong. I don't know if he's stealing. They're all old looking, scarred to hell. But he must be broke. We're all taking advantage of the insurance money. I shouldn't talk. But he's been here almost six months and he can't keep a job. I don't mind carrying him for awhile. We don't have much family left, Juney, and I'm sorry for that. For you, I'm so sorry for that."

He took a huge breath and swallowed all the heat in the room. I shivered. And then that life, that anger came back.

"Is he even family? Is he? That's terrible. If she can hear me, well, I know. I know. But it's not clear enough. It's not. He had planned to take the civil service exam in May. I know the city's desperate, and I believe the vets deserve opportunities, but we might be better off without him there. I was rooting for him. I was. But he has no plan, which is no sin at twenty-four, but I don't know if he's capable of making one. The dream keeps changing: cop, corrections, armed guard, post office, big-rig driver, Coast Guard. I feel like he's lying to me. He's probably just lying to himself. Something that matters, he said. But the problem is, when you've been lugging bodies around in a war zone, where everything is blown apart, with all those IEDs and walking bombs, do you believe that anymore? Can you? Sorry, June."

I was a little mad at getting treated like a baby. There were things he knew I knew. One of them was that Toby had been a mortician for the marines in Iraq. He did a tour in Afghanistan before that. He called himself a grunt. I talked about him for a school assignment we had at the beginning of last year. A friend of his had written to my mother. They were near the Pakistan border, hiking through the mountains in the afternoon, escorting about a dozen Taliban back to base. The sun made the sky white and the rock red, he said. One of the prisoners broke away and ran down a jagged decline. The marines started shooting. My uncle's friend said the bullets sounded like firecrackers. I made it clear in my report that he couldn't know what my uncle, or anyone else, thought. My teacher praised me for my insight. Toby watched until the prisoner reached some flat terrain. He leveled his rifle and fired. His friend, who was looking through binoculars, said you could see blood spray out from the man's neck as he fell into the dust. Mrs. Curtain also praised me for not being too descriptive. Teachers always have to contradict themselves: details are everything, but every detail isn't necessary, or necessarily in good taste. I wished I knew more. My mother did, too; she said, I think, taste could go to hell. I filled in the gaps with research about the Khyber Pass and on how Afghanistan had always suffered from battles between the Persians and the Turks. My title was: Civilization Kills. Mrs. Curtain called it provocative, but vague. I only got a B+.

Toby came home the Christmas before my mother died, but he wouldn't stay with us. We all went out to dinner once, to his favorite place, the Kowloon. He said the things you missed when you were in another country were shrimp fried rice the way you liked it, and those fake cows across Route 1, on the Hilltop's lawn, even though he hated that highway more than any road he'd ever seen. He barely touched his rice. Twice my mother had to send me to find him. He was at the takeout counter, staring out the window at those ceramic cows, or at the blur of headlights in the dark that looked like a windswept ribbon of fallen white stars. I touched his hand both times. Both times he looked surprised to see me. "It's so much darker in there than I remember," he said. He squeezed my fingers a little too hard as I led him back to our booth.

I remember that visit for what didn't happen. Toby avoided the war all night, until he announced that he was going to Iraq, and that he had requested to serve as a mortician. My mother already knew. My father and I respected his silence, but she leaned into him to dig up details about the man he shot in the neck. My father yelled at her after we dropped Toby off near a giant white gas tank in Lynn, at a girlfriend's apartment above a bar with a flashing neon Budweiser sign. Later he told me, in the attic, that the red light made him feel dead when he woke to it at night, but not always in a bad way. My father said my mother brought her own baggage to the dinner. She got so mad, and so quiet, which was usually how you could tell she was mad. And then she said: "You haven't seen yet. You have no right. You're outside and you hate us."

We almost never talked about the man who died in front of her when I was a baby. After she was gone my father opened up a little, in such a quiet voice, at first, you could forget to listen. He would start way back, with his bad feeling about her being an officer. She'd say he was sexist. He reminded her about getting too close to evil, how that proximity tore him up the first year, of what he witnessed—not the dying, but the beaten, the wicked, and the dead—and how she rescued him. (I wanted to hear all this, over and over, even when the facts started to change and I wondered how true any of what he told me was, but I felt weird, too, and guilty, when things got too intimate.) Family saved him. Home was a sanctuary where normal, right, and good seemed as real as shingles, beams, and doors. He grabbed my shoulders, as if he were going to pick me up and carry me away, and looked right through me while I was finishing my sandwich, telling me that I was conceived then, thirteen years ago this month, his first June on the force. "All I remember," he said, "is the heat—we put an air-conditioner in the bedroom and I still couldn't stop sweating—and the terrible, nonstop dreams about violence, everyone being violated, and your mother loving me, like she'd been commanded to keep me sane. Everything else is a blank."

After she thought he would be alright, and once I came along, she wanted what he had. Maybe she'd grown a taste for it. The mortgage was a pressure, too, even with the money their parents had left them. After a month on the job, with my father always mad and anxious, she got unlucky fast. She was called to a bomb scare just a few miles from where we lived. A son wanted his father dead, rigged up a device to explode under his car, but left the garage door open and got reported by a neighborhood jogger. My mother was at the end of the driveway, taking notes from an old woman in a housedress who lived across the street, saw nothing, but wouldn't stop talking. There was sudden noise, flame, flying and drifting pieces of things. They staggered. Two men my mother didn't know from the bomb squad were thrown out of the garage. One was on his knees, trying to press a hanging flap of skin back onto his throat with his wrist because his hand was gone. He lived. The other one lost his eyes. He crawled to my mother and murmured something about his wife and children. She knelt down, patted his sticky hair, and leaned into his breath before he coughed globs of blood into her face and died.

She was out of work for awhile. My father tried to pay her back for what she'd done for him. I don't think he failed. She saw therapists, too, and did get better for most of my life. There were dreams that made her moan. There was always too much quiet. And she didn't touch me, I think, for a long time. When she tried to bring up the day to my father, she called herself stupid for believing she could bear so much. She said she was willing herself to stare into the man's face, through the blood and the distortion, to prove to him she'd carry his words back to his family. She never thought that she'd be too weak, and she felt sick that she had to lie to his wife because she couldn't remember one thing he said.

When Toby came home before Iraq, she had already decided to give him a present: her mother's Bible. It was in the trunk of the car, wrapped in blue paper with a red ribbon. That's why I'm sure she knew he was going to be a mortician. She marked the book of Tobit for him. Tobit took care of dead Jews during the Babylonian captivity. He's not in the real Bible. He's in the books that usually get left out, but my grandmother had the one with everything. My mother never really mentioned religion. I was confirmed as a Catholic, but we didn't go to church much after the ceremony. When she gave him the Bible at the end of dinner, I might have seen what my father meant about my uncle's eyes. I noticed the neediness, what he called a shameful quality, as if a guest with no manners or sense of boundaries roared in a crowded room: love me! I still thought it might be easier and a little kinder to say they were children's eyes. Most kids didn't know yet about shame. When he got close to the candle on the table to look at the book, the wide open stare and all that white of the eyeball had a planet of shadow inside. My mother had an old black and white cat that she brought to the marriage. He went blind and his pupils stayed dilated, no matter how much light flooded them. I missed how the black orbs turned into thin slashes in a sea of green and yellow. Toby reminded me of our cat, even now, so it was hard to say if he looked different. The childish wonder, the neediness, and the dysfunctional pupils all merged with something detached, preoccupied, and frozen. My father said, with a half-smile, that the serpent on his neck was sucking the life out of him. I told him that Jewish prophets had burned-out eyes, and he nodded. But I lied. If they had really seen anything, I think they would have gone blind. The Word of God, which usually came through an Angel, just scorched their throats with fire. Nothing happened to their eyes, not from hearsay, which isn't even admissible in court.

My father had taken my tray away and left the table. He was running water over the plate, squirming in the sun pouring through the window over the sink. I was clicking the dead flashlight on and off. When Toby put his hand in my hair, I dropped the light. We were all so jumpy. Maybe, like my father said, the feeling was in the house, because my mother and father were police. But since she died, the stakes seemed bigger. Each bang of a door, every phone ring, the weak echo of a yell from the baseball field across the railroad tracks—what would be the next signal that something you never thought of before, like your mother leaving the world because she couldn't stand you and her life, would happen in a heartbeat? If I tried to tell my father what I meant, he called her sick. She couldn't make the right choices. Professionals said the same thing. (I had some of their studies in the Khyber Pass file on my computer.) Depression and psychosis were the usual reasons people gave—survivors, I mean. The ones who died were never any help. Tobit's daughter-in-law, Sara, is suicidal because of Asmodeus, an evil spirit that lusted after her. He kills all the men she marries. She's not weak or crazy. What keeps her alive is thinking about her father, and what the shame of her act will do to him. Then she prays, and God hears her. Maybe my mother prayed and God didn't listen. Or maybe family didn't mean as much to her as it meant to Sara. Or maybe God's gone too far away to hear anyone anymore, or family had changed into a burden you should shrug off, or a trap.

I must have let a noise escape when Toby touched me, because my father spun around and dropped the plate on the floor. Toby was already tracking the flashlight that was rolling away from me. He dropped to his knees in a weird, graceful way, and crawled across the cool tile toward the broken pieces, tucking the light into a side pocket on his tan painter's pants. My father flailed one of his socked feet at him, as if he were shooing away a dog. He was mad at being caught off guard. Toby sprung up and sat in my father's chair by the patio window. His brown polo shirt was too big for him. He kept tugging on the sleeves, and at the neck, hunching over, like the sun was melting him. Those eyes were focused, or not focused, just above my head. The grace he found on the floor was gone.

"Sandwich?" my father asked, over the crash of sky-blue ceramic chunks into the trash. "We didn't know you were here."

"It's all good, Matt," Toby said. "Thanks, thanks a lot, though, man. Thanks."

I knew the response would irritate my father. He either seemed like he was in a daze or was too positive—for anyone, not just a war veteran, not just someone in a family that had fallen apart. Sometimes I thought a professional might call him bipolar, that this odd, untimely happiness was mania, but I didn't want to think about what could come next.

"I have an interview, Matt, up the street. Two-thirty sharp, man, up the street."

He pulled a pair of sunglasses out of another pocket in his pants and put them on. He wiped at his dry forehead with his sleeve. Then he jumped out of the chair and rushed toward the back door, near the trash, into the only part of the kitchen that had any sense of shadow.

"I was wondering if you'd let me take Juney. Two-thirty sharp."

My father was back at the counter, rolling three flashlights under his palms.

"Where's the interview?"

"The nursing home, across from the pond. The Providence, man. Helping out, you know?"

"You mean bedpans, changing old people? Is that what you mean?"

"Whatever, man. Whatever they need. It's all good, you know? Really, just . . . Two-thirty, and I thought me and June could get some lunch. Or dessert—ice cream, maybe. The pond, you know, on a day like this—people love to be out. Everyone will be out."

We couldn't see Toby's eyes, but his head drifted aside, and my father stopped rolling the flashlights. Everyone will be out; people love to be out. We were united. No one was alone. For just a second, by accident, a shared thought brought us all together: the criminal released early from jail in April shouldn't be out. He planted the bomb that killed the man who died whispering blood to my mother. He was convicted. He had appealed. The District Attorney made a mistake. My mother might have had to testify again in court. I didn't understand. I should have asked my father, or looked the case up. The night we went for Chinese food, she had just been informed of what they called a travesty. If you didn't think she was crazy, or didn't believe in evil demons, or really just demons, since God let everything happen, from the serpent to the devil in the desert, or at least had to act like he did, so he wouldn't seem surprised, but blamed you at the same time—you could have concluded that she shot herself because she couldn't bear to relive everything for another useless trial. Mad or possessed sounded braver.

"What's going on with these, Toby?" My father pointed at the lights.

He took off his sunglasses and stared into my father's eyes. I thought he was angry. I thought this was the day we all awoke to anger. But he shook his head, blinked a few times at a shuffling display of the possible emotions any man might feel—rage, guilt, despair, bewilderment—said oh man, oh man, and wiped his face with an open hand. Then his eyes disappeared behind the glasses, a smile took over his mouth, and he swayed back farther into the corner. Even though I felt safer, I knew we'd lost a chance at something we weren't even aware that we might need.

"Thanks, man, for always helping me," he said, and then just stood there with his arms loose at his sides. I ran into the bathroom to brush my teeth. The job was the key. My father was in love with the normal, and the slightest chance of recovering it clouded his judgment.

Toby grabbed his faded brown book bag from the garage on the way out. He didn't ask my father if he could take the car. He didn't pause at a bus stop. We walked the entire way, almost two miles. I was hot, but felt good. I was anxious. Toby offered me his sunglasses. I said no. I think he was glad. He never let go of my hand, but he kept doing the other thing that made my father nervous: he wouldn't walk on the sidewalks. He stayed in the gutters, even through the bubbling water in front of Madam Dawn's, the out of business psychic with the dead, purple neon sign in the window, across the street from Papa Gino's. My mother went there once, near the end. I waited under that sign, in a purple armchair, while they took her upstairs. She came down in about twenty minutes, laughing as the young receptionist with a pierced eyebrow ran her charge card through. My mother told her to fuck off. She walked by me like she forgot I was there, and I'd sunk so deep into the chair that it took me a minute to follow her. If bikers or runners came at Toby, he didn't alter his course. I would tug at him, but he didn't budge. They swerved into traffic or broke their stride. He had put headphones on as soon as we left home, but he talked, too. He said he wasn't stealing. He told me he used to lift weights to Metallica in high school. He was smoking more than I thought he smoked, lighting half-cigarettes with pinched ends that he'd saved in his green pack and drawing their last life away. He said some soldiers listened to metal to get them going. He did in Afghanistan, but not in Iraq. He took his headphones off and handed them to me.

"I used to feel so young, man, like you must feel, June. Man, these guys—they can play."

I listened for a second. I liked Toby. I might not have loved him. But I was upset by how I smothered myself to be polite. I didn't like Metallica. I didn't like music much, period, but this was just noise, like engines, or hate. Why didn't I tell him? Why did I still act like there were rules I had to follow? What did I care what he'd been through, what he'd seen? I was alive. I could walk on my own. I deserved respect, too. I deserved freedom.

He stared at me while I listened. I dropped his hand. All I could see was my own distorted reflection in his glasses, a carnival girl, stretched out and too vivid. He cocked his head and took the headphones back.

"You don't need it, Juney," he said. "You're the real thing, man." But he didn't sound sure. He didn't about the stealing, either.

We stopped about a block away from the nursing home. I could just see the gazebo and the pond. A slight breeze we couldn't feel was ruffling the water enough to make rapid little waves that stirred the trapped sunlight into pretty sparks from a grinding machine or a fireworks display. The black Vietnam memorial on the grass, a human-sized glassy slab etched with the names of local dead kids, looked more like a tribute to shade in a bright time of burning, when coolness and shadow had been outlawed or forgotten. I could barely see, over the top of the stone, across the pond, through the haze, the middle school I was supposed to attend in the fall. I was sweating, even though I only had my pink tank-top on, and jeans, and maybe that's what made me panic and imagine blood on my thighs.

Toby was crouched in the gutter outside Masson's, tucking his iPod into his bag. Flashlights kept falling onto the curb. He stared at me a long time, I think, and I looked at myself where his eyes should be, afraid my fear showed. I wasn't brave enough to go into the café's bathroom. I remembered how embarrassed my father was a few weeks before when we had to buy my first tampons. I told him to stay in the car. I was glad he didn't. He walked with me down the side aisle of the drug store, read the backs of boxes, compared prices, paid at the register. I looked up menstruation. My mother called it her friend. Science couldn't tell you anything. She probably couldn't have done much better. All the blood was your body keeping itself ready for giving birth—whatever that meant. The sun burns away, too, and should destroy itself, but doesn't. We know nothing. People in charge must get so tired of pretending—parents, too. I do. Why did my father give in to my shame, when we had no reason to be ashamed? Why did I care what Toby would think of a natural condition? Why didn't I tell him I had gone as far as a weak, bloody girl could go?

He crossed the intersection when the light went green. I followed him. He didn't go towards the nursing home. I didn't ask him why. I didn't cry. We went straight ahead, passing Victorian homes made for huge families, with big trees looming in their front yards and a crazy absence of shade on the pale grass. We turned at the library, down Pond Street. The houses here were modern, low to the ground and vulnerable looking. If they were people, I would have wondered how they could survive, why they weren't devoured by the massive, hungry beasts surrounding them, even though you almost never thought that when you looked at small people, or children. You just assumed that everything lived. I didn't assume. I probably did, before; I couldn't remember. Now I think I felt amazement, even resentment, at the existence of the lucky or the resilient, or anything too stupid to die.

Toby stayed ahead of me, in the street. He kept glancing back. I wanted to be mad at him. I wanted to demand my freedom. I was surprised to discover I was wrong about my weakness. And something told me that he wasn't nuts, or if he was, he wasn't alone. I even left the sidewalk and joined him in the sandy gutter. My stomach was a knot. My legs felt like jelly. The baby-voice in my head wanted my uncle to carry me. But then we crossed a crispy lawn and invaded someone's backyard, slipping into a thick nest of green leaves, vines, and shrubbery. I could see the pond. Toby held branches so they wouldn't snap into my face. He didn't catch them all. Our feet slid in soft earth that sloped down toward the water. The wet smells of vegetation I couldn't name and wild flowers I couldn't see attacked me. I recognized a trace of lilacs, which reminded me of home and the purple cans of air freshener my mother used to buy. The sudden shade seemed miraculous enough to make me dream that my uncle was divine.

We descended onto a thin track of mud and stood beside each other. The pond water slapped against small stones, dead branches, and the thin trunks of weak trees lined up on the shore. They had enough leaves on them to conceal us from people whose only concern was their heart rate and longer life, trudging along the path that snaked past tennis courts and soccer fields and the empty student parking lot for the high school. Toby took his backpack off and sat down on a cushion of vines. I sat, too, and pressed my legs together. I was tired. I closed my eyes. The smells were making me dizzy. I was afraid I might sink into the leaves, or the mud, or pour into the water, but not really afraid, since I gave into the spell. We could see and not be seen. I knew that was a big part of it, but I didn't know why.

Toby had a worn, tartan blanket spread out on the mud when I opened my eyes. He was kneeling down in front of me. My feet were pushed up against his thigh, so I couldn't have been pulled into the pond. He was tapping my ankle in a soft, rushed rhythm. I recognized the blanket from our linen closet. I knew it had been with me forever. Since I had memory of a life, that blanket was there. Nothing was ever truer. I wanted more, though. When I half-awoke in that fragrant vegetation with those faded black and red squares in front of me, I prayed for something to come, something of my mother's, of me, something we'd done or felt on that thing that signified everything. Nothing came. Divinity died on the spot. I became as angry as I think I've ever been, but I can't be sure, since what the blanket showed me was how much I'd already lost of all I had ever felt. Why remember the blanket at all, then? Why be tortured with a door into nowhere that made you mad with the comforts of home and the terror of the strange at the same time? If we hadn't stopped in the mud, if we had run together through the branches, bleeding, our clothes catching and tearing, and we drowned in the pond, sinking, defying the science that said dead bodies floated, and someone found the rags we left behind, somehow preserved forever in the trees and vines, a thousand years later, an orphan who lost his family because there were no families anymore, or societies, and who could barely believe there ever were—that's what that blanket was like.

A long, dirty, black leather bag was beside Toby. My mother's Bible was between his knees. He handed me a heavy pair of black binoculars. His sunglasses were off. That must have been what made me think of orphans.

"Your mother wrote me all the time, June, when I was in Iraq." He kept checking his watch, pulling wet leaves out of the thick black straps on the bag. "She wanted to know everything, man, about what I did. I'd get dozens of letters. They were the only ones I got. It's all gore, June. It's all inhuman. And that's what she wanted."

You could hear the breeze you couldn't feel lifting the leaves, flicking the water. The honk of a horn or the screech of tires would waft over the pond and fade at the wall of trees, like a message that didn't matter anymore.

"She asked what the heat did to flesh. She asked about smells. When I didn't give the right answers, she filled in the blanks herself. For pages and pages she'd describe things, man, that if you hadn't already seen them, you couldn't take. But her last note just said she wanted her book back."

Toby ran his fingers over the rippled leather cover of the Bible. When he came home after my mother's funeral, we were up in the attic, kneeling in front of the window, watching snow fall. That was the first time I went past the stairs, and that I remember thinking he was cute, like a little boy. He told me to think of him as a good friend. He told me about Tobit, about how important he was, and that he was in a secret part of the Bible that had to do with the end of the world. A soldier told him he was wrong once, that he was mixing things up. He held up the heirloom and told him to walk away. I didn't say anything.

"She wanted to rip out the New Testament. She bought her own copy, and hated what Jesus said about leaving the dead for the dead. Man, she went red over that. I didn't understand. There are lots of things I don't understand in here. In shooting, June, you go for center mass. Go for the most you'll get, by the numbers. People outside think that's cruel. They want you to wound. If they shot, man, they'd know the comfort. With words it's the same, but different. Center mass changes all the time. In the Marines: no one left behind. So Tobit feels right to me. But Jesus does, too. I wouldn't send her the book."

He unzipped the black bag and told me to focus on the gazebo on the other side of the pond. I had to lean toward the water. I could see the nursing home in the background, over traffic, and remembered his interview. We shouldn't have been in mud and vine. I adjusted the lenses. A man in sandals, brown shorts, and high, white socks was standing inside the gazebo, a hand over his eyes like he was saluting me. He was blocking the sun, following something into the pond. I tracked his gaze and saw a little dog, his knotty fur wet and dark, a leash dangling off his collar as he trotted back from the water to his master: a terrier, maybe. Then clicking noises close by made me think of machines.

Toby was snapping a rifle onto a low tripod at the far end of the blanket. He stretched onto his belly beside me, kicking a filthy flashlight out of the way, and looked through what seemed like another flashlight on the top of the gun.

"Vera had to believe in law, June. She couldn't get how a new law could be no law—how God could send the Son to change it all. At least she couldn't get it at the end. Me, I won't get lost in that shit, man. I can't. I did."

I didn't know what to say. I was sick. I would be sick most of my life. I always wanted to hear about my mother, but what I heard never fit anymore with what I knew, or what I remembered was changing so much that there was nothing real to fit the new stuff into.

I slid down the hill, onto the muddy edge around the blanket. My pants were wet. I was sure I was bleeding to death. I got so mad that I didn't care.

"You see it over there, June, what people will die for. In those places it's more obvious. I mean, smart people are saying Jesus is still in the tomb, man, with a family and everything. Jesus Christ. If he were like the rest of us, you'd say, nice, good for you, man, good for you. Someone buried you with your family. That's the most, man. That's center mass. All those soldiers I carried: that's about what I thought. That's just about all of it. Some guys called them angels. That was a lie, man. Lies keep coming; they keep coming. But Jesus was God, too, so you're supposed to hold your breath and rethink everything, and they know, man, the smart ones who throw that stuff out there, that most people can't. They can't, but if you don't . . ."

"They're cowards," I said.

"No, June. Come on—no. People do what they think will make them sleep, or what will keep them awake in peace. You pick a thing, or a way, and you pray, or you don't. No one can do everything, but you have to do something. They told us not to personalize the dead. Don't look at pictures too long. Don't take anything from the bodies. That was their rule, not mine."

"Is that the man they set free, Uncle Toby? Is that the one to blame for my mother?"

He put his sunglasses back on and stood up. He raised me up and slapped leaves off my jeans. I wasn't embarrassed.

"I watched him, June, for a long time. Routine makes everyone seem so dull. But that is him. I had to keep remembering. That is the bomber."

We were fused together. Everyone was out today, except for my father. I felt bad leaving him behind, like a traitor, but not enough to cry. I took the steps to the gun, with my uncle's hand on my shoulders, and knelt down onto the blanket. Toby crouched across from me. He called the flashlight a scope and told me to look through it. He put my fingers on a ring that I spun until the man was a god standing on the water in front of us. His thin, receding hair was flapping in the breeze that moved the leaves. A cigarette was burning in his mouth. His skin was all pockmarked. Maybe the father he wanted to blow up never told him not to pick his pimples, and he hated him forever. My mother told me, I think, before she died in the car with the engine running in the gutter, with blood and skull on the front seat, and the windows, and in her hair. Maybe she told me on the tartan blanket under a shady tree.

I was crying in Toby's glasses. He took his hand off me and pulled a camouflage flashlight out of a pocket. A dead soldier's name was scratched onto the shaft. He pressed the end. The light came on: a dim, yellow-white circle in our cave of imperfect shade. He leaned over the gun and put it beside me, grazing my cheek with a kiss.

"I can't do it, Juney. I just can't."

I wiped my face. Toby pressed an eye against the scope, turned the ring, and leaned on his elbow and the gun. He put a hand on the barrel and lodged his shoulder against the stock. His face was right next to mine. He waited. I reached for the trigger and flexed my finger. The crack of the gun made me wish I was deaf. Toby's arms shook. I banged my head against his. I picked up the binoculars. The man was gone. I stood up. The thin trees swayed. He was a small, twisted line hanging off the edge of the gazebo. The dog was a black smudge rolling back and forth. The echoes of his yelps reached us late and seemed artificial. The leash I couldn't see made me feel terrible.

Toby was already disassembling the gun. He put the flashlight and the Bible into his backpack, contorted his arms through the straps, and wrapped the rifle in the blanket. I dropped onto the vines while he stuffed the bundle into the long bag. I watched the people across the water, toward the school. Nothing had changed. They were running, walking, talking. No one noticed. Someone must care. Maybe we had become the invisible breeze. My uncle slung the black bag over his shoulder. He swept the mud clear with a leafy branch he tossed into the pond. We crawled up into the stranger's yard and walked out into the middle of the street in the hot sun, toward the railroad tracks. The sudden wail of sirens reintroduced the normal, the law, my father. We passed a dozen people waiting for the train. I was almost glad they noticed us. Toby stared up at an island of soft, cool blue in the sky. We stood at the end of the platform so long that I was certain we were escaping. I felt nauseous. I sat on the hardtop and hoped my pants would dry before my skin burned.

He stepped toward the tracks and looked back at me. We were going home. I couldn't move. I don't even know if I tried. He came over, bent down, and picked me up. The long bag shifted off his shoulder. I tugged on the strap and hugged his neck, my face against the winged snake. I don't remember much of the trip. If I opened my eyes to look forward, the shimmer that liquefied the horizon made my nausea worse. I kept thinking he'd have to rest, and then they would catch us. He never stopped. He just carried everything, even when a train roared past. He moved over—he never touched the rails anyway, and he stepped over most of the ties—but he kept going. The noise and the breeze woke me up a little, enough to believe that Toby was holding me back from being torn out of his arms.

We finally stopped at the dead end of a street that led to my house. A white truck was idling by a receiving dock in the old brick factory that used to make radios during World War II. Ancient ivy thick with shadows crawled up the face of the building and scurried away from windows and doors. Dozens of companies were in there now. One of them was a yoga studio my mother thought about joining. My father said the papers were talking about knocking the place down to build condominiums. I could see our driveway from here. I wished we hadn't sold my mother's car. Toby dropped me and his bags in some high, yellow grass. I heard bugs shriek, or birds. He wiped sweat from his forehead, unzipped the backpack, and put on his headphones.

"I had some white kid from Texas tell me that I liked Tobit because he was a slave. Other guys got mad. Other guys got violent. I didn't care. Like I said, it's a trap I'd been in before. Your mother just got stuck, June. She just forgot; that's all. Remember. Tell your father thanks, even when he won't want to hear my name."

He hugged me so fast that he crushed my arms at my side before I could decide if I wanted to hug him back. I didn't feel sick anymore, just irritated, like when you wake up too soon. He picked up his bags. The animal screams were drowned out by the alarm beeping and beeping on the truck backing up. Toby returned to the tracks, balancing on a rail with his arms out like a boy pretending he was walking a tightrope. He'd stumble off and jump back on. I stood watching him. I thought I was crying again. I was wrong. The heat burning out of the ground ate him up. He got small and didn't look real. That's when I stepped out of the grass to go home, back to my tomb of sandwiches, clean clothes, and familiar things that couldn't keep the truth.

SLUMMING WITH LAZARUS FREDERICK LORD

Now that you're rich with death, relax:
Lazarus has taken you to HEART—
that's <u>HEA</u>ven's <u>R</u>apid <u>T</u>ransit to you, pilgrim.

Now leaving "Valhalla," next stop, "Nirvana."
The doors will open to your right.
Change at "The Great Good Place."

Through all the boroughs of Paradise,
you'll rock until you jerk to a stop
deep in the Ghetto of God.

At Elysian Fields Housing Project,
fingers spread over barrels of burning money,
they free-base God's Grace.

In the only rain that's eternal,
matted Nazarene poking through
the hole in a green trash bag

worn over two rotting sweaters,
a reeking spirit shambles up to you,
mumbling for any large change.

And always through your broken soles
vibrates the afterlife's underground,
rippling the Ripple in your cup.

Or is it because, at last complete
with you, the last of the blessèd damned,
this New Jerusalem now descends?

COMMUTING THROUGH THE RAPTURE FREDERICK LORD

The Weather Channel reported high levels of apocalypse—
the ocean turned to blood—so I skipped the beach for work.

Houses whose cooks had been snatched up by an invisible Hand
burned like heretics on every corner.

The unheard sermons of pilotless planes droned on
past their airports, with panic in First Class.

Rattling up to God like Legos™ up a vacuum cleaner hose,
the True Believers swarmed the sun,

abandoning us True Sinners: televangelists,
Massachusetts drivers, Yankee fans,

divorce lawyers, insurance lawyers, lawyers,
and those who once voted Republican in a weak moment.

Now everyone knows who the real bastards are: us.
My whole department had perfect attendance.

SUBVERSIVE MARYANN CORBETT

Lately, these soggy summer mornings,
yanking myself across the yard
and fumbling to fit my life to the times
of buses grinding the gridded streets,
I wonder about the wan half-smile
of the resin saint on the lawn—Francis,

the garden standard, yes, but a poet.
The surface meaning of his measured line
is not the point, and the visible signs
mislead the mind. For although the sculptor
has fitted the hands with slender finches,
little palmfuls of tractable junco,

the birds the *poverino* preached to
in legend were battle-carrion ravens,
blood-faced with thirteenth-century death.
And here he is still, palming God's love—
the love that loves before anyone bothers
even to wipe the guts from his face—

to raccoons who come up from the river at night
and gnaw the rubber trashcan lids,
to woodchucks who smash the tufa birdbath,
to birds and squirrels who ravage the raspberries.
He stretches his faux-stone hands out: *Fratelli!*

And I suspect that my fenced-in life
is a bad fit for his welcoming smirk,
this poet who spoke to the ravening wolf,
to the leper who stank, to the Saracen.

MID EVIL MARYANN CORBETT

Fortuna rules us both. We're both unhappy.
Someone fell ill, and so I have this course
to teach—I should be glad for this first crack,
but bristle at the absence of control.
You, too, feel like a pawn of random events:
your credit count, your schedule, your last name,
the prodding of advisers. Neither of us
planned on *Intro to Lit. of the Middle Ages*,
but here we both are, hauling ourselves to class
at eight, three times a week.
                            God knows I've tried
to woo you, show you how it's often spring
in Middle English, wintertime in Old,
and why, in so hard a time, someone took pains
to string together words for singing's sake.
And *pains* is the proper word. It was *labora*
and *ora* too: the calves slaughtered for vellum,
the skinning, scraping, chalking, scoring with lines,
the cutting of pens from quills. *Pain* is the word
for what it cost, for the years the words have waited
for you.
         You, who are always painfully there,
hard at work ignoring the four-stress line
and the notes of *Sumer is icumen in*.
You make a point of filling classroom space,
near horizontal, legs stretched front, head back,
arms folded, as if to make a narrow target
for the babble I pour over you, as if
to aim it right between my eyes: your boredom
with low-tech words in a language you don't speak.

MARYANN CORBETT

And the last blow is this, your final exam,
in which, over and over, you call the course
mid evil literature. Yes, I suppose
for you that is the word. We both are learning.
In future I expect I'll be more guarded,
teaching the poems, holding back the heart.
You'll claim your paper. Mild civilities
will be exchanged, and then you'll lope away,
a sad C minus in your grip ensuring
we're done. It's mid-December. Snow will fall—
hrim ond hrith, but no one says that now,
since this is the sphere of Time, beneath the moon,
where everything must change, and where the poems
evaporate like hoarfrost in the sun.

READING THE FIRE CODE MARYANN CORBETT

Words as dry as kindling—*shall, shall not*—
    The aisle width shall be measured from the seat back.
    The required width of the aisles shall not be obstructed—
Like Deuteronomy. A rigid text.

Lift up the page and feel your nostrils flare.
They pull away from the sharp burnt-offering smell:

These twenty lines of new and amended law,
the permit rules for indoor pyrotechnics,
are the ruins of a nightclub in Rhode Island—
yes, you remember now: the foam on the walls,
the spark, the flashover.

                        These old provisions,
law that has stood for years, with its command
Doors to remain unlocked during business hours—
these are the ash of mourning, these are the sackcloth
for a bar in New York, the last cry of the trampled
at the padlocked exits.
                      And threaded among the words
that dictate the maximum distance from the hydrants,
that insist on the fire escape, the means of egress:
sounds of a poem (the Triangle Shirtwaist fire,
the seamstresses falling into eternity)
whisper to those with ears to hear.

                                 The lines
are calm on the page, their nerve ends burned away.

THE DEATH OF NEW AURORA DAVID BOROFKA

IN THE SMALL HOURS OF A MORNING IN 1978, the Clackamas County Sheriff's Deputies raided the home in which my wife and I were living. We were not the only ones dragged away in handcuffs since we lived with twelve other couples, three single men, four unmarried women, and a mixed assortment of children and newborns, dogs and cats and chickens and goats in an old barn some distance east of Oregon City, Oregon, where we called ourselves the New Aurora Colony and answered to the leadership of Bonner and Rachel Sidwell. Maybe you've heard of them?

    A barn is not much of a house, I'll admit, but that's no reason to arrest everyone living in it. I had lived there for five years, and it was the home that I knew. When the deputies came, I was fogged with sleep, and I'm told that I kept asking, "Why? Why are you doing this? I don't understand." Over and over and over again. As it turned out, the reasons were more complicated than the deputies had patience, and if you read *The Oregonian* in the days following our arrest, you wouldn't have been any better informed either since the raid occurred the day after the bodies were discovered in Jonestown. We looked through page after page of *The Oregonian*, expecting to see our names exposed and our reputations ruined, but all we saw were photos of South American jungle with body bags lined up like a boardwalk. An inventory of the deceased filled an entire page. What were we, a mere thirty-three pilgrims, that anyone should take notice or care? Evidently the powers that be had decided we were a threat they could not afford to let materialize. Jonestown was a cautionary tale and the authorities put themselves on notice. Later we heard the rumors that the police had acted on: Satanic ritual abuse, corruption of minors, white slavery, drug abuse. How could anyone have believed it of us, small and mostly happy family that we were? Who could have told such lies?

That night, after the evening confession, I had taken off my glasses and brushed my teeth, washed my face and inspected my gums. Tammy wore a flannel nightgown, a present from one of the other women in our group, since the nights of November were cold and the barn had no insulation. She touched me on the shoulder, my child bride, and hugged me around the waist. That touch and hug could mean many things, but that night we decided that it meant we were happy and content, glad to be part of a larger family, which even now we could hear snuggling into their beds, and—in one or two instances—snuggling into each other. For it is impossible to be discrete inside rooms not much more private than the stalls built for the original inhabitants of our barn, just four-by-eight sheets of plywood nailed together like a house of cards. Why, the walls did not even come close to the roof! There was all that airy space above our heads, and sounds drifted willy-nilly among the rafters. We turned the lantern down, slipped under our blankets, and huddled against one another for warmth.

Only to be awakened five hours later by the sound of yelling and the beams of flashlights and electric lanterns pointed directly into our eyes.

"Let's go, let's go," the shadows were shouting. "Outside. Now."

Beds were overturned, babies were crying.

I held my hand in front of my face. Half a dozen men wearing helmets and armored vests had circled our bed with their rifles at the ready.

"Yes," Tammy said, holding her hands up. "Okay. We're getting up."

"Why are you doing this?" I said. "I don't understand." Over and over. "We've been invaded," I said when the fog had lifted slightly. "This is a declaration of war. Where's Bonner?" I said. "Where's Rachel?"

"Shut up," one of them said, and he used his rifle butt none too gently against my shoulder.

They marched us outside into the ghostly half-light before dawn. Mt. Hood bulked in the eastern distance, a darker silhouette. In an hour, the sun would rise behind it, but by that time we had been searched and handcuffed and loaded into vans for the slow, winding trip to Oregon City.

"This is an outrage," I said. "Why are you doing this?"

The officer sitting next to the driver turned around and looked at me through the mesh. He had a mustache that looked like the grille of a 1956 Pontiac. "You don't need me to tell you," he said. "You tell me what you've done," he said as though to scold me. "Confession is good for the soul. Follow the leader." And then, "I'm not the criminal. I'm not the one being arrested."

"I'm a college graduate," I said. "I teach seventh grade math. That may be a fool's errand, but it's no crime."

"Whatever," he said, turning the back of his head to me.

"We don't have to stand for this," I said.

"Whatever," he said again.

Tammy leaned her head against my shoulder. "*Ssh*, let it go for now," she whispered. "We'll get it straightened out. It's just some kind of mistake. A terrible mistake." She tapped on the mesh. "We're Christians," she said to the back of the officer's head. "Each and every last one of us. And it's a sorry state of affairs if that's a worry to the police."

"You're the oddest bunch I ever heard of," he said, not bothering to turn around and face us. "For Christians, that is."

What did they have on us anyway? Last I heard being poor in this country was no felony, just a misdemeanor. We may have been rich in love and long on education, but as a group we were as poor as trash—there was no denying it—so I suppose our place within the community had suffered accordingly. Someone had brought false witness, so there we were.

Oh, Jesus, Jesus, Jesus, I prayed silently, *what have we done to deserve this? We paid our bills, the ones that I know of.*

But that's the point: all those unpaid bills you never know about until the due date is past and gone.

So you hate us that much. Is that the way it is? I prayed, but evidently, not wishing to abrogate the position of faith, the King of kings and Lord of lords was silent, and I had no idea what His answer might have been.

Meanwhile, the van twisted and turned along our sluice of country roads. The cops kept to themselves, and when rain began to fall as it does so often in that green paradise, the windshield wipers slapped back and forth, back and forth. In the beam of the headlights the drizzle looked like a curtain of sequins. Tammy fell asleep with her head on my shoulder, and my back was beginning to cramp, but I was loathe to shift her away. I've discovered that you can push people away for your own comfort, but then it starts to become a habit. So when the van pulled to a stop, I walked into the Clackamas County Courthouse as twisted and arthritic as an old man. There was a photographer outside the courthouse waiting for us, and he caught me trying to unkink the muscles in my shoulder and neck, and the picture made me look like a flamingo cleaning under its wing. Since they were still running photos of body bags, *The Oregonian* didn't run the picture right away, and after a week I thought I was in the clear, but then a month after our arrest, I opened up a copy of *The Fresno Bee* only to see myself as the product of syndication: crippled and in the handcuffs of a previous life. I was stunned by the doubleness of seeing myself in two places, two times, in two disparate circumstances, for by that time Tammy and I had been relocated to the dusty, barren heart of California and told to begin a new life.

WHICH WE DID. WE DID. Thirty-three pilgrims wearing our handcuffs along with our confusion. It was illegal what they did to us, we knew that even as it happened, but we were all too tired to argue. It makes me wonder if we were so happy in our barn, after all.

Maybe we were looking for a change, and we were glad for the intrusion of an authority outside ourselves. Who knows? No matter what, they scattered us like the nation of Israel, banished to remote outposts around the country. Some went south, others east. I heard that one couple, Aaron and Brenda Caldwell, were given bus tickets for Lubbock, and when they arrived, Aaron had to be hospitalized, his depression was so severe. Tammy and I traveled to Fresno, which was bad enough, and moved into the apartment that had been arranged for us, a one-bedroom, furnished, courtesy of the authorities who had taken our statements and found us to be mostly truthful if not the most cooperative of witnesses. We were very disoriented. Seven hundred miles south of what we knew. We had come from a place where the rain is constant and the land is green. As we dropped lower and lower on the map, Tammy wept each time the bus pulled into another depot. Dust boiled around the tires and rose past the windows like unanswered prayer. There were fewer and fewer trees, and everything looked parched. Even the asphalt was cracked. And this was late December! By the time we arrived in Fresno, the shock was still setting in.

"Oh, honey," she said, "this can't be. I didn't find my life just to lose it all over again."

"It's what we've come to," I said, "and there's no going back. We'll just have to make the best of it."

The air inside the depot smelled like diesel and sweat. We called for a cab. Forty-five minutes later a black station wagon the size of a hearse pulled to the curb. The driver looked at our shabby plastic suitcases and didn't bother to lower the back window. Everything we owned fit on our laps in the back seat. He drove us from the diagonal streets of downtown while he whistled "The Daring Young Man on the Flying Trapeze" and watched us in his rearview mirror. The address was on North Fruit.

"What do you think of that part of town," I said, "where we're going to live?" We had passed entire blocks of pawn shops and adult book stores, all down at the heels. Nothing that some fresh plaster and paint and a new economic structure couldn't solve. "It's okay, isn't it?"

"Could be worse," our driver said. "Could be better. Take your keys out of your car, if you know what I mean."

"We don't have a car," Tammy said.

"Well, then. You see? You're better off."

The Tropics, our apartment complex, was a circle of two-story buildings around a miniature pool. A liquor store slumped on the nearest corner. I paid the driver with a collection of limp one-dollar bills.

He thanked me and said, "Life is a banquet, you know, but you can't be afraid to eat."

"There's no going back," I said, giving him another dollar, "that's true enough. Even if we could. There's nothing to go back for." For by this time, we already knew that the deputies had torched our barn; they had been more than happy to tell us about it: how they had ignited it with an army surplus flamethrower, and in thirty minutes the fire had done its work.

"There's nothing to go forward for either." Tammy eyed the faded green stucco of our new home. "This is not how I pictured paradise," she said. She stared at the palm trees that rose thirty, forty, fifty feet into the hazy air. She was a child of the Northwest, and her vision of Eden included fir trees, dark rainy skies, and a smattering of snow. Bonner and Rachel Sidwell had been part of that vision, too, of course. They had told us what was right and what we were to do. They had loved us and cared for us as though they were the mother and father that Jesus had intended for us all along.

THERE'S NOTHING SO BAD, IT CAN'T GET WORSE. Then again, it can always get better, and if Christianity is built on anything, it's built on grace and the notion that things can get better even if there doesn't seem to be a reason why that should be so. And since no one gets a guarantee one way or the other, what's to be gained by pessimism? Even when the great teacher of experience says otherwise. We prayed for the health of our extended family, but we were raided like gamblers in the middle of an illegal game. We prayed to be reunited, and they loaded us onto a bus bound for the dusty and forgotten heart of California.

Oh, we were hard shelled optimists! And we were persistent. We prayed, and we hoped, and we planned our family even after we were told that Tammy was not likely ever to have a baby.

We were still reeling from that news—the status of Tammy's fertility—as well as the raid, the day we stepped off the bus in Fresno. In the wake of our eviction from New Aurora, there had been doctors and counselors and psychologists as well as law enforcement, and it was during her medical examination that an OB/GYN delivered the bad news. He wore a white labcoat with a pocketful of pens, and he spoke as though commenting upon the weather. "You know you'll never have children," he had said. "An embryo wouldn't stick there with suction cups." He worked with women every day, and he must have enjoyed abusing them, especially someone like Tammy who was wearing the county-issue jumpsuit. She was just another felon to him. What a sensitive soul, he was. So then Tammy broke down, and out came the shrinks. We were fascinating for a while, and when we weren't any longer, they put us on the bus for Fresno, and I suppose that's when we began to explore the dangerous territory of our own imaginations. We were just playing around, I thought, inventing a more bearable alternative. We let ourselves pretend that our move to Fresno was the result of a job transfer. We didn't ask questions, we invented answers whole cloth. We manufactured histories as complex as case studies for the children we didn't have and the families that we did. We imagined that the stranger next to us in our bed at night was someone that we knew.

* * *

But to get back to our new, unwished-for life: our landlady at the apartment complex was a fifty-something widow named Phyllis Garabedian who knew everything about us, every rumor, down to the last mistaken detail.

"There will be no rituals and no animal sacrifices," she said when she handed us the keys to our apartment. "Not here. I will not tolerate it. And no kinky sex, you get me? No children, no threesomes. What I see, I report to the authorities. No reason to let this go on."

She was a woman who didn't stand for any nonsense, and she addressed every issue directly. If she didn't like someone, she wrote an eviction notice, no matter what a tenant's rights might be. And it wasn't just the behavior of others; she didn't like the five gray strands at either temple, so she dyed her hair as black as night; she plucked her jagged eyebrows and drew them back on again as perfect curves.

"I don't understand," I said. "I don't understand at all. We were the victims of false accusation. By whom, I will never know nor understand. The police moved in, they threw us out of our home, and then they told us to go elsewhere. Those charges were never proven. There was nothing to prove."

"If I believed that there was," Mrs. Garabedian said, "you wouldn't be here. But I figured a warning wouldn't hurt. Know what I mean?"

Our rent was paid for three months, and we had been given a small settlement, though by our communal standards it seemed like an enormous windfall. They did that so we wouldn't sue, I guess. Pain and suffering, the loss of our barn. The disruption of our lives. The forced deportation that none of us ever questioned. None of us ever took the bastards to court, unfortunately, just to see them squirm. The county was embarrassed, but so were we, and we were easy to buy off. I suppose that on some level we felt guilty about something, even if we weren't. We were so used to confessing every evening we must have believed we *had* done something wrong.

And after five years in a barn, our modest apartment seemed the height of luxury. We bought food from a grocery store where the produce was set out like jewelry, and the winter weather in Fresno was so mild as to seem a mistake. But, oh, how miserable we were! We moped inside during the day, having nowhere to go and no means to get there, and for the nights we bought a television, a thirteen-inch reconditioned motel set with a pair of rabbit ears. With our government funds we could have bought something new, but we were creatures of poverty and thrift, old habits being what they were. We brought our purchase home, plugged it in and left it on for two weeks straight. It burbled even while we slept. We watched *Three's Company* and knew we'd been abandoned. Oh, Jesus, what a world, what a world!

One morning Tammy turned the dial to *Sesame Street*; I showered and brushed my teeth to the sound of Elmo and Oscar, and when I sat down for breakfast, there was milk puddled on the table and Tammy's hands were over her face and tears were leaking between her fingers.

"What's the matter?" I said. "It's just spilled milk. I'll get a towel and it'll be gone this quick."

"It's the children," she said. "I miss them, and I can't stand the separation."

I didn't understand her meaning at the time because I thought she was talking about the distance between ourselves and the children we might have had.

A few weeks later she invited Mrs. Garabedian for dinner. In the meantime, Tammy had insisted that we have our photograph taken at a studio near our apartment. The photographer specialized in portraits and period costumes. I wore a suit that must have belonged to Wyatt Earp while Tammy looked like Lily Langtry and the brown photograph an artifact; anyone looking at it would have assumed that the figures in it—the man sitting in his brocaded vest, the woman with her hand on his shoulder—had been dead for years. "It's a death mask," I joked when I saw it. "We're not bad for a couple of corpses."

But when Mrs. Garabedian sat in our living room, Tammy began to give her a new version of our history, one that even I had not heard before, and she brought out the photograph as proof, claiming it was from our wedding album. Our two-year-old twins, she said, were with their grandparents—her parents who loved the chaos of a large and happy family and didn't mind taking care of them while we got ourselves settled. Mrs. Garabedian would have had no reason to doubt Tammy's story except that she already knew our biographies from the police report. Besides Tammy was a terrible liar, as though she wanted Mrs. G. to know the lies for what they were. Every whopper was as obvious as she could make it.

"We were married in a meadow by a Methodist minister," Tammy said.

"It's a tongue twister more than the truth," I said. "If you can say that five times in a row, you're a better man than I."

Tammy ignored me. "He married us at dawn, just as the sun was coming up behind the mountains. The sky was streaked pink and gold, and it was the happiest day of my life," she said to Mrs. Garabedian who looked more than a little skeptical.

"But now," Tammy said, "my babies are seven hundred miles away, and I miss them terribly."

"That must be difficult," Mrs. Garabedian said, looking carefully into Tammy's eyes. "It's so hard to be so far away."

"It's awful. We talk on the phone, but they're not old enough to understand."

"Yes," I said, and I was also looking hard at my wife. "We're lucky that Tammy's parents are so kind. Because we know how well the children are cared for, since they're such wonderful people."

"It's a blessing," Tammy nodded. "God is good."

Tammy had made a meatloaf, her one specialty, and Mrs. Garabedian had brought two bottles of wine, and we talked and talked. Our conversation, however, could have been scripted, it was so constrained by current events and political topics; we managed to steer clear of the more controversial subjects such as marriage and children, religion and the law, concentrating instead on interest rates and the failing presidency of that lust-filled Christian, Jimmy Carter. Tammy, whose previous drinking had been confined to the odd beer she and her sisters had stolen from her stepfather's cooler, gulped three glasses of wine and passed out at nine on the sofa.

"Oh, my," she said, crawling onto the cushions, "I'm sorry to be like this." A moment later we heard her snore.

Mrs. Garabedian set her glass down and covered my hand with her own. "I don't know what you're doing, robbing the cradle like this, but this little-girl wife of yours is going to need some help. That much is clear. She's sweet and kind, but she's a child and mad as a March hare. You can see that, can't you?"

"It may seem that way," I said, "but there's a reasonable explanation: we've been under quite a bit of stress of late. What with the move and all."

"Bullshit," Mrs. Garabedian said. Have I mentioned that her late husband had been a union machinist, and she had picked up his salty way of speaking? "Bullshit," she said again. "She's nuts. And the longer you wait to get her help, the sicker she's going to get. This isn't something you can ignore."

"Well," I began, "I'm not sure—"

"Come outside with me."

We put on our jackets. The weather may have been mild by Oregon standards, but there was a chill in the air, and the damp made haloes around the street lamps. I opened the drapes in the living room so I could see Tammy stretched out on the couch while Mrs. Garabedian pulled a pack of Kools from the pocket of her jeans. She stuck one of the mentholated cigarettes between her lips and used a disposable lighter to get it going.

"I'll never understand how people can get so messed up," she said.

"I don't understand it either," I said. "You knew our marriage was arranged, didn't you? She ran away from a terrible home, and I was available. Bonner thought it would be best. One day I'm single, the next day I'm married. So what if she's sixteen? God's will be done. One day we're having a prayer session, the next we're in jail. It's a crazy mess all right, and I can't even try to explain it. I give God the praise, but some times I wonder if even He knows what's going on. Tammy is just trying to comfort herself. She's telling herself a story, and maybe she'll feel better for it."

"It was more than Jesus ever did for us," I added, betraying my own sense of bitterness. Let's face it: Mr. Lord and Savior never bothered to return a call.

"Why blame Him?" Mrs. G. said. "It's not like you're the first ones to take some heat, you know. Face it: Jesus got sold out for thirty pieces of silver. You're in good company." She blew smoke from her nose and pulled her jacket tighter. "You kids are feeling beat up, you wouldn't be human if you didn't, but at some point you're going to have to rejoin the world. A job would be good. You need the work more than you need the money. And you need something to occupy your time other than that lousy TV."

She thanked me for the dinner and retrieved her purse from the living room. "I don't understand much about your lives," she said, looking at Tammy on our couch, the rise and fall of her breathing, "but this isn't healthy. Not to my way of thinking. If I've offended you, don't mind me."

"That's okay," I said. "I don't understand anything either."

"I'm serious."

"So am I," I said.

When she was gone, I knelt beside the couch. Tammy was still asleep, or so I thought, and I took pleasure in watching her. And pain, I can't deny it. Pain was there too. She had dressed up for the evening, putting on her best flannel shirt to go with her newest pair of jeans. At New Aurora, she could have been accused of putting on airs. For that matter, the scent of her drugstore perfume still lingered at the base of her throat, where she had dabbed it three hours earlier in such quantities that I couldn't help coughing, the bathroom was so full of the scent. Gardenia, honeysuckle, I couldn't tell. "Sweetheart," I said. "Honey. Dear one. We're in trouble up to our eyeballs if this is the way it's going to be. Mrs. Garabedian thinks you're a loon and fading fast. Fun is fun, but there's the truth and then there's fiction."

"Jes' foolin'," Tammy mumbled with her eyes closed. "You know me."

"We have no children, your parents are rotten to the core, and we were married in a barn underneath a brown army blanket."

"No kidding," she said. "I had no idea."

"This is no time for fun and games," I said. "It's time to face the facts."

"The Miss'sippi River is seventeen miles long," she said. "Seventeen hundred? Thousand? None of the above? How about them facts?"

"More jokes," I said. "Why are you being like this?"

"Being like what?" she said.

MRS. GARABEDIAN WAS AS GOOD AS HER WORD. Better, in fact, for that good woman had a heart that was more suited to social work than property management. She arranged an interview for me with a private GED school, catering to the failed offspring of the wealthy and dissatisfied. A friend of hers, a druggist, offered Tammy a part-time job two evenings a week working the cash register at his store three blocks away from our apartment.

Tammy was especially grateful, and when she woke up the morning after our dinner party, she vowed never to touch alcohol again, her headache was so vile, and to apologize she baked four pans of brownies, one of which she gave to Mrs. Garabedian, and the rest Tammy distributed to the elderly women in our complex.

So we settled into the routine of our new lives. The newspaper arrived in the mornings, I went to work with my lunch in a brown paper sack like any other wage slave, and we watched the news at dinner, governing ourselves against sloth so that the moment the news hour was over, we unplugged the set and put it back into the closet. On Wednesdays and Fridays, I walked Tammy to the drugstore at seven o'clock, kissed her at the doorway, and returned to pick her up again at midnight. She was paid minimum wage, but one of the perks was a twenty percent discount on any of her purchases, so each morning after her evening of work, I found new bottles of floral-scented perfume lining the counter of the bathroom sink.

Now and then, we heard from a few of our brothers and sisters from New Aurora. Brenda Caldwell wrote, saying that once Aaron was out of the hospital they planned to move back to the Northwest, Seattle preferably, where Aaron had friends and the possibility of a job. She included a list of names and addresses, the ones she'd been able to find after a month or more of searching phone books and directory assistance. One of the couples whose address or phone number she hadn't been able to find was Bonner and Rachel Sidwell and their son Joshua. Did we know anything about what might have happened to them? No one else had heard a thing. It was as if they had vanished along with our barn. Their absence was dire and foreboding and an intimation of dirty tricks, the disappeared, and unmarked graves. The morning of the raid had been so chaotic that no one remembered seeing them loaded into one of the vans or processed at the county courthouse, but then it was all so dark and disordered. It was funny, Brenda mused in her letter, we had all been so close to each other and sanctified for service to the Lord—we were so special, unique in His sight—and now look at us: so distant from each other and no different from anyone else on the face of the planet.

At the end of our second Fresno spring, I had a week of vacation time and money in my wallet, a fact which still took me by surprise. Tammy and I took the train to Portland, and we rented a car, so we came back to Oregon as private citizens rather than as wards of the state. Still, we felt as disoriented as we had when we left, maybe more so. Like looking through the wrong end of a telescope. We drove to Oregon City through brilliant sunshine, turned east, and then fifteen minutes later, we were turning off the highway into the rutted New Aurora driveway. We were looking for something in the charred remnants, the bits and pieces of what had once been. What we found was our barn. Well, it looked like the same barn, but this barn had a fresh coat of red paint, the shingles and windows repaired, and a neat row of rhododendrons and chrysanthemums flanking either side of the door.

"Did we make a wrong turn somewhere?" Tammy said, looking behind us toward the highway.

"I'm sure we made several," I said, "but who would know?"

Just then the door opened, sliding across on its tracks to reveal Rachel Sidwell carrying an infant in a Snugli against her maternal front while she held the hand of a stocky, tottering toddler. She looked up when she saw the car, guilty thing that she was, but then she put on the bravest of hostess smiles and walked toward us with her arms outstretched.

She was alive and healthy and apparently no worse for wear.

"It's the both of you," she cried. "And here. You get a chance to meet Elizabeth." She pointed to the pink knit cap slumped against her chest.

"And can that be Joshua?" Tammy said, pointing to the toddler who had dropped to his bottom and was drawing with his fingers in the dirt. "That big boy over there?"

"In the flesh," Rachel said. "And who would have ever thought the two of you would come back?"

"Not me," I said. "As devastated as we were? I never would have believed it. Not in a million years. But time has flown, that much is sure."

"The barn looks nice," Tammy said. "Nicely rebuilt."

"It's a funny thing," I said. "No one knows where you are because you never left home."

"There's a story in all this," Rachel said, "if you have a mind to listen."

She offered us coffee and a chance to talk, so we followed into the darker interior. Gone were the plywood walls and the chinks of light from the poorly mended roof. There was an up to date kitchen fit for a restaurant with a stainless steel oven and a four-burner gas stove. A high chair stood at the end of a new dining room table and chairs.

She and Bonner had made a deal. They were property owners after all, and we were merely squatters. So after the raid, when the vans had taken the rest of us away, Bonner and Rachel were left behind, negotiating with the Sheriff and the county's legal counsel. It took three days of bargaining, but in the end they had the legal advantage since no crimes could be established. They agreed not to sue in return for capital improvements to the barn—which was never burned, that was just a story they put out so that we wouldn't be tempted to return—and a sum of money larger than they had hoped to imagine, although it was much smaller than a potential court judgment might have been. So said the lawyers they consulted after the fact. So even then we had been cheated. They also agreed not to contact any of us or to start another community. New Aurora was dead and there was to be no resurrection.

"The settlement you received," Rachel said. "We negotiated that."

"And did you tell them to send us to Fresno?" I said. "That garden spot, where it rains every seventh year?"

"Look," Rachel said, "we did the best we could. Given the circumstances. After all, they raided us looking for horrors, but the two of you were the only crime they found. Statutory rape is serious, you know."

"I warned Bonner," I said. "You were there."

"We were lucky that they were willing to overlook an indiscretion here and there. Bonner said if they weren't so embarrassed, everything might have been different. As it was, they wanted to wash their hands of us."

"So where is he?" I said. "Where is the old horse trader?"

"Bonner is at work, if that's who you mean," Rachel said.

"Bonner at work?" I said. "This must be the first job he's ever had."

"He's in marketing."

"Okay, so he's still not working," I said. "Just selling another illusion."

"Baby," Tammy said. "Don't be mean."

"It was awful for us too, you know. We died that day, to see our family leave. But we did what was best for everyone's sake," Rachel said, sniffling. And then in that way of babies, Elizabeth woke to her mother's grief and began to cry as well. "We did what Jesus told us to do."

"I'm sure you think that," I said. "And meanwhile, here you are—in Paradise with babies and barn of your own while we're eating the heat and dust along with the rest of the Dust Bowl survivors. Just another pair of Okies, trying to fit in."

"Isn't that the way it is?" Rachel said. "We all have to grow up, don't we? Some time or another. We all have to move on with our lives. Even New Aurora gets replaced by something else. Look at the old colony. Wilhelm Keil. All those pious Germans. So serious and hard-working. No fun whatsoever."

At that point Tammy and I must have looked a little glassy-eyed because she asked if we knew the story of Wilhelm Keil. We did not. Why should we? I had lived at New Aurora for five years without a thought of what might have gone before.

"What's the point of being the New Aurora then, if you haven't heard of the Old?" Rachel said.

This Keil was a tailor and dressmaker, and depending on his audience, a pharmacist trafficking in patent remedies who insisted he be called "doctor." Despite his vocational shortcomings, he believed that God had better things in store. In 1855 he gathered a group of like-minded believers together and they traveled from Missouri to the Pacific Northwest. He had promised his son Willie that he would lead the caravan of God's people to their western paradise. But then with the inconsiderate nature of youth, Willie contracted malaria and died. Believing that a promise is a promise even to those no longer among the living, Dr. Keil ordered a coffin built. Lined in lead then filled with whiskey, the coffin was mounted on the foremost wagon of the caravan and Willie was interred. For two thousand miles Willie Keil's pickled body, sloshing in its coffin, led the colonists through plains and mountains.

"And do you know what?" Rachel said. "After all that, after two thousand miles of hauling Willie's body over mountain and plain, they buried him in the wrong place."

Briefly settling for a time in Willapa Bay, Washington, Dr. Keil buried his son on the road between Raymond and Centralia. They sang a song of his own composition, "Das Grab Ist Tief Und Still" ("The Grave is Deep and Quiet"). Then, disappointed by the rain, the densely-forested hills, and the site's remoteness from any other settlements, Dr. Keil led his followers back east, then south to the site of what would become Aurora Colony.

"Half an hour from where we're sitting," Rachel said. "Aurora thrived for thirty or forty years. Until Keil died that is, and then, the colony fell apart. But Willie's still in Washington."

"That's your Wilhelm Keil," I said, "or your Bonner Sidwell. Snake-oil salesmen like all the rest. He couldn't even sell whiskey without calling it medicine or embalming fluid. Another form of marketing."

"Bonner will be sorry he missed you," Rachel said. "I'll tell him you were here. I would invite you to stay for dinner, but . . ."

Her voice trailed off. We stared at Elizabeth who had settled down against her mother, at Joshua who was playing with a truck on the kitchen floor.

"It was you, wasn't it?" Tammy said. "I just figured it out. God, I am so slow." She had been silent for some time listening to Rachel and me talk across the table, and now she was tapping her forehead with her fists. "It's taken me all this time. You were the one who called. You were tired of being the mother of a brood. Isn't that right? You were tired of having so many children. Babies your own age. How could you?

"Did we know you were unhappy? How could you not tell us?

"How could you abandon your beloveds?"

AGREEMENT JENN BLAIR

And the people changed their mind.
They said only give us potato logs and bacon slabs
and not too many Baptist churches set back in the trees.
Give us clean hearts and even cleaner restrooms.
Let the heron in flight pause until
the children in the backseat have a chance to see it—
Do not bother us overmuch and Sundays
we will lavish you with the coins we have saved all week
give you any inheritance we can scoop up off the top
of the nicked dresser, counter corners.

Let us wander Sinai forever, with oversized drinks.
Give us gas stations evenly spaced
and let the road kill be not too distressing.
And we—we in turn—will fling out a praise
over the wheat fields and silos we swiftly pass
—loudly bless those who pin themselves
down long enough to wring bread and vegetable
sweat from the thin, pinched furrows.

NOTE JENN BLAIR

The tall woman stood at the front and told us
about how faith existed on the far ocean
as a poor woman would receive a piece of
scripture and bake it in a loaf of bread
to keep it safe from the soldiers already
knocking down the door. Sitting on the shag
green carpet it was easy to lower my head
and pretend I was a martyr, hiding
down in the catacombs singing a song
of praise to pass the days full of night,
trembling underground in Cappadocia
as the horses' hooves rumbled over my
pale altar gathered visage, unsettling
but not snapping my bones.

Then a thin man stood and said something
was eating his organs but that he still
wanted to thank God for his life and
the way that early morning fell down
inside the leaves of the Oaks running
along the edge of his backyard fence
and when I slept that night I dreamed
I wrote him a note and tucked it away
in the soft fleshy curves of the dough.
But when I awoke I was scared I had
left the paper blank or that the words
maybe had all burned off in the fire.

CATHOLIC WORKER RICK MULLIN

The painter, Georges Rouault, finds human texture
in the metal part of Sainte Chapelle,
in the neglected fraction. Red lapel
stigmata and the carbon-capped prefecture
tie his jurist to the man of sorrow,
and his harlot to the aged clown.
A dutiful apprentice, he might drown
in misery today, in light tomorrow.

Delivered to the bombing of the Commune,
baptized in the radical vanguard
of modern art, he wandered on the street
of refugees, a witness to the brickyard
and that constant echo in the blood-strewn
alleys: Take this, all of you, and eat.

MAN NAILED TO CROSS IN PHILIPPINES CHRIS FLOWERS

was the headline that caught my eye,
printed in no-frills font above a pixilated
photograph of a contemporary crucifixion.

His body was dark and gaunt, both arms outstretched,
bound tightly to planed wood with clean lengths of rope.
It turns out he had miraculously survived a fall
from a twelve-story building as a construction worker
and this was his way of thanking God.

Long spikes, polished silver, disappeared
into the whites of his palms—
a spectacle that hinged on illusion—
a modern-day Houdini that executed
his grand finale in the presence of thousands,

their jaws clenched, hands frozen in mid-air
struggling to raise him as gently as possible.
His loins were covered with a starched cloth:
it reminded me of a painting that hung top-heavy
in the narrow room where I attended confirmation class.

Men in pastel robes flocked to a Jesus
that looked oddly familiar in the Sunday morning light,
red beard, blue eyes, fluid hair—
skin the color of talc. *An Irish rock star?*
Blood snaked from his hands in symmetrical ribbons.

Stark cherubim hovered, trumpets in hand,
wings glowing florescent in a backlit haze,
their eyes distant and unintelligible, as if dreaming
of the days there was something to see.

DEBORAH MEG SEFTON

WHEN CURTIS WALKED INTO THE LIBRARY straight up to your desk and your high forehead bent over a reference slip he knew what he was getting, being a man of few illusions. He wanted help with something simple but hard and this called for straightforward zeal. To demonstrate this, he wore black jeans, t-shirt, shoes. He needed a disciple, strong and true. He was not a man who would waste his efforts on some woman who had too much to lose by loving him. He had a cross with a wheel on it that weighed one hundred pounds. Would someone follow him and wipe the sweat off of his brow and refresh him with drink while he hauled it through town? He was going out to the places where women sold their bodies. Your Filipino boss who wore the flower on her dress twitched her bottom between the stacks. You left your desk to follow Jesus. Curtis had all the fire as in days of old when your father stood from the pulpit and the power and the glory showed and a tingling went over your skin like gooseflesh, except when this preacher was done he wheeled his cross to a hotel room and kissed you like you were his water. He laid you out and you were sure. He left the cross in your room. You were pure and intact. Dreams of white drifted down. A dress like snow, a crown of flowers.

YOU WERE NOT GOING BACK TO YOUR WORK at the library, where the homeless talked about electricity in the air, all around. It was strange how they always used to ask you for books, out of all the librarians there, and to you they spilled out their theories about invisible charges, as if you were some kind of conduit. Maybe your father made you that way when he shot you through with the Spirit and then left you empty or maybe Jesus made you vulnerable. It was the sad people who felt the love in you. You saw them coming, down a long row of books, their clothes slipshod and soiled, eyes darting like fish. No matter how high you piled the books on your desk, they found you and then they got you into the stacks and told you, forced on you, what they believed about the material world, its qualities visible and invisible, its causes and effects, existences and essences, their voices climbing to fever pitch, until you slipped them the thunderstorm book, somewhere between 551.5 and 551.6, the cover a dark sky and lightning bolt. That quelled them as if someone had wrapped them in a restraint.

You would not go back there. The tiny librarian who wore a polyester flower on her dress every day did not know anything about how you witnessed the words of the Holy issued from your father's mouth in a church just down the street. She only knew that you didn't fill out your reference request forms neatly so that the other librarians could read them. She's worked at the library for five years and just took her first vacation last year when the library forced her to. Some of the librarians said she still came in her jeans and did some paperwork but this was hard to imagine—the jeans part, not the part about coming in during a mandatory vacation. Every day you knew her, she wore hose and vinyl pumps and dresses with different patterns on them, sometimes a suit jacket if she had a department head meeting. She stood over you some nights and made you rewrite the reference slips. When she was not looking you slipped away to look up books on the Outer Banks, where your parents retired.

How bitter you have been. How you have despised the thought of your father playing golf with your mother in North Carolina. The indentation in the carpet where he used to stand and say goodbye to his parishioners with you was occupied by someone else every Sunday, someone you had never met. When you were the golden girl, you knew the secret place where your father kept his cup, a cup he would sip out of when everyone bowed to pray, right before the sermon. You used to feel its cool smoothness when you went up to the pulpit to play preacher. Who filled it before the service? Only that person and you knew of its existence. You pretended to sip and there was nothing there. Maybe it was a foretaste of what was to come, that you would get nothing, only air and memories.

Why was it that you held onto these dreams of when you were a girl? Was it because it was the last time you remember Jesus that solidly, as solidly as your father's knobby fingers, and his brown eyes kind and soft? You used to meet the copper Jesus in the columbarium on your lunch break and look for your father's face in the burnished cheek, the hollowed out eyes. Copper Jesus stood, no lap for sitting, and the hand he extended was far smaller than your own. You sat on the stone bench in front of the place where your brother's ashes were kept and wondered how your father could be thinking of his chip shot. You grabbed a knot of flowers from the feet of Jesus and scattered them, roots and all, at the foot of your brother's remains. There was no container for the flowers and you wished he were laid out in the ground, like people used to be. Your father helped design the columbarium and you had complained about the lack of flower holders, although by then it was too late.

A redesign would involve a removal of the ashes and hence all kinds of permits and procedures. Perhaps no one had complained of it but you. No wonder no one had been winking at you when they came down the aisle, as a father might his daughter, or a groomsman his bride. You were always such a complainer.

ON THE SECOND DAY OF YOUR DISCIPLESHIP, Curtis offered his mouth to yours. His breath was milky and sweet. You were lying on your back and in the hollow of your neck he placed something metal and small: a tiny silver ring with two hands clasping. More than the promise of marriage, it was a promise that bound you to the God of his mission. He held you like a lover, like Christ loved the church, and yes, you say, yes, yes. No longer were you the golden girl holding the sweaty hand of your father, sweaty from the long exertion in the high pulpit, sweaty when he shook the hands of the parishioners in the narthex.

You called your parents to tell them the good news. Your mother seemed not to hear. She did not know Curtis, did not recognize an engagement ring without a diamond. She described for you a party on a boat where there had been fire-eaters, magicians, a four-tiered chocolate fountain into which the guests dipped cake and fruit. Your mother, you were sure, had pulled your father into this. She had leaned on him until he no longer pounded on pulpits. It's called retirement she said when you complained, when you said he had a calling to preach the Word. You and your father, she said, with your notions and your dreamy dreams, your unrealistic expectations. You reminded yourself that she had lost a child, and sometimes you excused her. In the weeks after your brother's car crashed into the tree, your mother laid her head down on the spot where your brother had been found. She collected bits of glass and looked for small things that might have flown from the car.

On the day of your wedding, Curtis wore a tuxedo and his mother came too, dressed in soft pink, and so did his father, a man with a flat top, still from Navy days. Your parents did not come. It is all done improperly, most improper, objected your mother in that small mincing way. I love you honey, said your Dad. Then your Mom made him get off the phone. All the librarians were there except the Filipino who was likely adjusting her flower, somewhere in the stacks. Ms. Filipino would never marry, you heard the librarians saying, not if Deborah manages to pull this one off and that woman is trying so hard, twitching her backside around and laughing for the good looking men, taking her glasses off for them as soon as she sees them coming. I mean, Deborah of all people, they said, that forehead and that face, not trying to look good at all and then, boom, like grace, someone whisks her away.

The minister by Lake Eola wore a white robe, just like in your dreams, with a stole of intertwining vines. After you exchanged rings, the minister laid his hands over yours and they were warm and sweaty and his exertions made this more than his blessing on the marriage, but a testimony. Jane, the children's librarian, was baptized in the lake afterwards by her own request and this was proof to the minister that the ceremony had been more than the joining of two hearts but a sign of the Holy. Everyone had cake and sparkling grape juice. You were filled up and warm and sat around talking on the amphitheater stage close by the lake, you and your colleagues never having been close until that day—and now you could call them friends—and then someone got the idea to rent the swans that were really paddle boats with a swan facade and you with your new husband, you paddled around and then when you got to the fountain, you jumped in, your white dress floating around you, your feet slipping free of your shoes and everyone jumped in and you all laughed and floated and lost your shoes as if you were ascending.

You took up the cross when Curtis died. Someone avenging the trade of prostitution shot him. You sat in the dim apartment you shared with him for a scant three weeks. You ate the last can of vegetables and then you took the cross to the place where your father had once breathed out the Spirit. On Sunday morning, you wheeled it by the windows so that the parishioners would look out. The cross had a squeaky wheel and was not easy to listen to. You called your parents, the last call you made before your phone service was cut. You told them what you were doing for your Lord, your husband's mission. Your mother complained that you never call early enough, always when they were in bed and yet you were beginning to see what she was about and what she was up against and you told her no matter what, you would always be her daughter. She had been trying to rid herself of you, to be free from pain.

At three months, you could not ignore the change, the cessation of cycles, your growing stomach. Your parents came and you were in their good graces again. It was painfully transparent why: You had fulfilled their desires for a grandchild, but you didn't care anymore about your principles and battles. The hormones and God made you giddy, and you made the Filipino with the flower the godmother. Why not? You knew she will do the right thing by your child. She was so thrilled, she cried and became serious and gave up her twitching. A man finally fell in love with her velvety cheek and the large dark eyes behind her glasses.

You and your parents stood by the baptismal font, along with Angelina, Phillip's godmother. On the other side of a long row of windows where you used to wheel your cross was the columbarium. After the service, you took the cup that was in its secret place behind the pulpit. When no one was looking, you filled it with water from the font, asking God's forgiveness. You poured it on the flowers at the feet of the once ineffectual copper Jesus. Small though he was, he seemed more of a comfort.

Your fire will be a cooling one and in the stone court, your brother will reside in a believer's sleep.

INTIMACY KATIE MANNING

I have known the connection of crackers,
crushed between teeth, marriage of wine and whistle,
all the bonds between body-bread and berry-blood,
a white table cloth wet with purple drops
from a gaudy goblet, wrinkled hands on a child's head,
pink and purple Advent candles lit precariously,
melted wax on the freshly shampooed carpet
inside the white, suburban church.
But I have known intimacy in an old building,
mid-city, where the corner store sells
hot dog buns and cardboard grape juice boxes,
where my neighbor holds *el cuerpo y la sangre*
and never spills on the orange, duct-taped carpet.

SUMMER BURIAL HANNAH E. FRIES

We scraped the bird from the road with sticks.
Bicycles thrown aside, we worked
lost in the self-denying focus of children,
intent on the matted mass of feathers and gore.
Only the beak—whole, hard, uncrushed—
told us for sure. So it was not wings,
not flight at all, but the tiny sharpness
of the mouth that had ceased to sing
that held fiercely the essence of *bird*.
Strange task for the summer holiday,
this claiming of the neighborhood dead—
little undertakers, we lifted them
to sandy ground between wood and road,
covered the mangled forms.
Two twigs tied with grass—our cross—
leaves, pebbles, dandelions to decorate the mound.
This was all we knew: the quick,
the uncatchable, suddenly still on the black tar,
the dimming of a dark round eye, the secret
of the body spilling out,
and the simple acts that smooth the edges of an ending,
gather what's broken to a semblance of order.
Oh crumpled messes of fur or skin or feathers,
poor ruined bodies, endure our little crosses,
forgive our yet unyielding voices.

OCTOBER'S ORCHID JOYCE MAGNIN MOCCERO

I COULD HAVE BEEN NICER, right from the start, but Christ, she pissed me off.

My sister checked herself out of the funny farm A.M.A. with three days worth of meds and a screaming orange ID bracelet strapped around her wrist, then showed up at my house at 2 a.m., sopping wet, carrying a small backpack slung over her left shoulder. She stood there like a shivering stray cat, the porch light reflected in her dilated pupils—the shimmer of a drug-induced, temporary calm. The last time I saw Rona she was wild and manic, painting large wide strokes on a large, wide canvas like a monkey with a brush would. Painting nothing in particular and everything in general with bold, bright, psychedelic colors, ranting and raving about the loud voices, bugs, and God. Swirls of confusion and light coming from arms and legs and disembodied purple petals on the canvas.

To be fair, Rona had a gift—a beautiful gift. She paints—she used to paint with delicate, exacting, sane strokes that made me both jealous and proud—orchids, mostly, dainty velvet petals with sensuous curves and barely distinct folds in stunning colors of purple, orange, and yellow on lanky green stems. Now the orchids are entangled in her brain, and she can't stop being crazy long enough to tease them apart.

"What are you doing here? Haven't you caused enough trouble?"

"Please, Georgia, can I come in? It's pouring rain out here, and I . . . I got no other place. We're still sisters, right?"

"I thought Doctor Schmidt had you committed."

"She did, but I couldn't stand it there any more. It's a terrible place—" she shivered—"Please, let me in? I'm cold. I . . . I walked the whole way."

"Rona, the kids, they're asleep. They've had a rough couple of weeks."

She put an index finger to her lips. "I'll whisper. Promise."

I blocked the doorway. "Look, call Mom. Tell her you want to come home. Tell her you're sorry."

"I can't call her, Georgia. You know she hates me."

Our mother washed her hands of Rona six years ago, the day she crashed the Mercedes and then showed up at the country club wearing nothing but a bra and panties, ranting some nonsense about everything being our mother's fault, bugs and speed limits—ruining my wedding. I watched her skinny body quiver on my porch like a sapling in the chilly October wind. "I'll get you a towel," I said.

It was the least I could do.

When I got back from the laundry room with a warm, blue, terry towel fresh from the dryer, Rona was sitting in my leather sofa leaving a rain puddle on the Persian rug.

"Shit, Rona, look what you did."

"I'm sorry. I . . . I didn't mean to." She wiped the spot with the towel. Then wrapped the towel around her shoulders, still shivering.

"I'll get another one."

"I'm thirsty," Rona said. "The drugs. They dry me out."

"There's water in the fridge."

She returned with a bottle of Deer Park and the towel around her shoulders.

"I got a change of clothes in my pack," she said, "Or are you gonna throw me out?"

"Get changed. I'll call Mom in the morning."

"She won't care, you know. She won't."

Rona came out of the bathroom in a pair of jeans two sizes too large and a red sweatshirt that looked like it had been the former plaything of a pit bull. She threw the pack on my couch and I cringed at the sight of the filthy, worn bag on my upholstery.

God knew where it'd been.

"Geez, you look like shit. I'll get you something decent to wear." Five minutes later Rona was in front of my TV wearing a pair of my jeans—still too large but at least they had a brand, and my striped sweater, an old one I never wore anymore, drinking my water. I gave her a pair of fresh socks and then tossed her clothes in the garbage.

"I couldn't stay there, Georgia. It's a fishbowl. You don't know what it's like, the people, the smells, the . . . awful nurses handing out pills like they're all so superior, watching every move, every step. I know. I watched them watching me."

"But you can't stay here. Isn't there some . . . what do they call it? Halfway house?"

"They're just as bad." Rona clicked on the TV and started flipping channels.

"Keep the volume down," I said, "The boys . . . your nephews, asleep upstairs."

She muted the television.

"You'll find a blanket and a pillow in the hall closet. Sleep in the den. The sofa folds out."

The next morning I found her, curled like an armadillo on the kitchen floor, rocking back and forth and whimpering about bugs.

"Where's your meds?" I asked urgently. I searched her backpack and found a small watercolor—an orchid, four delicate blooms—smeared by last night's rain I thought. Rain-smothered, but otherwise, a perfect flower. Oh, Rona.

She snatched it. "It's not yours."

"I'm sorry. It was right there."

She wiped it with the back of her hand against her thigh—hard, harder. "Damn rain, goddamn rain. Ruins everything."

She looked at me, and then at the painting. I thought I could see inside her mind as she tried to rein it in. "I . . . I tried, Georgia."

I grabbed her hand. "Rona. Stop. It's just a painting."

She stopped moving her hand over the paper. "It's a phalaenopsis—my favorite."

Then in an instant her eyes grew wide, and she drew a huge breath and smacked my shoulder. "Get it off. Get it off."

"What?" I patted my arms and chest.

"There." She pointed to the fridge.

Dappled sunlight danced on the floor through the window. Nothing else. I went to her bag and pulled out three prescription bottles. "Rona, take the drugs . . . you'll feel better."

She smacked them out of my hand.

"I hate that shit. They don't make me feel better. Don't you get that? They don't make me feel . . . anything—the brushes, the strokes, the colors—they all become black like . . ."

Colby, my oldest son, six years old, saw her and heard her.

I grabbed him by the hand and took him to the den and turned on Nickelodeon. The bed was pulled out with its skinny, blue mattress exposed like a tongue. She didn't bother with a bottom sheet, just a bright yellow blanket, no pillow. I straightened the room up, tousled Colby's hair. "I love you." He smiled and went back to his cartoon.

"You have to leave, Rona. Go back to the hospital."

"But . . . but it's so awful there. Choking, suffocating, the others . . . they cry all the time. Please, you're my . . . my sister."

As she sobbed, she swallowed the pills, hands shaking. How could she ever hold a brush? My sister. I loved her once, years ago now, years have passed from drawing cartoons on the basement walls, from running to the park on New Year's Eve to bang pots with our mother's wooden spoons, and from the promises we made to always be sisters and friends. I loved her—once. But now, I didn't know.

She covered her face in her hands, trying to gather herself. Her next words were almost in a whisper. "They hate me, you know, the paintings—those arms and legs, twisting about and around, but they don't stand still. Georgia, they keep moving in circles . . . circles."

Shit, why can't they help her? They put a man on the moon but can't keep the bugs out of my sister's head. She couldn't resist them. Her bugs weighed her down. They weighed her down so much she refused to let the nurses at the hospital put her on the scale. *They'll find out*, she had claimed, *I'll weigh too much and they'll have to dig them out of my brain with a shovel*. I knelt down and put my hand on her shoulder. "Geez, Rona. They . . . they aren't . . . real."

She rocked. She rocked and hugged herself. She rocked and cried. "Make them stop crawling, Georgia, please."

Jackson, only three, appeared at the kitchen door rubbing his sleepy eyes. "Mommy, there's a bug in my room."

"Shit. Rona. You're scaring the boys."

I took Jackson to join Colby, got them both Lucky Charms in snow white bowls and called my mother. "No," she said. She hung up before I could protest.

"See, you didn't have to call her."

"She's busy, too, Rona. The country club and—"

She pounded her thigh. "You always side with her. Why?"

"Rona, stop it. We can't take care of you—nobody can. Not even you."

I didn't want to say it but I didn't take it back. It was too true.

"He's here!" Jackson shouted.

He was my ex-husband. I looked up at the clock. Eight-o-five. Time for school. It was the arrangement—one week out of every four—for now. He divorced me, married Tammy, and started wearing sandals. It's been a year.

"Why is she here?" Sam asked when he saw Rona. "I don't want her here with the kids. I swear, Georgia, I'll fight for custody."

"Go to hell."

Jackson clung to his father's leg like a boa while Colby stuffed a teddy bear into his backpack.

I got dressed—ready for work—a Donna Karan suit the color of lentils, a mid-length jacket with three buttons and a matching pleated skirt and a white blouse. I finally made partner after working myself nearly to death and giving Frank Johnson, the senior partner, a blowjob under his desk. I got the position just like he promised—last week, finally. It was either Stewart Constable or me and since Stewart wasn't about to do the old gizzard, well, it was six minutes out of my life and it paid off. I told Sam and he called me a whore. I told him so I could watch him squirm. The marriage was pretty much over before then.

He doesn't really want the boys. It's all about staying in control.

Rona was drinking coffee and picking at what was left of the Lucky Charms in Jackson's bowl. She plucked a green clover and popped it in her mouth. "Here's to luck and pharmaceuticals. I'll take my medicine—everyday—promise." She crossed her heart.

"Rona, I can't keep you . . . it's too much." I glanced back at the clock. "I'm late."

"I'll sleep. I can sleep now. See? I can sleep all day, just like in the cracker box, only no bars on the windows. I hate those bars."

"Should have thought about that before you stopped taking your medicine."

"You got no right to say that!" She exploded. "You got no goddamn right! You don't know what it's like. The stinking drugs, the way they make my brain float. I can't think. I can't paint."

Her eyes glistened—no telling why. I felt a twinge of sympathy, and then remembered something about not helping those who wouldn't help themselves. She pushed her thin fingers through her short-cropped hair, so thin now, and I blew air out my nose, exasperated, late. "Okay, but just for today, and just because the boys won't be here. Just . . . sleep."

I buckled my watch and slipped into a pair of black pumps that made my calves look sexy. I grabbed my briefcase off the dining room table where it always landed and stayed.

"If I find one thing out of place when I get home tonight, I swear, I'll call the police—understand, Rona."

"Sleep. I will Georgia. I'll go to sleep."

Rona dumped three pills in her palm and held them toward me, her hand shaking like an aspen leaf. A blue pill. A pink pill and a small white tablet. "See, I'll take them," Rona said. She popped them in her mouth and swallowed, no water, as though taking the pills was like breathing. Then she picked up the cereal bowl and drank the milk, wiping her mouth with the back of her hand. "See, Georgia. I can do it."

"Good. Now go to sleep."

I MET A CLIENT FOR A THREE-MARTINI LUNCH at Friar Tuck's Steak House. He was a bore, a loud-mouthed bore scheduled to testify the next day about some shady investments. It was my job to prepare him, coddle him. "So, I hear you're a partner now, Georgia." He reached across the table, tapping my hand with his fingertips. "I hear you really got what it takes." I pulled my hand away and sipped my iced tea. A moment later Carson, our overly gay server, brought me the bill. I signed and left my client to suck down the last of his courage before getting grilled like a salmon the next morning.

I parked my Volvo in the garage and waited until the electric door slammed shut.

The smooth sound of Oscar Peterson drifted near when I opened the door to the house. I thought it might be a good sign. When she was lucid enough to like anything, Rona liked jazz. It reminded her of our father. But it was dark inside.

"Rona?"

I stopped, cold, in the living room as an odd smell hit me—earthy, organic.

"Rona?"

Maybe she left. Maybe she went back to the hospital. Maybe our mother with her permed gray hair and dark dress with dots of color, took her home, combed her dirty hair, and tucked her into bed with chicken soup and *Elle* magazine. Maybe. Instead, Rona was at the dining room table. Her head rested in the crook of her arm.

"Rona, I'm home." I waited for her to lift her head, to move, to moan, to scream. But she didn't. I shook her, and her other arm fell like dead weight against her thigh, knocking a bottle of Vodka to the floor. I grabbed the pill bottles—all empty, all three. Drained.

"Oh, Christ, Rona, wake up. Wake up." I shook her again and again until she fell onto the floor, free from her bugs and pills and nurses and orchids and all the other things of this world that taunted her, betrayed her, called her names, and made her sick.

The Vodka was mine. I had it in the kitchen since last Christmas. All these months untouched, just waiting for what? Another party?

"Oh, Rona," I said, stroking her hair. "I'm sorry . . . I'm sorry but you . . . "

I called the police, like I promised.

AFTER THE FUNERAL I DROVE MY MOTHER HOME. I parked in her driveway.

"I thought the reverend did a fine job," Mother said, 'a fine job. And he was so . . . sweet, 'So sorry about Rona,' he said. Did you hear him say that?"

"I heard."

"And I do think he was sincere, Georgia, don't you? He did seem to understand how hard it was for us all along, you know, with Rona."

My stomach tensed. I took a shallow breath.

"And weren't the flowers nice?" She touched the side of her face with her gloved hand. "Mr. Saki out did himself. Where do you suppose he found such luscious orchids in October?"

"Phalaenopsis," I said.

"I'm sorry?"

I paused, considering, then answered: "Yes. Yes, they were pretty."

Mother's lips turned up to a slight smile. "Yes."

"Now, will you be all right? I need to get the boys."

"Oh, yes, dear. I'll be fine . . . now."

I picked up the boys at their father's. Jackson poked me on the shoulder. "Daddy said Aunt Rona is dead."

I nodded into the rearview mirror, making certain he saw me.

A week later I had Rona's October Orchid framed. I hung it in the dining room and stared at it for a few minutes—even smeared it was beautiful. It still mattered.

IT ALL COMES DOWN TO LAUNDRY MICHAEL MARTIN

She certainly knew how to remove a stain from a sheet
menstrual blood   semen   meconium   milk
the incontestable evidence of our impending death

> *In the river everything is green*
> *pale ropes of light hang from the surface*

In time, she could read a person's fortune from the stains
the marriage to a wingèd man
a journey by sea
the inevitable death by fire

> *Your grandfather pulls you by the hair*
> *flops you on the creaking dock*
> *to draw the river from your breath*

She removed them through the most common of agencies
vinegar, beer, sweat, and the incomparable solvent of her own tears.

> *Et effundam super vos aquam mundam*
> *et mundabimini ab omnibus inquinamentis vestris*

The bedclothes, suspended from a silver cord,
captured the terrible freshness of the wind
as if rising from the dead.

CARDINAL'S EVE SALLY ROSEN KINDRED

What did God give Mrs. Jackson
who took bright pills to keep her joy
at Christmas safe? Their failure

brought our sacrament: candles she lit
in our hands on the wet street
before she sang and had us sing

for the child she knew would come.
In two days she'd be
in a white bed, whispering

to the devil on her left shoulder
and kissing the devil on her right,
but tonight we were singing to the glory

of brown bags of sand
flaming Tallwood Drive from Beth's house
all the way to iced Watauga Creek.

Her notes bristled red birds of light
and the big girls' soft coats frosted them in pink,
but Mrs. Jackson loved my cheek

with her tweed suit jacket scratch,
loved me, the runt, with her North Star heat,
for which my weak mouth

keened to the December crunch:
cold-glass mystery of birth, dark
path, our grass. Greensboro,

Bethlehem: her wild cardinal call
drew them both to warm foil
dripping wax into snow that like song

took dark flight. I remember leaving her one year
for the still front room to play
wrecked chimes of discovery

on my home keys. Mother frowned me
to bed. Midnight which I'd never seen coming
was clear. I did not know

about her doctors then—a mercy
that I'd not yet had my own.
Unholy pills, your impotence

turned the front yard snow to cathedral glass
and brought me wildest bells
that like sickness or salvation

God did not take away.

LOOK UP J. STEPHEN RHODES

THE COUNCIL RING, 1959

EVERY MORNING FOR FIVE WEEKS, I woke to the sound of the mess hall bell down the hill from our cabin at Camp Sequoyah. I was twelve. After dressing, making up my bunk, and a quick trip to the bathroom, I headed for the council ring. I carried the leather-bound Revised Standard Version Bible my grandfather had just given me.

Morning watch was voluntary. Sequoyah was not a church camp, but the camp leaders were committed to liberal ideals of manhood and ecumenical religion. The nature counselor flew a United Nations flag next to his cabin.

Rough board benches stretched in concentric circles around a large fire pit. White pines shaded the council ring, making it a dark place except for the circle of brightening sky above. Fifteen or twenty campers and counselors sat scattered around.

I read the Psalms: The heavens are telling the glory of God. I will lift up my eyes to the hills. From whence does my help come?

No one ever said a word.

IN THE AUDIENCE, 1964

MY FRIEND LINDA AND I DROVE TO DOWNTOWN ATLANTA to hear the Mormon Tabernacle Choir in the old Municipal Auditorium. One hundred forty voices sang Holst's setting of the 148th Psalm. Throughout the hymn, I could not take my eyes off one elderly tenor whose face seemed brighter than those of the men around him. While he was careful to look at the conductor, his eyes kept drifting upward.

Burn lamps of night with constant flame,
Shine to the honor of His name.
Thou sun, whom all the lands obey,
Renew his praise from day to day.

Whatever he had going on inside him, I wanted.

Crawford W. Long Memorial Hospital, 1970

During my first year in the Central Supply Department, my supervisor ordered me to rotate through all three shifts each week. She did not think highly of conscientious objectors. I ran the autoclaves, washed and sterilized surgical instruments, cleaned suction machines, and set up most of the tractions in the hospital. I hated the hours, but loved the work and my dozen co-workers, all women. They liked having a man to tease: "You're going to get corns on your ass if you keep sitting down all of the time—get over here and help me wash these pans."

The best perk of the job: I had the run of the hospital. When I felt stifled, I could take the elevator to the roof. Atlanta's skyscrapers stood a mile to the south. Overhead: Orion, Cassiopeia, and Ursa Major. The only sound was the traffic on the streets far below.

Steve, 1982

Gail, the kids, and I were staying at a beach house in Florida. Through sliding glass doors we looked at the blue sky and the equally blue ocean beneath it. When I answered the telephone, Susan said Steve had killed himself—had driven out to the county airport at night and shot himself in the head. Would I come home and officiate at his funeral?

So many flowers surrounded the dais that I could only see the full congregation when I stepped up to the pulpit. One of Steve's daughters ran around the sanctuary before she finally sat and fidgeted by Susan, who held her other daughter in her lap. I spoke about our hurt and about God's grace: "I have a vision of Steve right now. His tears are being wiped away. Most of us know that Steve loved to look at the stars through his telescope. I like to think of him now, closer to his stars."

* * *

Memphis, 1993

I asked Lucretia—my spiritual director—"Do you think it is legitimate to move somewhere solely because you want to be near the mountains? Can God call a person to be near green hills and open sky?"

Lucretia grinned and nodded.

Christmas Ridge Farm, 2005

While I walked around our pasture, I yelled at the sky about the death of our youngest daughter. Suicide. "I hope you're listening Rebecca. I hope you know how much I'm hurting here."

"And you, too, God."

The sky was silent and cobalt, with wisps of cirrus clouds.

Saddle Mountain, 2007

From my desk, I can see Saddle Mountain to the west. The sky and mountain bump up against each other. At dawn, the sun makes the mountain seem closer. At dusk, it seems farther away. The line where sky and mountain meet says different things. One time, "Sky!" Another, "Mountain!" Sometimes, "Both!"

I have lived below Saddle Mountain for fourteen years—the longest I have lived one place since I was a boy.

I lean back in the chair and read: I will lift up my eyes to the hills. From whence does my help come?

MISCARRIAGES BRIAN G. PHIPPS

I've thought it would be a relief if you should happen
to miscarry. Baby, you are two years too soon,
unexpected, skewing our expectations. Soon
you will lie in my grandfather's cradle, rocking
in your first dream, some of my dreams, perhaps,
bundled under the blanket with you.
There's a picture on the wall by the cradle,
an ad from *Bicycling Magazine*.
The bike in the ad's on layaway. This is
one dream I choose to grasp before you
arrive, in case your mother's labor complicates,
the midwife rushes her to the hospital,
and I'm suddenly in debt, struggling
to close the gap. Every night
I dream about the bike. Once,
in the middle of a dreamride, receiving
blankets nuzzled my legs, lashed my ankles
to the frame, and tangled in the spokes.
The bike kept rolling somehow until
the pothole on Willow Highway
pretzeled the front wheel. Once,
during a road race in a middle dream,
my water bottle blew its rubber nipple,
and I got off my bike to warm milk for you
in a mud puddle boiling in the sun. You suckled
in my arms, and sweat rolled off my face, tipping
down your cheek as we rocked in a roadside chair,
the clicks and sticky whirr of the race
decrescendoing away from us.

WINTER SOLSTICE BRIAN G. PHIPPS

Low and wan, the midday sun
hangs over a stand of trees somehow
substantial in their slenderness,
casting shadows over a field of unbroken
snow. Approaching the middle of
my life, I want to be
as staunch as those trees. And maybe
I am. Maybe this deepening
cold is a kind of thawing, a giving
in to the season, giving myself
over to my life.

THE INSTITUTE OF TRANSCENDENCE KIRSTEN EVE BEACHY

SHE WAS GLAD THE MONK that the Institute of Transcendence sent to the airport didn't speak, just held a card that said *Donna*, because she went tongue-tied staring at the bulges of his skull under his bare skin. She guessed he didn't speak English or was under a vow of silence, if they had those at the Institute. Perhaps he simply was shy. She could make cards like his when she got home: *Excuse me. Hello, isn't the weather delightful? Oh, it doesn't matter about my day—tell me about yours.*

The monk had two more cards, so they waited for two more planes before going out to the van. *Greg* and *Howell*: young men, tall and healthy. As the van cut across the floodplain towards the foothills, she kept her eyes on her lap and listened to their conversation. Greg said he was tired of chaining himself to redwoods. "So I'm thinking there's only so much action you can do before you get burnt out, ya know? Unless you take time to think as well as act—that's why I come up here two, three times a year."

Howell, a Religions student, said this was his first Peace Retreat. "I want to be more exposed to some of the areas I'm studying. I hear the Institute personalizes and Westernizes these concepts so you can grasp them in a short time. I've always wanted my own guru—" he laughed deprecatingly. "Not my own, but one I can talk to firsthand. *Disciple.*"

"Oh, yeah," said Greg. "You can have your own. At least, you can get the one you want. I always sign up for Nori's weekend. He's cool. Very cool. Like Yoda." She imagined Nori. He would be short, arthritic, and bursting with cryptic advice. Perhaps he would be slightly green.

They turned to her. "Why do you want a guru?" Howell asked.

She blushed. "My daughters thought I should come. I'm trying to do community mediation. I'm not very good at it." It was what she'd decided to tell anyone who asked, far less embarrassing than explaining her spells, how they'd struck with increasing frequency in the past few years, even last month at John's recognition banquet. His boss threw the party, the man for whom John worked late nights and some weekends, correcting mistakes and clearing up misunderstandings. John claimed he kept Mr. Eiger afloat. Mr. Eiger said as much himself, late into the party, just before he confided loudly to the gathered secretaries that he'd bring John into partnership if he'd trade in his wife for a lighter model. And even though Donna knew he was intoxicated and that they owed him everything, when Mr. Eiger approached her, she couldn't bring herself to admire the photograph of his new great-grand-daughter. She remembered a picture she'd once seen of a grandma in KKK robes crooning over an infant, and as she grasped for words, the temperature plummeted, the air exploded out into the vaccuum, and she gasped like a fish in the alien atmosphere. John snapped in her ear, "Quit breathing!" a cordial smile still plastered to his face. She succeeded after a few shuddering breaths, clamping down so thoroughly on her instincts that she couldn't remember how to inhale at all, and as Mr. Eiger inquired, "Is anything wrong?" the merciful darkness closed across his face and she sank down, down, down.

At the hospital, they said it wasn't asthma. There was nothing wrong at all.

Later, she noticed a flier tacked to the bulletin board in the GasMark: *Find PEACE as the rhythms of your breath echo the rhythms of the universe: a weekend of renewal in the Rockies.* When she showed her daughter Ruby, Ruby yawned and said, "It couldn't hurt." Jessica told her she'd have to get her ass in gear—why not this way? John was surprised, but when she explained she'd already frozen a weekend's worth of suppers, he said, "You really ought to have some kind of hobby." He even took off work to drive her to the airport.

What she'd told the boys was almost true: She tried community mediation once, but had one of her attacks during her first intervention, a dialogue between a sullen kid who'd stolen an Eternal Flame from a grave and the outraged husband of the deceased. Aura, her mentor, had said "Maybe you should contribute some other way."

In the van, Greg patted her shoulder kindly. "A Peace Retreat will be just the thing to center your mediation." Then he turned to Howell and for the rest of the trip they discussed dietary preferences, leaving her to herself. She grimaced inwardly while they argued whether it would be ethical to eat fish if someone could develop sustainable aquaculture, glad she'd finished her double cheeseburger before their flights arrived.

They turned off the road and followed a gravel lane for several miles until they drove up to The Institute of Transcendence, which was nestled against the flank of the mountain. Greg turned to her. "They call this the Mountain of the Gods." The name reminded her of her childhood El-Shaddai, the God of the Mountains, the god of Genesis. How strange to have your phrases turned inside out. Would it appall Papa to know she was far from the fold, about to dabble in eastern mysticism?

Through the van windows, she couldn't see much of the mountain itself. The building, though, was long and low, like a motel, and built of cement blocks. No landscaping at all. What had she expected? Rock gardens, pools and waterfalls? Pagodas? Maybe an onion dome? But Nori, when he darted out to greet the van, exceeded her expectations in his saffron robe and wire-rimmed spectacles, the bare skin of his olive head. He rolled back the van door and cried, in clipped British English, "Welcome! Welcome, children!"

Unfolding herself from the van into the afternoon heat, Donna found that he was, after all, at least as tall as John. She felt the impulse to bow, but he thrust out a hand and shook hers heartily. His knuckles were smooth as a child's, his eyes a hundred years old.

Inside the institute, thick carpets, lamp-lighting, and a honeycomb of open chambers quieted her disappointment at the exterior; in one room a small fountain burbled out of the floor. Nori led them past other saffron-robed monks in the halls and students leaning on cushions in a section full of books, reading. They entered a room where two young women waited. The one with the long blond ponytail bounced up and introduced herself as Morgan; the other had henna-red hair hacked short and bushy eyebrows. She acknowledged them with a nod. "This is Sondra," said Morgan. "She's an *artist*." And then Morgan turned to Donna. "Do you do art?"

"Well . . ." she looked at the floor. At home she sang in the Holy Mountain Church choir. She thought of it as art, but it hardly bore mentioning.

"Now we are all together," said Nori. "If you will excuse me, I will prepare to go up the mountain." He nodded to them and trotted out of the room. Moments later, he returned, wearing blue jeans with a sweater knotted around the waist. He carried a large sack over his shoulder, which he dumped out on the floor: a canvas knapsack for each of them, cups, spoons, bags of rice, and rolled-up mats. "Each of you will also bring a change of clothes, extra socks, and a blanket. Howell, you look sturdy. You will bring the cooking pot." He told them to bring any books from the library they might care to read, but Donna's pack felt heavy enough without them. Morgan loaded up on books, and Greg strapped a collapsible guitar to his pack. "I had it specially made for hiking," he explained.

The trek across the mountain reminded Donna how little she used her body. She leaned forward against the weight of her pack, thumbs hooked into the straps, the flesh of her arms hanging heavily on her bones. She fell back at once and soon lost sight of the others. When she got home, she'd see about a membership or a program or a trainer; expensive as they were, John would be pleased. In spite of her exhaustion, she couldn't help appreciating the golden afternoon light, the gentle breeze, the quiet broken only by birdsong. She'd rather be back here than with the others anyhow. They were so content with themselves, Morgan already jostling Greg and picking on Howell's haircut, Sondra in serious discussion with Nori about the local geology.

After a time, she began to fear losing them, though the packed dust of the path cut a clear line through the low grasses. She picked up her pace. Across the meadow and through a stand of trees, she found Nori, sitting on a boulder with an open sketchbook. "That fir down there," he said, pointing, "all twisted with wind, I had to get it." She peered at the tree and then at his sketchbook, but all she saw were a few bare lines. He snapped the book shut and jumped up to hike with her.

"Perhaps you will allow me to carry something?"

She shook her head, but wished he would. He had been waiting for her, the last little duck, the lost puppy.

"At least we can fix your shoulders," he said, circling her and then, from behind, lifting the weight of her pack. Freed for a moment, she felt herself almost float. "Good! Good! Up with your shoulders!" As he settled the pack back against them, he gripped each shoulder and said, "Keep them back, now. Remember, you are no twisty tree."

"Thank you," she said. The pack did seem lighter, her shoulders wider.

But in a few steps, he stopped her again. "You are not letting yourself breathe. You are trapping your air here—" he tapped her breastbone—"When you should fill up your wonderful belly." He placed his hand over her navel, as if feeling for a baby's kick, and said, "Breathe into my hand." Donna tried. "No, breathe!" he commanded, and the air flowed down through her lungs and out towards his hand. "Better. You must breathe well. Up here, the air is thinner."

As they started down the path together, she stole side glances at his straight figure, his crow's-feet. Her stomach was warm where he'd touched her, the air in it golden. They found the others waiting at a fork in the path. Sondra hopped from one foot to the other, like a jogger at a busy crosswalk waiting for traffic to clear. "We thought you'd fallen off the mountain," said Howell, and the rest laughed. Kind laughter, she told herself. These were good people.

Nori pointed up the left hand path, "Not far now, chickens!"

Before they reached their camp they had to cross a wide, shallow cascade, cold from snowmelt. The others stepped across a string of stones in the water, barely breaking stride, but Donna stopped at the edge, glaring at the first wet rock. She couldn't force her foot forward. Nori, and then the others, stopped to watch. Feeling all their eyes, she wished herself away; the air in her lungs went slippery and fish-cold. Before the fear could take her, Greg waded into the water to offer his hand, and Howell joined them halfway across, soaking his white-as-new Adidas, to support her other side. When they reached the bank, the boys didn't hear her murmured thanks underneath Morgan's enthusiastic applause.

The shelter was barely more than a roof with a fireplace at one end, where they boiled rice for dinner. If nothing else, I'll lose weight, she thought, picking at the brown rice in the fading light. It had more texture than she cared for; the occasional hulls broke under her teeth like beetle shells. She washed it down with water from the stream, which tasted of iodine.

After the flight, the drive, and the hike, she could barely sit up. She unrolled her reed mat and tried to get comfortable. It wasn't fair, she thought, to have so much padding and still feel the concrete floor of the pavilion. The others would have no trouble sleeping; they were talking themselves into somnolence. Greg strummed his guitar while Morgan read out loud from a book called *The Nations* and Howell interjected his thoughts. She guessed they were in their twenties. Sondra, building an urn out of a globs of native clay, might be creeping into her thirties. But Nori, with his legs tucked under him, sketching in the flickering light of citronella buckets, could be any age at all.

Eventually he held up his hand to stop the reading. "I must tell you, that book was quite important when it was written. Now, however, the nations are waning in power. Their people know each other, and there is greater knitting of the human soul. This is the problem now: that a handful of people, six or seven, could choose to destroy us all. The technology is there. We have one hope, and that is to put peace in the hearts of all people, starting now, starting with ourselves. Every hour we must receive now as a gift. We will be lucky if we are given a generation."

Donna hoped this was the signal for bedtime. It was. Morgan's book fell shut, and Sondra began to scrape up her clay. The aspens shivered in a breeze off the mountainside, but the single wall of the shelter kept its chill breath out, left the candle flames steady. As the others picked up their mats, Donna hoped they wouldn't group on the far end without her; she didn't want anyone too close, either. What if she snored? She peeked through her eyelashes. The disciples were spreading out all along the pavilion, spaced widely except for Morgan who unrolled her mat just near enough to Greg's to make Donna chuckle.

Nori bent over the last citronella bucket, and the orange fire danced up his cheekbones toward his bare skull, making his eye sockets stand out in relief as he said, "Rest well. Tomorrow the real work begins. The work of silence, reflection, breathing. You will get very tired." He clapped his hands and blew out the candle. The resulting shadows were almost blue, infused with moonlight.

He dropped his mat right beside hers, and as the others settled for sleep, he rolled towards her, propping himself up on one elbow. Infinitely gentle, he touched her cheek and then her hand where it curled under her chin. "Are you asleep, little one?" His shaved head dipped close, and she could smell the spice, like cardamom, of his breath.

"No," she whispered. "Just trying to process it all."

"You are a processor?" he asked, then touched her cheek again, lightly, with the side of one finger. "What if we go off for a bit by ourselves?"

At first she couldn't understand why. To her, still starving, the wrapper he pulled from his pocket looked just like a ketchup packet.

The earthquake of realization remade her brain.

For once, there was too much air. She found herself saying, in a perfectly natural voice, "I'm married."

"I didn't know it mattered," he said. "You seem quite separate, so singular."

She didn't know what to say.

"So you don't want to . . . ?"

She shook her head slightly, trying to look calm, to smile a little, as if she were asked all the time, as if she practiced fidelity regularly, as if she wasn't melting into her mat. She'd been a virgin when she married, more by default than by choice (though she'd made promises to Papa and to God). Her few boyfriends and then John had been ridiculously respectful of her purity at a time when the rest of the world seemed bent on discovering all the pleasures of love. No one had ever asked her—John didn't count.

"Wait," Nori murmured. "Stay just as you are." He crossed the shelter and returned with his sketchbook. "I was trying to draw you all evening. You're perfect now."

She let her eyes close, the moonlight filter through. Here I am, almost fifty, round as a turnip, and here is this man sketching me in the moonlight. She fell asleep listening to his pencil-strokes, and when she woke the moon had set. She heard him breathing on the mat next to hers, thought she could feel his air on the back of her neck. He lay curled towards her on his separate island of reed.

The next day, Friday, they all breathed. Lying on their backs with their eyes closed. With them open, watching the clouds, watching one cloud move all the way across the sky. They breathed while examining a square inch of grass, breathed blindfolded, trying to memorize the contours of each others' hands. Breathed on *ahs* and *oms* and *ohs*, breathed alone with the midges on separate patches of mountainside. Her body felt larger, lighter, shot through with air like an angel food cake. Nori neither avoided her nor singled her out. She couldn't help watching him jealously, but nothing passed between him and the other women—blond Morgan, Sondra with the clay plastered on her cheek. She was sure he hadn't asked them, sure he wouldn't. What if, she thought, I am the only one he's ever asked?

They ate only two more times, brown rice, but it didn't occur to her to be cranky about her hunger. In the evening, when their work was over, Greg played his guitar and Sondra convinced Donna to shape clay, too, and she built a lopsided bowl that someone would crush in the night on the way to the vault toilet. They were supposed to fall asleep counting their breaths, but Donna gave up at four hundred, flattened her hands on her mat, stared at the roof. She did not feel herself at all, wondered where Donna had gone and what she would think about all this, a fish out of water, its drowning gills bursting into red.

"You are all so aware," Nori said the next morning. "You have fallen asleep counting your breath and listened to it all night. You are ready for the next step." He sent them off to separate corners to sit cross-legged and watch their stomachs rise and fall.

This is it, she thought. This is where I'll gain control of my breath. Here I will learn the secret of my vascular system. She had tried counting backwards as she did years ago in Lamaze, and all that did was make her cry, remembering. She had tried counting forwards, slowly, to ten, as Aura taught her to calm rushes of anger in mediation sessions. But her breath was unruly, didn't care about numbers. This was the time to pin it down, command obedience.

Her belly filled and emptied under the thin knit of her t-shirt, and she watched, fascinated. It was like the flank of some animal, collapsed in exhaustion from a long run, its side rising up and down, the bellows at work to cool the blood. And then there crept upon her the knowledge that the air itself forced her lungs open, then drained, then forced them open again, an outside agent squeezing her belly in and out, in and out; raped by air! Before the terror could seize her, she squeezed her eyes shut and commanded her brain to think of something else, of the girl who might have signed up for this weekend if Donna hadn't filled the spot: a twenty-something mystic, brunette, with a Guatemalan cap pulled over her hair, who would have played flute in the evenings and known some trick to keep blood circulating (Donna's thighs were tingling as they lost oxygen), a series of muscle flexes or an herbal infusion; who would have wandered off into the mountains and returned with handfuls of wildflowers and tales of taming marmots. Who would have known what to do with a monk and his gas station condom.

Finally Nori called them. "What did you see?" he asked, when they returned to the circle.

"Oh," sighed Morgan. "It was wonderful. I was breathing out darkness and breathing in light. My lungs were filling with light!" Donna shuddered, but Nori nodded, fingertips pressed together, and turned his eyes upon Sondra.

"Very gut," was all Sondra said. Greg didn't want to talk about it; he said he'd make a song in the evening to express the experience, but Howell had been bursting to share since they sat down:

"I've read about this, but I didn't believe it. A shift in vision occurs, and you see that you are not breathing: breath is breathing you. Your breath is a participation in an outside force, your breath is that force entering you . . ."

Donna stared at him in horror.

". . . that gentle, benevolent force."

Suddenly she was on her feet in thin air, spitting out a whisper: "You don't know a thing about breath. How it takes you, ungentle, and fights your will, how it stops you when you need it most!" She was shouting. Donna the fish looked on, surprised. Donna doesn't shout, she thought. Donna is a fish. No, better, she's an opossum whose brain shuts down when it's terrified, a possum collapsed, unappetizing to predators.

She struggled on, trying to explain with words that wouldn't line up, trying to describe the shape of helplessness: a cussing juvie, a man expecting justice, a woman unmourned, her flame snatched away. She was babbling. Donna stopped, hot with embarrassment. These people with pepper spray and dissertations and God-knew-what in their lives, real problems. These good people. But it was better, after all, to be vertical than horizontal. The others looked at their hands, the ground. Only Nori watched her, a broad grin splitting his face. He nodded encouragingly. She glared back, exhaled.

"I'm done," she said. "See you later." She grabbed her pack and headed for the path. There had to be a bed, a real bed, down at the Institute for her last night here, and anything but brown rice for supper, whatever she had to pay, would be worth it.

They put her up without a fuss, gave her curried vegetables and cottage cheese and a room to herself. In the morning, when the others returned from the mountain, she joined them to turn in her pack. They welcomed her gently, with pats on the shoulder and squeezes of her fingers, these good people, and promptly turned back to their farewells. Nori only nodded.

Before they left, he presented them each with sketches he'd drawn. Hers was the one he drew on the first night: her face smooth and peaceful, the eyelashes alive upon the cheek as if ready to wake into a blue-lit dream; the face that was both a slumbering Madonna's and her own; her hand curled under her chin, cupping a blessing. When he passed around a sheet for their addresses, she left hers blank, but she didn't mean to leave the picture behind.

Sometimes still, the face settles across Donna's mind, the face that Nori gave her, while she's crossing the street or chopping vegetables, commonplace things. She remembers the picture in color sometimes, or in shades of gray, deep blues. The eyelashes are always right, she's sure, but the fingers curl a new way each time, subtly, like smoke waiting to rise.

BEYOND MAUREEN DOYLE MCQUERRY

After a painting by Wolf Kahn

The arc of river leads the eye
to a distant bend. Everything near is grey,
land and water, sky's bleak extension,
but there, behind the dark-treed isthmus,
the sky ignites.

You cannot help but send your heart
paddling forward, a wary scout,
into the vanishing point.
The painter promises so much,

try as you might, you cannot
strain into that future. Everything narrows
to a single stroke of intention,
one bold, dash of gold.

CONVERSATION MAUREEN DOYLE MCQUERRY

If there is a word
at the end of it all,
it might be said here in the small red café
that clings to the cliffs
near Bonnie Doon where a thousand pumpkins
rush to the sea,
lettuce green vines and the fog,
always the fog, muffling
the bright intrusion of day.

We would sit at the redwood table
overlooking the sea with a glass of good wine,
below us a coast of small beaches
turned out like a giant's pockets,
spilling sand and stones, glass and shells,
a random assortment
of things found and loved.

It is a good place, at the end of land
and the beginning of sea, for conversation.
The geography of my heart
mapped here years ago, carried still.

We would lean in like old friends
conspiring together, eager to hear
each other's news, and later I might ask
for an explanation of the difficult things:
the neighbor's child who died too young,
plagues and dark ages, the way men's hearts
are drawn to war, but by then

CONVERSATION

the sun will have bested the grey,
and on the horizon one small boat
like a gull's wing,
rides to the end of the world.

EROSION BARRY L. DUNLAP

She rebukes me for
building this house,
for making a hill
where a year ago
white swamp
lilies bathed
under a rain
like this one
that is leaving
deep scars as it
moves dirt back.

THE LAST GOOD DAY JEFF E. BROOKS-HARRIS

THE WATER WAS SMOOTH AS GLASS. Without trade winds to ruffle the surface of the ocean, Kailua Beach was calm and inviting. Carolyn and I sat in beach chairs within a small grove of trees. Her brown braided hair draped across her shoulder and down to her waist. Carolyn's long hair was the first thing I noticed when I met her eleven years earlier. Her braid was her trademark.

My wife looked in my eyes and said, "Jeff, I don't know what's worse; to be the one dying or to be the one left behind."

Even weakened by cancer, Carolyn still looked like the woman I married but her body had already begun to change in subtle ways. Her skin had yellowed as her liver weakened. Her stomach expanded as the cancer grew.

"I think it's worse to be the one dying," I spoke slowly. "I know I'll have a rough time after you're gone but I'll get to watch Genevieve grow up." My mind flashed ahead to my daughter's graduations, her wedding. I saw myself sitting alone without my wife. I looked away from Carolyn as my throat tightened. I reached out and held her hand, trying to communicate more than words would allow.

Eight years earlier, Carolyn and I spent a quiet January day at Kailua Beach, very near where we now sat. Because it was Super Bowl Sunday, the beach wasn't crowded. A few children played in the sand, their parents watching nearby. There may have been some little boys at the beach that day but we saw only the girls. I gently rubbed my wife's pregnant belly, wondering if the baby was feeling cramped.

"Hang in there, little Genevieve," I said. "You'll be out in few more days. I can't wait to see you!"

As Carolyn and I watched the girls play in the gentle waves, we imagined bringing our own little girl to Kailua. We dreamed about all the ways our life would be different, starting in a few short days, when we would begin our life as a family of three. We wondered if we would be able to buy a house in Kailua. Could we build our dream here?

In March, a month after the baby was born, we stopped at the beach to let her nurse before meeting a realtor to look at houses in Kailua. In April, Carolyn's parents visited us to see the new baby and we stopped at the beach after showing them the house we had just purchased. We bought a Baby Jogger in June and began to run on the beach with little Genevieve bundled up inside. Our baby girl was introduced to the salty ocean water in her yellow "floaty boaty." When Gen was one, she would walk on the beach and fall, landing on her diapered bottom. She would hold up her hands in the air and say, "Hep me, hep me," not wanting to get sand on her hands. When she was two, a little boy reached into his bag of Cheetos and offered one to Gen. Cheetos became part of the ritual. Kalapawai Market became the "cheeto store" and we would stop there on our way to the ocean. Every year, on the Fourth of July, we would all watch the fireworks from Kailua Beach. When my extended family came to visit—just months before Carolyn got sick—we rented a beach house and Genevieve got to share the white sand and blue water with her six cousins.

Carolyn and I raised our little girl on Kailua Beach. We made our dream come true.

All of these memories swam together that quiet morning as we talked about our life together knowing we would soon be parted by death. When I married Carolyn, we were both already in our thirties, and I anticipated planning for a baby right away. I had not imagined saying goodbye to her when I was forty-three, only nine years after our wedding. I kissed Carolyn's forehead and told her that she was my one true love. I noticed that the taste of her skin had changed over the last several days. Her body chemistry was different. She already tasted like death.

When we were ready to leave, Carolyn wanted to walk down to the water's edge. Cancer had weakened her enough that she needed support to make her way through the sand. It was important for her to feel the cool water wash over her feet. That's what you do when you go to the ocean. She wanted to leave her footprints in the sand one last time. In this simple act, Carolyn affirmed that she was still alive.

THAT QUIET WEDNESDAY MORNING at the beach was Carolyn's last good day. More than any other moment this was when we celebrated our life together and said goodbye. That day was the dividing point of my life, the pivot from which I looked back fondly at the past and looked forward only with fear and confusion.

The intimacy of our conversation that Wednesday would not be repeated. She was very tired the following day. On Friday, she had a hard time following the story when I read to her. On Saturday night, Carolyn lost control of her bladder for the first time. On

Sunday morning, when everyone else in the grocery store was buying chips and beer for the Super Bowl, I stood with tears running down my cheeks trying to decide what kind of Depends to buy. Carolyn was too sick to attend Genevieve's eighth birthday party that afternoon and I just wanted to get through it as quickly as I could. On my way home from Build-a-Bear Workshop, I stopped at the pharmacy to pick up liquid morphine.

Carolyn died at home Tuesday night after Genevieve went to sleep. This was just six days after we sat in our beach chairs, remembering our life together and imagining our family without her. Our dream was gone.

The funeral was the following week and it began to rain. After the service, people had a hard time making their way from the church sanctuary to the parish hall because it was pouring so hard. It kept raining for forty days. It was the rainiest winter on record. Rainy days do not make you think about walking on the beach.

The things people said to comfort me were not always helpful. They searched for a silver lining in a way that felt obscene. One friend said that she didn't complain about having outpatient surgery a few weeks after Carolyn died. Another friend from church pointed out what meaningful conversations they had all had about life as a result of my family's loss. Perhaps Carolyn's death was a way for our community to learn valuable lessons. Maybe this is why she died. For me it wasn't worth it. I wanted my wife back. I wanted my daughter to grow up surrounded by her mother's love. I told my friend I didn't care what they had learned. Screw you for thinking God would sacrifice my daughter's mother so you can value your own life a little more.

In the blur of comforting words that didn't comfort, someone said to me, "You and Genevieve will be so close." What the hell did that mean? Was it worth losing my wife so I would be dedicated to my daughter? I knew that how well Gen survived this trauma was dependent on how well I could nurture her. We had always been close but this shared loss put extra stress on our relationship. At first we both felt lousy all the time so it was easy to share the same pain. At other times, Gen would direct her anger at me. Once she accused me of not praying hard enough. If only I had believed in a miracle, her mommy would still be alive. When we fought about homework, we were not just fighting about homework. Gen seemed to strike out because it was me—and not Carolyn—who was helping her with her lessons. For over a year, all of our conflicts were injected with hidden feelings of rage and pain. How could I be an adequate parent when my life felt like such a mess? Was I supposed to be strong and hide my tears or was it okay to model appropriate feelings of grief?

As Carolyn was dying and for weeks after her death, I would pray the twenty-third psalm over and over again: "Though I walk through the valley of the shadow of death, I fear no evil; for you are with me." But this prayer did not always ring true. There were deep feelings of fear when I didn't know if I could make it on my own. There were brief moments when I felt God's presence but longer periods of time when I felt abandoned and angry about the burden that had landed on my shoulders. I would resent my friends' wedding anniversaries. Why do you get fifteen or twenty years or more with your love when mine has been ripped away from me? I felt cheated when anyone over fifty celebrated a birthday at church.

AFTER THE RAIN STOPPED, GENEVIEVE AND I RETURNED to Kailua Beach for the first time since the funeral. It had been two months. I surveyed the same beach but it felt completely different. It was no longer a place of beauty and hope. An older couple walked up the beach, leaning into the wind. As Gen ran ahead of me along the water's edge, the couple joined hands and spoke to one another as they walked. I looked away with a bitter taste in my mouth. Why me? Carolyn should be here with me! Why did she leave me? Why do other couples get "happily ever after" when our dream was wrecked and drowned?

Genevieve and I walked past the small grove of trees where Carolyn and I sat that last good day, only two months earlier. Where we sat eight years ago, feeling our baby in her crowded womb, dreaming of living in Kailua and raising our daughter on this beautiful beach. Could Gen and I still walk along the beach as a family of two? As I watched my eight-year-old run ahead of me on the sand, I tried to make sense of it all. How could I connect my past and future?

I wanted to believe that I could somehow manage to maintain the same dream. If Genevieve and I kept coming to the same beach, the dream would remain alive. Wouldn't it? As months and years pass by, I realize that my hope of carrying on our dream alone was naive. I can't bring the dream back to life now, without Carolyn. Everything is too different. I try to pick up the pieces of my shattered life and put them back together but there are chunks missing and the glue in the cracks stains and wrinkles the smooth, beautiful surface I remember. The dream is gone.

A FEW MONTHS AFTER THE FUNERAL, someone told Genevieve that her mommy was happy now in heaven. These words upset us both. Why would someone tell a grieving child that her mother doesn't miss her? Genevieve asks me how Mommy could be happy without us. After struggling with this question for a while, I tell my little girl that maybe Mommy's experience is different than ours because she is closer to God. But I want to believe that Carolyn misses us as much as we miss her. Maybe God can comfort her better than we can comfort one another. Thinking that our loved ones are with God at last—and out of pain—works for an eighty-year-old grandfather but little girls still need their mothers. For me, the idea of heaven feels like a chasm, dividing me and Genevieve on one side from both Carolyn and God on the other. Sometimes, Genevieve tells me she wants to die so she can be with Mommy in heaven. I tell her I cannot bear the thought of losing both her and Carolyn. I need her here with me on this side of the divide.

A Christian friend tells me that the book of Revelation says there are no tears in heaven. Does that mean Carolyn doesn't miss Genevieve or me? Doesn't Revelation also describe the New Jerusalem as a giant golden cube? I can write off John's revelation as an old man's hallucination but I always put more stock in Jesus' words. Perhaps I can find comfort in his description of the afterlife. In Mark's gospel, Jesus tells the Sadducees that "when they rise from the dead, they neither marry nor are given in marriage, but are like angels in heaven." Damn! So much for that comforting image of my wife waiting for me with open arms at the pearly gates. For a young widower, it's a profoundly sad idea that the afterlife is so different from the here-and-now that earthly love will be irrelevant. Can Carolyn and I at least be friends? Can we sit on a cloud together, playing our harps? The idea that even if we meet in heaven we won't be united in the same way is another dream shattered. I feel cheated that we didn't make it to our tenth wedding anniversary. Now I can't even hope for more time together after I die.

"I can't live without you," sounds like teen anguish after a young lover's first big loss. The more painful reality is that life continues. Widowers in their sixties or seventies often die within a year of their wives. In my forties, as a single parent, I am not afforded this luxury. I am not allowed to lie down and die. I have to continue because there is no other choice. Even if I stay up late watching David Letterman and Conan O'Brien, eating too much ice cream to distract me from the empty bed in my room, I still have to take my daughter to school in the morning after making her lunch.

I most often wrestle with, "Why me?" late at night when Genevieve is asleep in the next room. Sometimes I think about Gethsemane and Jesus struggling with the same question when those closest to him slept nearby. I feel some comfort in knowing that when Jesus faced death, he didn't easily accept the strange obligation that stood before him. I am not alone in wondering why things feel like they're falling apart and questioning whether this could possibly be part of some mysterious plan. I think of the discouraged followers on the road to Emmaus struggling to understand why someone so full of life could have been taken away so quickly. Unfortunately for me, there is no resurrection to answer my dark questions three days later. I am left with the conclusion that, in this corner of the universe, chaos still triumphs over order; light has not yet conquered darkness.

There are times when Kailua Beach feels like a place of comfort and others when the water feels poisoned with grief. Forty days after Carolyn's funeral, the winter rains had filled our beautiful blue water full of brown mud. That's what my life felt like. What once was pure and lovely was now contaminated and stained. For a while, Genevieve would refuse to walk on the beach with me because it reminded her too much of her mother. It didn't feel the same without her. Yet, I longed to return to Kailua Beach, so I could try to hold on to a fading dream.

Of the many things that people said to me to try and make sense of my loss, one came to ring more true months and years later. It had seemed trite and empty right after the funeral: "You and Genevieve will be so close." At first, this had sounded like another profane justification for Carolyn's death. Almost two years later, I hear these words as mere observation and try to embrace them as a simple truth. Genevieve and I *are* closer and we have a different relationship than before we encountered cancer and death.

When Genevieve experienced a growth spurt and was almost as tall as one of my adult friends, I let her begin riding in the front seat of the car. This changed our relationship in a subtle way. Suddenly we were talking side-by-side as peers during the ride to and from school. Genevieve now sat where Carolyn used to. One day she pointed at my pants and asked, "Are these khakis?" My little girl was growing up and now she had my undivided attention.

Even though Carolyn's death is a fading memory for others, our loss is still at full volume. Genevieve is the only person I speak to every day. I realize, in a surprising way, how interesting a kid can be. There are moments when we feel like the Dynamic Duo. The first summer after Carolyn's death, Gen and I traveled to eight states visiting friends and sleeping on lumpy hide-a-beds and futons around the country. In the fall, we bought a tandem bike and began riding to Kailua Beach on Saturday mornings. The second summer, we traveled to Paris and Athens together. At other times, when things do not feel so good, we give each other permission to be sad and to cry whenever we miss Carolyn. Genevieve and I have become a different type of family than we were before.

Could it be that my wife had distracted me from the love I now feel for my daughter? Had *eros* diverted me from the potential depths of *philos*? Now that I am accustomed to the intimate one-on-one connection, I wonder if married parents know what they are missing. I wonder if parents with more than one child appreciate their children the way I cherish my one-and-only.

I REMEMBER WALKING ON THE BEACH with Genevieve after the rain stopped, two months after the last good day. I didn't recognize it at the time but the pattern in the wet sand foreshadowed an eventual, tentative answer to my painful questions: Could we move through life as a family of two? Was this enough?

Carolyn is gone but Genevieve and I are still here. The dream is broken and we are the tattered survivors washed ashore. Where once three lives entwined, now there are only two. I have to keep putting one wet, sandy foot in front of the other. But the small wet prints in the sand alongside mine tell me that I am not alone. Gen pauses and lets me catch up to her as the water swirls around our ankles. She squeezes my hand hard, letting me know how lost she feels. I squeeze back, trying to tell her that she is not alone. We walk together in silence. As I listen to the low roar of the ocean, I notice Genevieve's long hair blowing in the wind.

FORGETTING GRACE MEREDITH STEWART

I can no
    longer remember
        the name
of the street
    across from school
        where the sycamore trees thrived
and colored
    themselves
        beyond their own lines.
What other names
    will wander past
        the borders of my mind?
My best friend
    in the whole wide world
        of fifth grade.
The make, model
    of the car I drove
        in high school.
The man in my church
    I prayed for
        as he died of cancer.
The five children
    he left behind.

Oh help me,
    it's grace, I know,
        to forget.

MEREDITH STEWART

The name
        of the character
                in the Borges story
who never forgot
        and died of it.
                He died, didn't he?
What grace.

JOHN CHAPTER TWELVE KATHERINE NICOLE LEE

You say, "Unless a kernel of wheat falls to the ground and dies, it remains only a single seed."
But I am not ready for Gethsemane—
Nor ever will be.

You have called me to this place and said, "Bloom where I have planted you."
But I know to do so, my self must be unsheathed—
You tear me even now.

I say to you that I am betwixt and between your revelations and my blindness.
But you promise eyes that see in unseen places—
Your mud and spittle placed upon this, my blind soul.

Still, "my heart is troubled, and what shall I say? Father, save me from this hour?"
Yet for this reason we both have come—
You to destroy my kingdom,
And I to establish yours.

WHISPER NEW ORLEANS JUSTIN WHITMEL EARLEY

From top an abandoned hotel, seven months after hurricane Katrina
—March 9, 2006

The sky was a sheet of music punctuated by stars and the horizon, speckled with a few lit windows, was a piano singing slow jazz to the Gulf of Mexico.

You and I sat in the giant curve of a chalky-white satellite dish on the rooftop of an abandoned hotel. We were voyeurs confident and brave, as if it were our right to watch the city line lay down gently on top of the Mississippi river, kissing the waters goodnight. "More then conquerors" perhaps? (But I've never quite understood what that means.)

If we could kneel on the round edge, and whisper some words into the giant dish then they might be heard—from Lake Pontchartrain, around St. Charles and to the parish at St. Bernard's. In a throaty voice you would say *it's high and deep*. In quiet harmony I would say *but not enough to separate us*, and the words would echo gently out of the dish and across the city—barely undulating, barely audible over the soundtrack of the sky.

Suddenly the people on Bourbon Street would drop to their hands and knees at the sidewalk drains. *I see*, they might say—not forgetting just finally understanding. Lapping at the clear stream of water in the streets they taste the way it gives and it takes—the way it does no wrong.

The water isn't so different from love—which isn't so different from whiskey. It's only that you understand your troubles so well you forget them. The guitars still play as if they were alive themselves and speaking in tongues. Just at that moment, the blood separates from the water.

SOMETIMES IN SHANGHAI JUSTIN WHITMEL EARLEY

sometimes in shanghai, just east of the sunrise
just after the fall of the city streaked moon
i hear to the beat of a 5/4 tune
—one loud, one lonely cry.

it shrieked in its pain that still far off high-rise
alone and obedient in its blocked off platoon.
it creaks with the weight of the oncoming noon
—heavy light just east of the sunrise.

walks in the man who's lost his disguise,
back to work after nights spent touching *nanjing lu*.
there's no dark to hide under suits what we do
—that's his loud, his lonely cry.

as the smog mingled clouds all roll through the sky
a young girl becomes lost searching for brother's room.
but he was a dream and so was his room
—she's still alone just east of the sunrise.

one lonely *laoren* brushed off by a housewife
stares with the whites of his eyes—
he looks down the street block and under the lamp clock
raises his cry to the skies . . .

"Must we all be just like my *arhou*?
One lonely string on a dying machine
Solo odes, just east of the sunrise."

THE SIGNIFICANCE OF PLACE ALLISON SMYTHE

From the window of my study, beyond a row of cedar trees, I spot the rooftop of the only neighbor's home we can see. It's begun to sink in that we will not be packing our bags after a rousing rural experiment and going home. After several years of toying with the idea of fleeing the cushy but manic urban domain we'd established in Houston, my husband and I held hands and took the plunge, relocating kids and business to ten rural acres 900 miles north of, and 4.5 million people shy of, the city in which we'd met, run a successful graphic design firm, and begun a family.

For several months now, I've been waking up smack dab in the middle of America, where just the walk down the winding drive to our mailbox surpasses the distance I strolled to the corner Taqueria, sushi bar, and twenty dollar manicure salon for almost two decades. I lived off one of the busiest streets of a city known for maddening traffic, requiring a series of strategic lefts just to get in and out of the neighborhood. Now we are at the hidden end of a long gravel drive off a gravel road—days go by before anyone knocks on our door. Only the UPS man shows up unannounced.

We bought our house in the chill of February, when trees were bare, the grass brown and dormant. Looking out the back windows we could see our backyard dip low toward a row of trees before swelling into a wide, hay fringed hill. Above that, only sunset. When we showed up with the moving van six months later, the land was so overtaken with dense, exuberant vegetation that everything we remembered was obliterated from view—the hill in the backyard, the neighbor's house, the driveway, the creek, the horizon. Thick walls of green trees closed claustrophobically in around us. We'd left a city that had surgically removed most remnants of nature like the appendix evolution forgot to discard in its march toward fittestness. Apart from extreme temperatures experienced reluctantly between dashes in and out of air conditioned buildings, the consciousness that we dwelt within a natural environment was as antique a notion as full service gas stations. Symmetrical rows of palm trees lining vast asphalt seas of retail serve as nostalgic reminders nature once flourished there, though the trees are bound in thousands of miniature white bulbs and thus converted into carnival glowsticks. But nature in Missouri still runs rampant, if not amok. What overwhelms one here is not the jangle of too many cars in too little space, or endless corridors of lit signs begging entry and consumption, or the tangle of highways, overpasses, and ubiquitous construction zones. Instead, with little else to interfere, the landscape looms large. Foliage overtakes anything that's sitting still, the landscape threatens to swallow you whole. From thick swaths of underbrush deer, rabbit, fox, turkey, snake, raccoon, possum, beaver, turtle, and the occasional bobcat parade. The hills brood, the sky broods, steep bluffs along the Missouri River collapse centuries.

"Do you want to come see the dinosaur egg now, Mommy?" my youngest pleads. Though she was trained not to cross the street alone in Houston, here she's already inventoried a section of our property I have not yet investigated. I'm happy to see her skipping through grass with room to run, in air safe to breath. I catch up to her and bend to see what sort of nest she's discovered. Nestled behind thick undergrowth I spot the silver exterior of our propane tank.

What opportunities did we lose in leaving a large, diverse city, and what have we gained in coming to live in a tiny, rural town in the Midwest? Our desire was to move to a place where our daughters would unravel the outdoors, the seasons, the stars, to appreciate their connection to the physical world before it's trumped by the siren call of the Galleria. Our earliest geographies, like DNA, are inherited; we grow up wired in ways we had no vote on. I wonder how this place will imprint their psyches, how will it influence who they become, or, for that matter, who I become. Each successive generation is more likely than the one before it to live in multiple locations; the once definitive designation of "Home" becomes ever more complex and elusive. Where are you from? No longer a one word answer. What priorities should inform the choices we make about where we spend these blinks of time we call our lives? And how do we anticipate the consequences of finding ourselves in this place and not that?

Neither the cityscape I left in Texas, nor the one unfolding itself daily in Rocheport, Missouri, felt like home upon arrival. I had arrived in a foreign environment and it felt like it. However, there have been other times when an initial encounter of a place has produced instant resonance, a sort of homecoming. I experienced this keenly for the first time as a junior in college when my father invited me to join him on a business trip to Boston. Finding this an excellent excuse to skip a few days of fall classes, I booked a flight from Lubbock to Logan and while my father saw to his obligations, I roamed Boston and Cambridge with an all too soon to be extinct lack of agenda.

I still recall that first ride on the T, rumbling from Back Bay to Harvard Square, peering out smudged windows at decidedly non-Texan streets and houses whirring by, yet feeling overwhelmed by the sensation of being not so much at home as *Home*. For the next couple of days I wandered autumn tinged streets and neighborhoods as if reacquainting myself, not with a place I'd been before (sorry, Shirley McClain), but with a place I strongly sensed, that in some real and physical way, I belonged to.

To what could I attribute the acute sense of correspondence, the deep familiarity and comfort I experienced on arrival in an unfamiliar destination? How could a place I'd just discovered evoke a sort of wrenching homesickness? A feeling different to the pleasure evoked by lovely or dramatic settings and different, too, from the thrill of an environment's contrast to the settings to which one is most accustomed: the ultra congested or the rural, the foreign, cold, distant, tropical, or vacant. No, what I felt in walking the old, twisting streets of Boston that fall was a profound sense of "geographical" family reunion, minus, perhaps, the baked beans.

I have noted a similar sense of homecoming, if in lesser intensity, in other places I have visited: in Lubbock, Texas, but not Sarasota, Florida; in northern New Mexico but not Spain or Mexico; the entire country of England but not New Zealand; Cadillac Mountain in Maine but not the cliffs of Malibu or the heights of Hong Kong. Sometimes recognition sparks upon arrival and sometimes it's a gradually unfolding revelation, though the rapport is derived neither from the features of the terrain nor the inhabitants of a place. The gravitational pull of the place as a whole exerts a draw greater than any of its parts, yet that is not to say that its mountains, plains or coasts, or the energies of a city, do not exert particular charms. God could have created the whole world as one big Hawaiian Island but instead we're presented a vast range of topographies: the Arctic, the Serengeti, rain forests, the Alps, the Everglades. Nebraska. The landscapes to which we are attracted for their drama, or lack thereof, may or may not correlate with terrains that resonate deeply and uniquely within our own interior landscapes.

Nonetheless, we forge some sort of relationship with any place in which we find ourselves jabbing the alarm clock and fumbling for the door keys day after day. Before I'd had any say in the matter, my parents had introduced me to the world in Long Island, moved me to central New Jersey as a toddler, and whisked me off to the Southwest at age ten, when my father's job relocated him to Dallas. "Who wants to move to Texas?" he'd asked casually after work one night. Visions of cactus, tumbleweeds blowing across barren, unpaved streets, horses tethered to posts, wafted through my mind like the steam rising from the spaghetti on the table.

"Uh, I do," I volunteered (as if I'd ever had a choice,) having no conception of what it meant to pull up roots, to say goodbye permanently, to start all over. In a small town not yet swallowed up into the greater suburbia of the DFW Metroplex, my New Jersey accent was teased out of me before the end of sixth grade. Suddenly a memory were the woods where I found and lost turtles, squirrels, and baby rabbits. And the ravine we mined for clay, hiking along the stream through skunkweed and mud, careful to avoid the "quicksand." Now we looked out on a treeless yard we raked wheelbarrows full of rocks out of, trying to coax grass to grow. Now there were boys who chased girls with tarantulas on strings while the girls, fresh out of elementary school and already wearing pantyhose and blue eye shadow, chased them. Increasingly intricate and sophisticated variations on that theme resounded throughout my remaining school years, and after a cruel bout of exclusion in sixth grade, I learned to navigate the minefield of cliques and social standing that Dallas is known for. What kind of person would I have been had we not left New Jersey, how differently might my life have played out had I finished high school at Bruce Springsteen's alma mater?

One day in high school my art teacher escorted a group of select seniors to the art department of a nearby college where design students showed us the many rounds of drafts they'd produced in designing a beer can label. In the following Q & A and in admirable bipartisanship, the dean of the art department recommended that anyone serious about studying design apply to Texas Tech University. It struck me then that if one is required to maintain a job in life, this career looked more tolerable than most I could think of so I ended up applying to Texas Tech after a prolonged look at a map to discover just where the city of Lubbock might be.

And it was in Lubbock, an arrival I atributed to an afternoon of skipping algebra and biology, that a landscape, and one mostly derided by others, first hoisted a flag and claimed me as its own although I was not aware the deed had been done until I departed four years later. The years I spent on the Caprock reset my interior vanishing point, widening the capacity of my soul for space, silence, distance, for stripped down beauty, until they became essential. I walked the flat fields of my friend's cotton farm in Shallowater until the sun went down, until we emerged as black cut outs against the pinks and reds of a simmering sky, the only sound, the sandy soil crunching under our feet, a sound that still evokes an eighteen wheeler full of longing for an unfettered, wide angle horizon. You might imagine you determine which geography will resonate with you, you find instead geography decides for you.

After my last year of school in those windswept West Texas plains, where I learned sand invades even the most tightly closed windows and gritted teeth, I heeded my prior calling to the leafy, rolling, comparatively claustrophobic topography of New England. At my December graduation I stood at the dizzying pinnacle of all the critical choices I would make about my future and had been fortunate enough to have stumbled, a year prior, on a city with my name on it. Certain that Boston was where my future was to unfold, I arrived at the Backbay YWCA with two suitcases, my portfolio and resume, and shoes way too delicate for the slush and ice that greeted my frostbitten toes that particularly frigid January.

As much as I loved the energy and excitement of my new city, I suffered withdrawal from the empty Texas plains. When the trees, buildings and infinite renditions of the vertical for too long cut the horizon from view, when the noise and commotion pressed in too hard, I'd ride the public transit system all the way to its end in a desperate attempt to find open space. But the transit system, by design, couldn't take me out beyond congested areas. I craved sky like a boat pines for sea. On the way to my first job at a graphic design firm, housed in a converted factory in the Italian North End, I pressed my face to the cool windows of the city bus and imagined I wielded a huge sickle; as we drove along I decapitated every building, sign pole and blade of grass rising skyward.

Eventually I ended up with a car of my own and found my way to Gloucester where I could walk on the beach, ritual styrofoam cup of coffee in one hand and fried shrimp in the other, find a flat rock to sit on and ingest the far off horizon, the endless sea almost as satisfying as my relinquished plains. I carved out respites of solitude despite my options. After an hour long commute each night, I'd rush to my yellow and white striped canvas sling back beach chair, the only piece of furniture on the cement slab that was our porch, mere feet from the neighboring porch, to catch the waning rays of sun in the small square of sky caught between roof and tree tops. For those moments I could be anywhere: the sky, my constant companion in every place I have been and ever will be, a centering. I wonder, deprived of the blue, how long I could retain any semblance of sanity.

As had the Panhandle, the city, too, made its mark on me. Boston, to a girl arriving from a then still largely homogenous region, was a dazzling bazaar of ethnic enclaves and exotic tableaus: passersby speaking Italian on bustling streets of the North End, freshly slaughtered poulty curtaining the windows of Chinatown, its narrow alleys running and pungent in summer, the Boston Irish bus driver calling out stops, fish and vegetables heaped in carts at Haymarket Square, musicians on the corners with guitar cases open to coins, the homeless folded in doorways and sometimes in line with you at the ATM. Historic buildings tucked among glass skyscrapers, their domes and steeples poking above treetops but failing to alter the skyline. Old juxtaposed with new, the city was a constant reminder of the passage of time and that time moved quickly. Everywhere people were in a hurry: pedestrians, patrons, commuters, vendors, workers. Life in fast forward.

If I'd lost cotton fields by day and stars by night, I'd inherited great bookstores, restaurants, performance venues, and a diverse mix of souls with whom I spent long hours gnawing on the mysteries of life. On my own for the first time, walking the highwire with safety net removed, I was as malleable a person as a fresh lump of Play-Doh. Quickly morphing into an urbanite, I wandered happily anonymous in the crowds, absorbing their energy, indulging in an amped up solitude enhanced by the hubbub. In the waning moments before work or at lunch I'd observe the rushing world with the luxurious remove of a tourist, pretending I would not momentarily resume my position among the ranks of this running shoe clad, perpetually harried, hurried, and ever mobile workforce.

Despite the exhilaration of setting forth on your own uncharted continent, making one's way into adulthood involves the certain rupture of naive innocence and the first indications that the big, wide world is destined to disappoint, if not completely break your heart. I'd landed in Boston armed only with what I could carry on a plane—wide-eyed idealism and a tiny knoll of experience from which to inform the choices I would make. I hoped, in at least some small but significant way, to leave the world a better place than I'd found it, a conviction stemming from the religious faith which had sprouted in high school and bloomed fully by the end of my college years.

Coinciding with college graduation and impending move was, I concluded, a divinely orchestrated introduction to a ministry serving the universities in Boston and Cambridge. Considering this the answer to the question of my mysterious pull to Boston, I reported for duty on arrival, moving my meager belongings from the Backbay YWCA to a rickety third floor apartment in Central Square which I ended up sharing with several women involved in the same campus work. When not at my job virtually all my free time was unreservedly devoted to working with them.

For several years I was fervent in faith and joyous in ministry, certain I'd found my life's calling, witnessing astonishing, if not miraculous, events transpire among the students and others we served. And serve we did—time, talents, resources and, not infrequently, our beds and living room floor, were freely offered to others. We believed we were living the life Christ calls all his followers to rather than merely paying lip service to the notion of offering our lives as sacrifices to God. Because we'd so fully subscribed to the conviction that the things we were doing and the sacrifices we'd made benefitted not only the people we knew personally, but also the past, present, and future Kingdom of God, the ever deepening fissures created by faults in the theological foundation of the ministry went too long unattended. The inevitable ensuing collapse of the ministry was nothing short of devastating. To think that much of what we'd espoused, what *I'd* espoused, in the effort to serve and give, was in the end sideways if not downright harmful was almost unbearable. I not only lost faith in those who lead the ministry, but by extension the God who I believed had lead me to them. I was confronted with the lengths my own conscience had traveled to deny the obvious and the excuses I'd made for others in order to uphold the ideals I so needed to make sense of the world and my place in it. My bright hope of a meaningful future, of believing my life mattered in the world, was shattered. After having spent the better part of my twenties in Boston and with the bitter taste of ashes still in my mouth, I knew it was time to let go of my crumbled ideals and move on. Rebecca Solnit, in *A Field Guide to Getting Lost*, writes:

> The places in which any significant event occurred become embedded with some of that emotion, and so to recover the memory of the place is to recover the emotion, and sometimes to revisit the place uncovers the emotion. Every love has its landscape. Thus place, which is always spoken of as though it only counts when you're present, possesses you in its absence . . .

Boston and all it stood for sunk inside me like my own private Atlantis. For years after I'd left, artifacts from that lost city washed up on my shores, invaded my dreams, colored every new thing I did in shades of mourning.

I'd left finally for Houston, arriving as a weary refugee from the Land of Disillusionment. I had friends there, it was nearer my family, and it seemed as good a place as any to lick my wounds, sort things out, and decide what I might do next, and where. I did not bother to research the city, its landscape or amenities, on the grounds that I would not stay long enough for it to matter, giving it two years at most. But as much as I had not made the decision *to* move to Houston as much as to *leave* Boston, and against my persistent resistance to the idea, Houston became home for the next seventeen years. Beware of great escapes.

If Boston was the stage of ruined hope, Houston was the workshop where I eventually dredged up broken pieces and reassembled them, bit by jagged bit, and began to fathom the picture that emerged. I finally came to cherish the fact that the resulting mosaic of my life held a particular, ravaged beauty which would never have appeared had the pieces not broken as they had, with every one of their sharp and scarring edges.

Hardly anyone you meet in Houston is from Houston and most don't plan on staying long—it's a city of transients, a between place people come to in hopes of forging fortunes and futures before they settle in places they really want to be. Because of this, the city is a maddening juxtaposition of greed and grace—allowing itself to be strip mined by self interested entrepreneurs and at the same time extending an outstretched hand to anyone needing to start over, to reinvent themselves and the world they live in.

A fouled Garden of Eden, its tropical air choked with chemicals and lush green landscape buried under concrete, the city's natural beauty is foiled by economic expediency. Developments are thrown up and historic buildings razed without a nod to aesthetics, heritage, or land use. The designated "Strip Club Capital of America" aptly reflects a city mostly treated like a one night stand. Development spans so far in every direction that you can't outdistance it without a couple of hours to spare on a freeway. With no empty landscapes to easily access, the highway became my Walden Pond. Instead of the Atlantic, I was calmed by the whir of tires on asphalt. Movement without hindrance, speed eschewing destination. Consuming mile after mile with no aim to arrival. Sometimes I'd spend a good hour just driving the loop around the city. Going in circles, perpetually leaving.

In spite of its deficiencies, Houston has a way of getting tangled up inside you. Visitors who deplore the city inevitably love the inhabitants. There is something open and authentic, generous and gritty, about the people there. With the eradication of natural landscape, the people of Houston become the landscape. When I think of the city, I don't think of skyscrapers, highways, cars, and construction zones, though it was all of these. I think of flowering patios, courtyards, porches and decks, I think of chips and salsa, guacamole and fajitas, coffee and beer, under palm trees and banana trees and stars we could not see, peopled with chatter and laughter and stubborn belief in better days.

So it was in Houston that I began to grapple with the whys and wherefores of my personal history and dredged up the determination to shape my failures into something meaningful: I enrolled in graduate school, met and married my husband, started a graphic design firm, had two children, and then, later than most, became a grown up. Life took on shapes I could not have foreseen and would never have occurred had life in Boston gone according to plan. To my plan, anyway. I'd imagined my destiny was in Boston, and it was, only not in the way I'd envisioned. It seldom is. I thought Houston a stop on the highway to pull out the map, but it required I stay until its work was complete. All the places I've lived have served to make me this person and not that. But as I'm still not the person I will be, I stand now at the mercy of Missouri, wondering what this verdant land will accomplish in me.

THIS MORNING WE WAVED GOODBYE as the last of our family, in from Florida, Texas, and Louisiana for the Thanksgiving holidays, vanished from view beyond the curve in our drive. For the past week every inch of our new house has been broken in, utilized for sleeping, eating, and armchair quarterbacking. Unseasonably warm, sunny, picture perfect days brought highs of almost 80, amazing our guests who had packed with expectations of dreary winter weather. And the days do get dreary; since summer's end it appears the ratio stands at two to one—two days of gloom for each day of sunshine. When the sun retreats for days on end I wonder how a population endures such seasons, how it manages not to descend into wholesale despair, dread and pessimism. The moment the sun's rays poke back through the gray ceiling the earth perks up and trouble seems suddenly manageable, slated for improvement, restoration, reconciliation, the soul instantly buoyed and blessed. You have to try harder to be in a bad mood with the sun warming your face. My long stint in Texas ensured that no matter where I find myself I will forever yearn for long summer days, a stretched horizon, and the blaze of relentless light.

"Are you still a Texas poet?" asks my friend, himself a poet, editing a book on Texas poets. These days, how do you determine where you are from? So far I have been from New York, New Jersey, Texas, Massachusetts, and now Missouri. By far I've spent more years in Texas than everywhere else put together. How long would I have to stay here to no longer be a Texas poet? To become a Missouri poet?

"Who wants to move to Missouri?" I asked my kids. We are living in a tiny town that a year ago I had never heard of. Many dominos fell in order to bring us here—we would never have known to even look for a place like this. So many other places we could have ended up but didn't. Each day I look out at the rolling terrain in wonder that somehow we are *here*. The math doesn't quite add up but then it won't, life is not an equation. Somehow we find ourselves in the places we need to be, for as long as we need to be there. They wait for us, they keep us until they are finished with us; in significant ways they remain with us. I can't say now if we chose Missouri or it chose us—or what exchanging pavement for dirt roads, restaurants for trees and hills, bookstores and theaters for deer and fox will accomplish in us. What I do know is that it will make a difference, our being here and not there. That we will be different people for having been here. *Where are you from?* has lost its significance. The question has become *Where were you made?*

PSALM 19 HANNAH FAITH NOTESS

Last night I woke up on the roof to the sound of everything shouting.

The stars chanted loudest, hung so low in the sky
I could pluck them like fruit from a spreading tree.

I watched the skies unfold so long, I learned all the patterns
I ever dreamed of weaving along my coat's hem, so long

that the sun came up panting like those marathoners
who run endlessly from village to village.

I know the words are true, even if I can't understand.

I know it from the rich woody sounds of the old language.
One day their meaning will break over me,
a wave of honey coursing through my body.

The grandfathers rode these words, sturdy as an oxcart, into the land.
Words poured from the rock, and they drank their fill,
clean fear numbing their lips.

If you cover my mouth with your hands, O Lord, will it not burn?

If I lie back under the stars, O Lord, will you not appear among them,
the faintest speck of a ruddy comet?

A WRECK HANNAH FAITH NOTESS

for Heather

Fear might not be the opposite of love.
Remember that morning after a night
of driving home from our friend's wedding,
when the car slipped silent through Chicago,
the city so lit up the buildings seemed
painted right onto air? Actually,
you were asleep, I think, and I was driving,
alone with the city. I thought the world
was saying its name to me, that I
was so awake my soul could attach to God
with a string made out of light. I was wrong.
No premonitions, not even awareness
that I hadn't slept all night. What happens next
I'd rather watch from a distance, like this:

The car drifts right, across the white line,
hits the rumble strip, then fishtails.
Its front fender nudges the guardrail, then
it pirouettes to kiss the back bumper
against the rail, a few yards further down.
It rests in the median, easing in
to the June grass with its newly flat front tire.

This never works. I can't manage that trick
from the movies, where the camera pans
up, away from the disaster, then freeze-frames
on blank sky. Instead the string I'd thought
was mystical still tugs on me, a sense—
not of an afterlife—but of another life

A WRECK

in which fear never rises in my throat
all choked with love, in which I never stare
at the blood my boyfriend doesn't notice
blooming from the sleeve of his white t-shirt,
in which you never lurch from the back seat,
holding your broken nose, in which years later
we sit somewhere with coffee and the paper,
shaking our heads at news of a car wreck

not mine. And that is not my life. Not mine.
I'm stuck in this one, halfway between
right now and memory, out on the highway
gathering our clothes flung from the trunk
of the smashed car we'll never see again.
"Leave it," the cop will say. "Leave it behind."

THE DISASTER TOURIST HANNAH FAITH NOTESS

I was three hundred miles north
on the beach when the tsunami hit.

It foamed up gently around my belly,
soaked into my towel and the pages
of a ratty paperback.

*

When the boy's wrecked body came to the hospital,
plucked like a rag off the barbed wire,

I sat just downstairs in the front office
wrestling with the ancient Dictaphone.

Its heavy pedal kept rewinding
to a blank stretch of tape.

*

The morning the hurricane swallowed a city,
a bus careened around the corner
in a wave of rain, drenching my new clothes.

I arrived angry and wet, complained
to the girl, who, eight months later,
would misjudge a landing in the fog,

transfigure her small plane
into a breathtaking ball of flame.

THE DISASTER TOURIST

*

O stupid angel of death, I want to say,
you missed me again!

Watch me disappear into the train depot,
into the past, just before the bombing.

Watch me lean awkwardly against
the flashing height-weight-horoscope machine,
clutching my shabby luggage in the spot

you would have caught me, if the taxi driver
had taken four months to arrive.

SINGLE-POINT PERSPECTIVE HANNAH FAITH NOTESS

—*Jamaa Masjid (Friday Mosque), Delhi*

I walk along one of a picture's lines—
the kind I always traced and erased
in art class. What I measured with a ruler
was never this symmetrical. Look how

rows of red-edged arches open their mouths
to call *Allahu akbar*. Shah Jahan,
everyone loves your tomb, the Taj Mahal,
but in your Friday mosque, I become

a point in faith's geometry. My eyes
move along lines to a vanishing point
where they converge—somewhere outside
in the car parts bazaar or a chai stall.

Beyond that point lines open, all pointing
to other things—Red Fort, the Himalayas,
one woman on her face toward Mecca,
her praying body open as a mouth.

LITTLE PROOFS ROSS KENNERLY

LATELY I AM COMPELLED TO CROSS MYSELF, though I was not raised Catholic. I received no proper training on how to make the sign, how to answer the responsory with *Lord, hear our prayer*, how to take the stale wafers and taste of wine. These are congregational duties I never learned. I was raised Methodist in northern Michigan, in a traditionally Protestant community that eschewed the Catholic faith; my mother even forbade me to attend Christmas Eve mass in a neighboring town with my high-school girlfriend. Not long ago, I came across a makeshift grave-site near my home in Chicago and felt I had no choice but to bear the cross: A small memorial was being constructed inchmeal on the façade of the Blarney Stone bar from photos or brief sentiments scribbled on red stationary and bouquets of convenience store flowers taped to one of its green pilasters. Above the developing shrine, the second floor windows were boarded up with sheets of plywood, the gray stones scorched with flares of soot. It was misting; the fine rain bled the ink from the handwritten epitaphs: I'm so sorry I never loved you the way I should have loved you. This is wrong. This is bullshit. Another one, in masculine script, read: I love you, brother. See you on the other side. I looked in the photographs for a face common to all of them; I determined the kid in sunglasses and khaki shorts posing with friends on the fishing boat was the same one smiling thinly in the restaurant with cups of dark wine on the table. Him, he was dead. Later, I found out from the Blarney Stone bartenders that he had been a regular there; he burned up on St. Patrick's Day after passing out drunk on his couch holding a lit cigarette in his hand. It was too bad, they said. He was a good kid. I touched the petals to feel if the flowers were real, then removed my hat and said a small prayer for those to follow—paraphrasing a bit of dialogue I remembered from *Finding Forrester*. It was all I could think to say. Then I crossed myself.

Since that morning, the need to do this has popped up more and more, though I don't always make the actual motions with my hands; sometimes I just feel phantom fingertips gracing my chest. The first time felt awkward, like verbalizing a word you have only recently learned. My cross was so poorly made that I looked around to see if anyone was behind me who might call me a poseur, some Catholic passerby who noticed my sign's rugged construction and would call me out for a fake, a charlatan making an ostentatious display of piety.

Lately, though, it feels more awkward not to make the cross, not to touch my lips, my chest, my shoulder, my shoulder, not to praise the Godhead spectacles-testicles-wallet-and-watch: I cross myself for the woman on the number 22 bus whose osteoporosis has folded her over on her lap like warm pita bread; her hairline is shaved back to the crown of her skull, tennis ball-size cysts sprout below her elbows and knees and wrists (I see them when she tugs at her oversized pull) and her thick glasses are cobbled together by strands of Scotch tape. I cross myself for a toddler making her first steps in the playground outside of Hawthorne Scholastic Academy on a Sunday; her mother claps as she wobbles over a low wooden beam partitioning the wooden chips under the swing-set from the blacktop track encircling the yuppie sunbathers in lawn chairs. I cross myself for an amputee at the YMCA, a professor of English from the University of Illinois-Chicago who jury-rigs a strap from the remainder of his right arm to the cable crossover machine to exercise his biceps; I have known him a long time, and as he is leaving we pound our left fists together, amen.

I cross myself for a woman who walks by dragging on an unlit cigarette. I cross myself for young people in wheelchairs. I cross myself when a friend mentions his girlfriend has a benign tumor on her pituitary gland, and on Thursday they are breaking apart her nose to prod inside her skull and remove it. I cross myself when I think of a man I saw covered in ash from the collapse of the twin towers, sweating and drinking a can of Sprite; I cross myself when I think of my sixty-year-old father water-skiing. I cross myself sometimes when the sun sets, and when I lie down to rest. I cross myself for people sitting alone in bars, for butts in ashtrays on empty porches, for actors crying onstage during curtain call, for firemen hanging off the side of their trucks, for crumpled cars along the side of Interstate 94, for blown truck tires, for homemade posters of lost pets, for quintets of singing homeless men, for dolls abandoned on the sidewalk, for a squirrel shimmying up a maple tree with a flyer in its mouth. I cross myself for roadside fruit stands, for the tiny spiders (and their tiny webs) in the window of my shower, for the stars when they blink through the pervading canopy of orange over this city. I cross myself for the holy silence of a Michigan darkness, for deer sneaking across night highways. I even crossed myself for a coyote that wandered into a downtown Quizno's, after someone told me coyotes appear in the Loop if their mates reject them.

* * *

IN 2001 I VISITED CATHÉDRALE NOTRE-DAME DE CHARTRES with twelve other Alma College students studying abroad in Paris for the spring semester. The village of Chartres is two hours southwest of Paris by RER train, lonesome in fields of dandelions like most towns within a hundred miles of the capital. Leaving the big city, the banlieues drop off suddenly into farmland, as if you had walked off some sheer precipice and landed square in a meadow rife with wildflowers. The cathedral is the tallest structure between Paris and Chartres; it approaches like a great, distant peak, an errant manmade Alp.

Alma's affiliate office at the Alliance Française set up a private tour of the enormous structure with a guide who introduced himself as Malcolm, an urbane gentleman with Moses-white hair and a British accent who was the curator of Chartres and (according a video I watched in French 221 later that year) the foremost authority on its arcane lore. Malcolm led us up the narthex steps, explaining as he crossed himself that a midday choir performance was planned later inside the musty cool nave, so we were to keep our voices low when asking questions. Malcolm's expertise pertained specifically to Chartres' stained glass windows, so after briefly touching on (or walking over) the famous labyrinth sprawling across the stone floor, he gave us a tutorial on each one of the windows, stopping at one point to scold an eavesdropper. "This is a private tour," he said, and again waited patiently, hands folded like a monk's at the base of his vest, for the outsider to leave. When she failed to get the hint, he repeated, "C'est un tour privé," which seemed to do the trick.

I can only recall two of the windows and their respective histories: the first was located on the west face—which I'm sure was significant—and depicted the Tree of Jesse, white like limestone, sprouting from the sleeping Bethlemite's guts. The second faced south and featured the story of Adam from the book of Genesis and Jesus' parable of the Good Samaritan from the Gospel of Luke. Malcolm explained that the intent of stained glass windows was akin to a picture book, called a Poor Man's Bible—in the Middle Ages, most commoners were illiterate, and the parallelism between the Old and New Testament stories helped them conceptualize biblical metaphors without having to be able to read the Bible. The Good Samaritan, Malcolm explained, was allegorical for Christ's redemption. The panes, each illustrating a different scene like a medieval comic strip—Eve offering Adam an apple, the Samaritan extending a hand to the fallen Jew—were interposed to reinforce the point. This story is called la Chute in French; the Fall of Man. Malcolm's head was full of little eurekas like this: The Hebrew word for "apple" also meant "evil," and its usage was tantamount to a biblical inside joke. During the construction of Notre-Dame de Chartres, medieval villagers kept piss-pots outside the front door to their homes, to be collected in the morning so the window-smiths could use the urine as a color fixative before firing the glass pieces. Each color was created from a mineral whose chemical structure would alter beautifully under extreme heat: cobalt for blue, iron for red, sulfur for yellow. Malcolm also noted that not everything depicted in the stained glass and rose windows (glowing soft blue like a summer prayer) could be found in the Bible; only someone like him, who had spent most of his life studying Scripture, would know these things. Solemnly, he crossed himself again, tracing over the meridian of buttons along his waistcoat.

It was then that the sanctuary began to hum with female voices, in choir like muted horns, rising and falling and shooting across the rib vaults like magnetic embers tugged across the night sky by the secret singing of sunflares.

I DECIDED THAT IF THIS URGE TO SIGN THE CROSS was not going to subside, I should at least learn to make it correctly. I took a manila folder stuffed with instructional and historical information on the holy sign to the park at Hawthorne, the same park where I had seen the mother applaud the first steps of her daughter. I picked out a metal bench with less pigeon droppings than the others, outside of the 200-meter track and the few men and women sharing towels in the May sun. Behind them, two girls wearing oversized sunglasses were sitting on miniature post-and-lentil slabs tiled with black and white squares for chess or checkers. They were doing leg raises and talking about drinking somewhere the night before. A third girl joined them a short while later, announcing herself with, "God, I hate my life."

There is some discrepancy as to the proper way to position your fingers: Orthodox Christians extend the index and middle finger, which is bent slightly, and press the thumb, ring and pinkie fingers together. According to a Wikipedia entry, this position is representative of the duality of Christ, perfect in both divinity and humanity; the index finger indicates Divinity "since He came down from on high and saved those below." The middle finger represents Christ bowing the heavens, coming down to Earth for our salvation. The Catholic Encyclopedia states that this hand formation also indicates the abbreviation for IXC (Jesous Christos Soter), the index finger representing the "I"; the bent middle finger, the "C"; and the thumb crossing the middle finger, the "X". However, Pope Innocent III changed this position in the 13th century, to the thumb, forefinger, and middle finger pressed together, and the other two held tightly in the palm. Depending on which denomination of Christianity you ascribe to, both are correct. Similarly, it seems no one in the last two thousand years has bothered to make an official ruling on which shoulder to touch first. Latin Catholics, Anglicans, Lutherans, and Oriental Orthodox sign left-to-right, watch and wallet. Eastern Orthodox and Eastern Catholics sign right-to-left, wallet and watch. The best explanation for this is the original right-to-left motion made by the priest was mirrored by the congregation, which from their perspective was left-to-right.

You can make a large cross, from forehead to breast—or forehead to stomach—and shoulder to shoulder. You can make a small cross with your thumb, on your Bible, your forehead, your lips or your chest. You can touch holy water first. *The Lay Folks Mass Book*, an instructional tome from the 1200s, says that after Scripture you can trace a cross on a bench, a wall or a book, and then kiss it; you can cross your thumb with your index finger and kiss it in the same manner. You can say the Jesus Prayer, Lord have mercy, In nomine Patris et Filii et Spiritus Sancti, The seal of the living God, In the name of Jesus of Nazareth or O God come to my assistance. Members of the clergy can sign in the air to bless persons or distant objects. Some nuns in the Middle Ages signed with an open hand. St. Nino, the Apostle of Georgia, signed an ailing queen's entire body with a wooden cross and cured her. One Catholic historian, Sozomen, describes a bishop who signed the cross with his finger at an attacking dragon and then spat on the beast. My favorite variation, however, is that you can make the sign using your tongue, up, down, right and left, "in circumstances where it may be considered inappropriate, or as a means to hide the gesture from others, or to keep its personal character." I think this is my best bet.

Occasions for making the cross:
—First thing in the morning, last thing at night
—In response to blasphemy, to suggest the offense and ask forgiveness for the offender
—Against temptation, sin, or danger to the body
—When passing a church, in recognition and adoration of Christ's presence in the Eucharist
—For God's blessing before a sport competition or a travel (good for fifty days if saying words, one hundred days if you use holy water)
—As an outward expression of your faith, to physically reference the Sacrifice of Jesus in your surroundings
—Before making or eating food, especially bread (you may cross the loaf with the knife)
—To use as a weapon against the spirits of darkness

One of the documents I brought with me, from the Office of Catholic Publications, said "the smallest flower, a grain of dust, the tiniest insect, each and all reveal the wisdom, the omnipotence, the infinite greatness of their Creator, as clearly as the sun itself and all the glories of the starlit heavens." I paused there for a moment to digest all of this and consider my surroundings in the park: The three girls who had been exercising on the chessboards were gone. Thin robins were dropping out of the ash trees spaced evenly around the school grounds and culling whatever larvae were writhing below from the surrounding mulch. A breeze was blowing, and I could smell my skin reacting to the sun, that wonderful, been-at-the-beach chemical aroma. Behind me, a woman passed by on the other side of the park fence, part of a group of Chicago Cubs fans walking to the Cubs-White Sox game at Wrigley Field a few blocks away. "MAKE SURE YOU LOOK AT

YOUR PAPERS AND NOT AT HER ASS!" she squawked at me, obviously referring to the girl lying a few yards away on a bedsheet with her boyfriend. I waited until the woman and her group reached the end of the block, and then I made a little cross on my forehead to ward off evil, if not only mean, spirits.

ON THE RETURN TRIP TO PARIS, three of us shared one of the RER's four-person booths with our professor, Madame Savarin. Julia, my best friend from college, was sitting beside me. Julia was an English major and the assistant volleyball coach, and had no real reason for taking the spring semester abroad, other than for the pure experience of living in Paris before she graduated; it was a kind of gift to herself, a final hurrah, and a week before we were to leave, at the foreign-exchange program orientation, she had chopped off her blonde hair above her shoulders and dyed it dark brown. Seated across from us was Madame Savarin (to me—everyone else called her Marie) and a student named Tim, who I had nicknamed Tim Le Pieux (Tim the Pious). Tim was very active in the Alma College religious community, and had led some of the sermons at Fellowship of Christian Athletes—or some other similar organization's meeting circles. Tim was going to divinity school after graduation; he had a black belt in Tae Kwon Do and a Fred Durst goatee. I was the only French major in the group, there to take the Diplôme de Langue—an examination that would determine whether or not I would graduate—on Madame Savarin's recommendation. Madame Savarin and I, incidentally, shared a long history of butting heads—one semester, she failed me in French Literature just to prove she could. She was brilliant and wiry, her mind and body lean and mean; she was an atheist, wrote folk music for fun, and had married the college's German professor for convenience, not love. Her true love had been the heir to a spiced rum company from South America.

Julia, Tim, and I were discussing our host's earlier comment about how some of his Christian esoterica hadn't originated in the Bible, because neither Julia or I, who both spent our childhoods in Sunday School (my mother was an instructor), had ever heard it before; some of the information (according to Tim) must have been rooted in the apocrypha—unauthenticated, disputed books omitted from the Bible, usually because biblical scholars can't validate the author, or there are multiple authors, or the Vatican Councils simply decided that whatever is included in the text is irrelevant. Tim said that Malcolm's parallels between Adam taking a bite out of the apple and the parable of the Good Samaritan, as well as how "apple" is synonymous with "evil" in Hebrew, was knowledge that Malcolm could have gained in seminary, but most likely only someone versed in apocrypha, such as the Dead Sea Scrolls, could have known some of this stuff.

I countered with some fideist logic from Douglas Adams' *Hitchhiker's Guide to the Galaxy*, which I had read recently. In the book, there exists a species of fish, called the Babel fish, which one of the main characters sticks in the ear of the story's protagonist,

Arthur Dent. The Babel fish feeds entirely on human brain waves, and, as a waste product, it translates whatever language passes through Arthur's ear canal into his native tongue, in this case English. Everybody in the book's universe has this handy fish stuck in his head, and everyone is able to communicate regardless of his race or home planet. Arthur learns that the existence of the Babel fish logically disproves the existence of God. As *Hitchhiker's Guide* tells it, God refuses to reveal His existence to Man because proof denies faith, and without faith He is nothing. Man responds by asking God to explain the Babel Fish. Something so beneficial to the human species could not have come about purely by coincidence, Man insists, which proves definitively that You must exist; which, by Your own definition, You don't. God answers that He hadn't considered this and vanishes.

Madame Savarin laughed (one of the few times I ever saw her laugh) and said my Babel fish anecdote reminded her of her favorite joke: René Descartes walks into a bar. He sits down on a barstool and orders a beer. After he finishes his beer, the bartender comes back over and asks: "Would you like another?" And Descartes says, "I don't think so," and disappears.

One of Madame Savarin's requirements for the course was that each student was to keep a daily journal of what we learned or witnessed during our brief stay in Paris. Though she didn't bring it up on the train, Julia shared an anecdote with me later that night over a drink at Café Oz in Châtelet—something that she couldn't wait to include in her class journal.

> *Today at Chartres cathedral, we heard a choir perform in the sanctuary. It was beautiful; so beautiful, in fact, that Ross and I went over and bought one of their CDs after the performance was over. We each had only forty francs or so, and the CD cost over eighty, so we split it between the two of us. We arranged that I would have it first, but I don't know how I will ever get it back to him once we return to the States. Anyway, while he paid for the CD (and the other students and Marie were waiting for us) I saw one of the congregation walk over to a font on her way out. She dipped her hand in the holy water and crossed herself. Then she picked her ass.*
>
> *I wonder if that gave her the holy shits.*

Notre-Dame de Chartres had invigorated me, reconciled my intellect and spirit in harmony like penitent voices filling up empty chambers, or excited smiles in a train car awash with breezy sun; Julia said she had felt God sitting beside her in one of the sanctuary folding chairs, come to her assistance. I was there, too, imbued with an equally profound sense of eternal, prescient holiness. I said to her, "This place could turn me into a Catholic."

* * *

I CROSS MYSELF FOR LITTLE PROOFS of God alive and on the earth, here beside me and in everything I touch and see, which maybe are an indication that He was once but is no longer here, or maybe, like the Babel fish, prove that He never existed in the first place. I cross myself for good intentions and misfortunes, for health and illness, for the good and evil I see in every day, and you could see too, if you listen, and wait. I cross myself for the ghost that lives in my apartment, an old woman who locks and unlocks my doors, rattles my toilet seat early in the morning and once even washed my dishes when I wasn't at home. I cross myself for the two men I saw help each other in a Paris Métro station: two strangers, one on each opposing platform, each in front of a soda machine; one soda machine wasn't working, and both trains were coming. "Mec," the man called out to get the other's attention, and tossed him a ten-franc piece. "Qu'est-ce que vous voulez?" the other man called back; "Un Coca!" was the reply. The other man deposited the coin, bought the beverage and tossed it across the tracks; the trains came, the men waved, and most likely never saw each other again. I cross myself for the angel in a pink track suit who appeared to me and my friend Amy, after Amy had screamed from a phone cabin on Rue de Montparnasse that her carte téléphonique wasn't working, and out of a sea of black-suited, dour-faced francophone Parisians came this woman, this angel in pink, who handed Amy a new card and said, "Here, use mine," and then disappeared like a bird into gushing waterfalls. I pray I continue to find these moments, these little proofs, as clearly as the sun itself and all the glories of the starlit heavens. I see a homeless man bathing himself in a fountain on LaSalle Street, and I cross myself, with my tongue this time, the Father, the Son and the Holy Spirit small in my mouth, like bits of sunshine.

ELI BISON BECOMES AN ANGEL JEREMY BURGESS

My name is not important; I'm still fighting for my name. Right now all that's important is that I'm a boxer and I'm in the ring with Eli Bison, the greatest fighter that has ever shared my stage. He's in the opposite corner looking me over, wondering just what kind of feast his Lord has prepared. I stand in my corner with a different kind of appetite.

Eli Bison.

I feel like a kid again, like it's a Friday night and I've ditched my friends to stay at home and watch him, only he's watching me back. His short hair and his baby face might fool you, but that's just his natural-born defense, a part of the underdog mentality that's gotten him this far. From the neck down, he's all business. His taut white body is already shining with the first drops of sweat, and as he hops in place, his gold satin shorts sway back and forth, his gloves held steadily. From my corner, I can see the large holes in his ear lobes that are normally filled by a pair of small black halos. Unfilled, these holes make him seem like an unfinished puzzle.

He has a tattoo on his right bicep. You couldn't read it from a distance, but I know what it says. Psalm 144:1—Blessed be the Lord my strength, who teacheth my hands to war and my fingers to fight. Seconds before we are set to meet in the center of the ring, the former title-holder stops hopping. Instead of panning his eyes across the audience and pitching his hands in the air, Eli Bison concentrates on nobody but himself, standing perfectly still before turning around and falling down on one knee, facing the corner post. He places his right fist on the bridge of his nose, lost in the deep valleys of prayer. I stand rigid and wide-eyed, watching this ritual. I stare him down. He knows I'll be waiting when he opens his eyes.

His concentration breaks only when the referee calls us in. Eli rises to his feet, removing the white towel from around his neck before approaching the center of the ring. Four steps forward and I'm face to face with Eli Bison, our eyes like guard dogs on short leashes. We touch gloves, a brief peace.

Then the coming storm.

My grandfather raised me to be a fighter.

Mom and I lived in Rome, New York, in the same district as he did, just a few blocks away, because she could never live completely on her own. So whenever I got bullied in the schoolyard, I would skip classes and run home into her arms with a red face and wet sleeves.

But this never got me anywhere.

So I ran to my grandfather's house instead one afternoon when I was eight. I tried to throw my arms around him, but he just pushed me away.

"Son, what the hell do you think you're doin?" he said.

After I told him about my mother and how she couldn't do anything about me being bullied, he sat me down on his tattered brown couch, kneeled in front of me, and held his hands up. He balled them up into tough, weathered fists and held them up to hide half his face.

"Hold your fists up," he told me.

"You see these right here?" he asked. "If you use these, you won't have to run home to your mother ever again. *These* are your mother and father. Your food and your shelter. Your God and your Devil. You understand me?"

I sniffled and nodded. He gave me a glass of water, let me watch a half hour of television, and then sent me on my way back to my mother's house.

The next time I came home early, I had blood on my shirt. My mother was furious, and it just made matters worse when I told her that it wasn't my blood.

This trend continued through middle school and high school, and by that time my mother had placed the full burden of my misconduct in my grandfather's hands. They argued like never before, and a rift formed between them. Rather than turning to one or the other, I turned to myself. I dropped out of high school three months into my sophomore year and moved out of the neighborhood.

I worked odd jobs at restaurants and bars to pay the rent. My one-bedroom apartment was a shit-hole, but it was miles away from my mother and grandfather—far enough to keep them out of my hair but close enough to keep my mother from calling and crying. Aside from drinking with my co-workers, I was alone most nights. But I broke out of this cycle when I saw a flyer one afternoon for an amateur fight night at a run-down gym in Rome's downtown district. The fights there were never glamorous and only happened about once a week. The rules were flexible, the pay wasn't much, and the crowds were small.

But I was good.

Soon enough, I became a big deal in a small town. I fought all over Rome, and then began to travel across the state for fights—Rochester, Buffalo, Albany, even New York City. I kept working day jobs, but I took up boxing as a professional.

I kept going to that old gym in Rome, too. After seeing me fight so many times, Jay the owner allowed me to train there for free. He had a cozy little office in the gym with a cheap television that could sometimes pick up scrambled pay-per-view fights. When the picture was clean enough, I would sit in Jay's office and watch fights with him.

This was the first time I saw Bison.

"Oh, this cat?" Jay told me. "He's one of those corn-fed Southern boys. They say he's one of the risin' stars in boxing right now. Talks funny, but boy, he can pound the hell outta ya."

I admired the way he fought. He was scrappy, quick, smart. Not the biggest fighter—not even close. But with the way he would hop around the ring and then come down like lightning with a quick jab-and-right-hook combo, he could knock out guys a foot taller.

Years later he became a born-again Christian and started traveling to conventions and revivals preaching the Lord's name. This didn't take away from his skill level, of course, but it made him mentally weaker. Jesus can do murder on a boxer. He lost his guts, his fighter's mentality. He started doing unto others and all that shit until he lost touch with the warrior.

And I hated him for it.

I hated him because he sold himself short, failing to live up to the potential that he showed as a young fighter. I hated him because he took every bit of his raw skill and let it soften into mediocrity through the grace of God. He could've been the greatest, and now he was nothing more than good. I stopped watching his fights, but I heard all about his mediocre career from the papers.

In his younger days, though, nobody could stop Eli Bison. I kept track of every one of his fights and measured my progress with his. I watched him as he gained ground on the best boxers in the country, then the world. Those pay-per-view channels were colorless and fuzzy, but I swear I could see something in him, something that separated him from all of the other boxers I watched back then.

If I had to call it anything, I'd say that he shined.

THERE'S A DANCE THAT TAKES HOLD OF YOU when you're behind the ropes. Eli and I, we're doing nothing more than dancing. The winner of the fight is simply the one who leads.

Round One.

Eli's already got me caught up in his foxtrot. You would say that I'm struggling to keep up. You would say I've got two left feet, that Eli Bison is the matador and I'm charging forward at every flash of red.

But me, I wouldn't say those things. I'm just getting warmed up.

It's as if he hasn't aged at all. As if he's somehow channeled his former self. Boxers age faster than ordinary people. You can see it in our faces, hear it resonating in our throats. We feel it in every step. Even on the inside, everything ticks slower. Every morning I can feel the years under my belt, heavier. My once perfect vision has blurred to the point where I need contact lenses. I could tell you the date by my monthly nosebleeds (the kind that my doctor won't diagnose as anything real). I can't tell if it's my bones or the stairs that creak when I walk. All of this before my thirtieth birthday.

But not Eli. He's hopping around like in my fuzzy black-and-white memories. His appearance hasn't changed. And to my dismay, neither has his style. In fact, it appears as if God's son here has been bathing in the fountain of youth on a daily basis and the opening minutes make me painfully aware of what Eli is still capable of doing. He hasn't changed in the ring the way he's changed in my mind.

But I can use this against him. He's fighting the way he used to. He's not just a story that I've read before—he's one I know by heart.

All I have to do is fight like him.

I don't hear the bell through my clouded thoughts. I watch through my fists as Eli puts his arms down and turns toward the corner.

My concentration broken, I turn towards the corner as Danny, my cutman, throws a stool on the mat and steps into the ring. I sit down heavily, my mouth gaping while water is shot down my throat and a soaking sponge is flopped upon my forehead. I watch as Danny's tattoo-covered arms rub a clear salve across my eyebrows, touching up the procedure by taking a cotton swab to the lining of my nostrils. I sit silently through the thirty-second surgery as he barks out my weaknesses and his demands.

"You're scramblin' in there like a fuckin' egg, man!" he tells me. "He's actin' all high and mighty out there in the ring, and the way you keep swingin' like an idiot just makes him better."

I lean back against the corner ropes and listen. He rubs his hands across the plane of my shaven head while I stare at him, mouth wide open.

"You're usin' your right arm too much—throw your jab in there, he won't be expectin' it. You connect with that a few times then you come back in there with that right hand. You surprise him like that, you're right back in this thing. Make him come to you, baby! Now you need this next round, and he don't want you to have it. Get back in there and take it from him!"

I trust my cutman. I do as I'm told.

* * *

MY WIFE CAME TO ME as a young nurse's assistant when I was in the hospital. I met her when she was tending to my wounds and she's been doing it ever since.

She came not a minute too soon.

After a couple of years of amateur fights, I had established myself locally as the best boxer in Rome. This didn't earn me too many friends, though. One kid that stepped into the ring with me gave me a warning before the fight: "Boy, if you win this fight, you gonna regret it." I laid him out cold two minutes into the second round, and a few weeks later, he followed me after I left the gym and stabbed me in the left side of my gut. I awoke in a hospital bed. I glanced to my right to see a young lady beside me. Her nametag said "Lydia." I stared at her. She had a tear in each eye, but smiled when she saw that I was awake.

"You've been runnin from somethin, sweetie," she said, "you nearly made this bed collapse you were rockin it so hard. I don't know what was goin on inside your head, but you...you looked like you were tryin to escape from somethin. From somebody. The doctors told me to come in here and watch you, to make sure you didn't hurt yourself."

I looked around the room, the dull scenery. "How long until I can fight again?" I asked her.

"Baby, you just did."

We were married two years later, after she gave birth to our first daughter.

Lydia was always encouraging me to turn pro, which I did soon after our wedding. I began to travel out of state to bigger arenas. My big break came when I fought Curtis Herrera, a southpaw from Mexico City, in a 5-round opening fight at Madison Square Garden. I won by majority decision. Then, when my mother died of a heart attack a couple of years after our wedding, Lydia suggested moving to a bigger city so that my career could flourish. We chose Boston. I had a name back in Rome, but in Boston I was nobody. Everybody wrote off the Herrera fight because it was near the end of his career (he had lost three fights in a row before losing to me). As a boxer, I knew that I couldn't just make a name for myself—I had to take it from somebody. I had to make my name by ruining that of a greater fighter. I was determined to take mine from Eli Bison.

And I wanted God to watch me do it.

WHEN YOU'RE INSIDE THE RING, you have to stay emotionless. There's no fear. No pain. No anger. No hatred. You're focused. Driven. If you let your heart get in the way of your mind, you're a goner for sure.

Round Two.

See, I'm the victim of a curse that forces me to wear my heart on my sleeve. I've trained all my life not just to be strong and quick but to perfect my poker face as well. I'll spend hours in front of the mirror, holding the same face. One that reveals no fear, no frustration, no emotion.

But now I'm stuck, because I'm in the ring with Eli Bison. And even if he can't see my fear, he can smell it. I can smell it myself. And, to make matters worse, he's still nothing but a blank, white canvas. With every punch I try to paint over his complexion, to stain his blank determination with streaks of red. But every brushstroke I take leads me to the same whiteness.

I'm starting to make progress, though.

Danny tells me to use my jab, so I use my jab. Eli hops forward to get up in my face, leaning towards my left in anticipation, and then I bring my left arm around and meet him there with a clean hook. Not as strong as my right arm, of course, but it catches him off guard.

The judges score us by hits and misses, but the winner is always the one that controls the momentum. Now that Bison's beginning to realize my potential, he's guarding me on all areas so that he can keep control. When he comes back at me, I'm forced to pin his arms down with my own. Whenever he starts to break free, whenever his fists come at me, I can do nothing but wrap him up against the ropes.

But he's moving just a bit slower.

I wait for him to pause for a breath, to drop his arms in the slightest, and then I pounce. Out of nowhere, I take the lead. I break out of his foxtrot and now we're three-stepping to my waltz. He's struggling to keep up with the time change and I'm light years ahead of him. I'm leading him all over the ring, spinning him along my fingers, stringing him along as I please. I finish the second movement with another quick left hook as the bell rings.

"Stevie Wonder woulda gave you that round," Danny tells me as my forehead is greeted by the soaking sponge again. "That was beautiful. He's expecting your jab now, so you gotta mix it up. When he gets outta breath, hit him in his body like you did back there. Go for the ribs. You gotta fuckin dog-fight this guy! He's slowin' down out there! You're smarter than him. He's got everything to lose, baby, and you're here to take it from him."

Danny's right. Eli has everything and more that's here for the taking. His pride, his dignity—his name.

The Lord giveth and the Lord taketh away, right?

With help from my daughters, I was able to finally meet Eli Bison in person. But not in the ring—in the church. Sort of.

Lydia wanted to raise our kids in the church and, as much as I hated that idea, the idea of constantly arguing with my wife was worse. So Maggie, my six-year-old daughter, and Jessie, her three-year-old baby sister, were sent to Sunday school as soon as they could walk. When some of Maggie's friends from church told her about a convention in Cape Cod, she came home that day and begged me to take her.

Lydia had to work that weekend. I had no interest in going until she told me who one of the featured speakers would be.

Naturally, Lydia was far from convinced when I told her that I was willing to go. "Maggie just wants to have a good time," she told me. "You wanna go there and start shit with this guy, and it's gonna ruin the experience for her!"

"I'm not tryin to find Jesus, baby," I said. "I'm tryin to find Bison. I'll save his beating for the ring."

"Just promise me that you'll take Jessie with you. I don't want to hire a baby-sitter," she called out as I left her.

I gave her my word and headed for my gym.

When I got there, I walked past all of the other hopefuls and headed straight for a speed bag. Cooper, the owner of the gym and my manager at the time, noticed my swagger and lost interest in the sparring match he'd been watching.

"What the hell's gotten into you?" he asked me as he approached, his raspy, cigarette-stained voice reminding me why I quit years ago.

"I'm goin out of town this weekend, Coop," I said as I pounded the speed bag.

"Who the hell told you that you could go outta town this weekend?"

Cooper knew I had potential, so he was protective of me. I tried to ignore him.

"I'm goin to Cape Cod with my daughters."

"What the hell is in Cape Cod?"

I gave the speed bag a knockout blow and turned towards Cooper. "Eli Bison."

Cooper let out a rough cackle, exposing his missing teeth. "Bison, huh?"

"Yeah. He's there for this Christian convention."

"What, is he gonna fight Christ?"

"He's one of the speakers. He preaches and shit. And I wanna fight him."

Cooper let out another round of cackling. "You couldn't get his autograph."

"People have heard of me, Coop. People are scared of me."

"Nobody's afraid of you! Are you kiddin me?"

With this remark, I punched the plaster wall as hard as I could to keep from hitting Cooper.

"What do you want from me?!" I yelled. I hadn't yet noticed that I'd made a dent in the wall. "You'd be *broke* without me!"

"Will you calm your ass down?" Cooper growled, unphased in his old age. He threw his hands up in frustration. "I don't know what you want with Bison anyway. He's washed up. He'll be retired in a year."

"He's not washed up, Coop. He's only thirty-three."

Cooper laughed again as he turned back towards me so that he could wave one hand across my face. "Alright, kid. You talk to Bison." He walked back towards one of the practice rings to tend to the other fighters.

I kept swinging.

When you've been hit enough times, you begin to rise above the physical.

Round Three.

It's that point in every boxer where pain no longer does bodily harm. Not at that moment, at least. Each hit becomes a tiny motivator, a reminder that the other guy is there and that he's trying to wear you down to nothing.

Eli and I are trading hits now like boys with baseball cards. Our rhythms are intertwining so that neither of us knows who's leading. Oh, the crowd loves it that way.

But before I know it, I'm backed into the corner while Eli's throwing punches. I can do nothing more than lift my arms and duck my head. He's going to win the round, which will put him ahead 2-1, if I don't do something to stop him.

In desperation, I fight dirty.

I wrap him up to keep him at bay until the ref separates us. As I come at Eli with both fists, I throw a rabbit punch to the right side of his neck. He staggers back a few steps, thrown off from the cheap shot. The ref tells me I've lost a point, but I'm okay with that. Lose a point, gain back the momentum.

I can hear his manager yelling at the ref, but Eli just brushes it off with a quick shake of his head. It's as if my maneuver hasn't affected him at all.

And now I'm wondering if anything affects him.

The sweat on my back was causing my shirt to stick by the time we reached Cape Cod. We pulled into the parking lot while Maggie marveled at the colorful banners proclaiming the events and activities that she would be taking part in. It was early in the afternoon, hours before the first day speakers were scheduled to give their sermons, so they were sitting in the various booths and tents scattered across the field. Maggie wanted to walk around with her church friends and their parents, so I told her where to meet me for supper as I saddled Jessie onto my shoulders and made my way to the Eli Bison booth.

He had a modest set-up. Two tables were joined together where he sat with his wife, his two daughters, and a couple of representatives from the conference. On one end of the tables there sat a small television playing clips from Eli's fights (the fights that he won, at least), and the rest of the table was covered with books and brochures that meant nothing to me. I picked up a green pamphlet when I approached his table: "Do Angels Exist?" I smiled as I placed the pamphlet back in its pile.

When I looked up, we were face to face.

He sat behind the table wearing a plain white hoodie and jeans. His short blond hair didn't glisten like when he was in the ring. His earlobes were filled with those little black halos, and he was laughing with one of the volunteers. I took Jessie off my shoulders and pointed her towards Bison's daughter, who was busy with a coloring book.

Eli smiled at me. I extended my hand, he shook it, and I introduced myself.

"I know who you are," he said humbly. I was thrown off slightly by the tone of his voice, a voice I had never heard because of Jay's scrambled reception. He spoke in a kind of nasally tenor—not what you expected from a boxer. His slight Southern accent gave his voice a necessary warmth—a warmth that was able to ease my initial curiosity once I picked up on it. "I've seen you fight," he continued.

"So what brings you here today?"

"My daughters," I said. "They love this Jesus shit."

Eli glanced towards our daughters, who were happily coloring a picture of Jesus with a flock of sheep. His smile faded as he leaned forward and lowered his voice.

"Brother, you don't sound like you're here for the right reasons."

Here it was. I knew that I wouldn't be able to face Eli Bison without having his Christian message shoved down my throat. I kept straight-faced this time. "No," I said. "God and I aren't the best of friends."

Eli grinned slightly as he adjusted his seat. "Well," he continued, "this is exactly why I preach God's word. For people in your situation."

I kept staring.

He looked me right in the eyes. "I think it would benefit you a lot if you came to hear me speak today."

But I didn't want to hear him speak. I was fed up with listening to him speak about speaking. So I leaned onto the front of the table resting just inches from his face. "I think it would benefit me if we stepped into the ring together."

His wife turned away from the conversation she was having with one of the volunteers. Jessie and Eli's daughter held their crayons still and looked up at me.

Eli grinned again. "So that's what this is all about?" he asked.

I nodded once as I backed away a few inches.

He stuck his hands into the front pocket of his hoodie. "You remind me of myself when I was younger. I was just like you. I didn't need God's help with anything. I thought I was invincible."

Once again, I had no response. I wasn't leaving until he agreed to fight me.

"How about this," he said. "You come to hear me speak today, I'll fight you."

I stood up. "Good."

With this response, he pushed his folding chair out from under the table, stood up, and walked around until he was right beside me. "You'll be hearing from me soon," he said as he reached out to shake my hand again. "God bless."

I shook his hand as he walked away, putting the white hood over his head. When it came time to hear his sermon, I saw the big crowd and decided to skip the lecture. I figured that he wouldn't notice if I was even in the crowd. Sure enough, his manager called Cooper in a month to discuss my schedule.

It wasn't until later that I got the feeling Eli knew I wasn't there.

ELI GETS A FEW QUICK FACE SHOTS on me and I'm dizzy.

Round Four.

Eli has managed to take the baton from me, and now he's conducting the symphony. He waves his arms back and forth, up and down—the crowd is his orchestra.

But it doesn't feel like dancing to me anymore. We're in a dog fight now. We throw punches wherever we can get them. We tie each other up every chance we get, still throwing uppercuts as the ref is forced to pull us apart.

All of a sudden, we're caught in a snowstorm. I have him leaning against the ropes and the flurry hits us both like an avalanche. Exchanging one for one. Every hit that I land, another glove greets me like an angry boss and tells me to get back to work. We are blindly hurling our fists at each other, not knowing where each punch will land. Chest. Cheek. Ribcage. A hit to the face and my vision begins to blur.

I stagger backwards a few steps as the crowd is silenced for a split second. The cheering, chanting, and applause come back in a static rush. I'm standing up for the moment, although my legs are shaking slightly. He can see them shake. I watch as Eli Bison comes off the ropes and stands straight up. While I stand temporarily immobile, hands in front of my face, he looks towards the ceiling and raises his arms to the sky.

And then it happens.

My vision comes back all at once, and his entire body seems to elevate itself, his feet lifting slightly off the mat. Veins pop out all over his forearms and neck, and he tilts his head back further as he closes his mouth and eyes. A pair of magnificent white wings reaches out from the center of his back, unfolding and broadening towards the heavens, wonderfully accompanying his arms on their journey into the sky. Fully extended, his wings take up nearly a full side of the ring. The background of the audience is lost in the maze of white feathers, but it feels as if the audience was never there to begin with, although I can hear them cheering. I want to cheer with them, but I can't even open my mouth. I can't even move.

Those big, beautiful wings. They extend majestically, shining brightly as a marvelous white backdrop for his bright red gloves. A few feathers fall to the mat as his wings reach farther upward—large, elegant feathers like an albatross. Each feather is full of intricate designs that look like they were stitched into each one by hand, like thousands of tiny little rivers. And then I look back up at him, piecing the patterns together in my mind.

Those wings.

He lowers his head and angles it towards mine. Calm. Knowing. He looks straight at me, moving his left arm to the four points of the cross before sending his right fist to connect squarely with my face.

Forehead. Ribcage. Shoulder to shoulder.

One.

When you first hit the floor, it's comforting. Security. The feeling that you can stay on this floor forever, safe. Instead of onto the rough mat, you're falling backwards into the ocean. You hear the splash of applause as you're being submerged, but once underwater you can't hear anything. Only your thoughts as they encourage you to either tread water or drown.

Two.

Middle school. A fight with a bully. I walk up to him with my fists raised until my forehead is inches from his face. He pushes me down and then walks away as I'm back on my feet again. They send me to the principal. They send him to the nurse.

Three.

Hospital bed. A hot towel across my forehead and water dripping onto my eyelids. My wife whispering comforting thoughts in an effort to put me to sleep, but I've just woken up. I'm no longer tired. She's picking up my sheets off the floor.

Four.

My grandfather in his living room, proud owner of the fifth television in all of Rome. It's nighttime and he's in his recliner watching boxing. He throws punches into the air. He doesn't know I'm watching from the doorframe, but he's worked up just the same. "Give em hell, son!"

Five.

The gym. My trainer. I've finished sparring and I'm walking back to the locker room. As I take off my boxing gloves, I glance down at my taped-up hands. There's blood on the palms. I pause, then put my gloves back on and leave.

Six.

The park. My daughters building sandcastles. When they finish, they rush past each other and jump on each other's work. They smile at each other, and begin to build again.

Seven.

A fast-food restaurant. I'm eating alone. A man comes in behind me—homeless. He asks the lady behind the counter for a cup of hot water, and she gives it to him. Then he gathers up several ketchup packets, squeezes them into the water, and eats.

Eight.

My mother's funeral. I'm in the front row with Maggie and my wife. An adult choir is singing. *And God will raise you up on eagles' wings.* Maggie refused to wear anything other than her favorite white dress. She's two years old. Filing out into the foyer, Maggie pulls on my jacket. "I just talked to Grandma," she tells me.

Nine.

My senses come back. I see Eli again. He's standing over me with his eyes closed, wings scraping the ceiling. I can no longer hear the noise of the crowd. I can't hear the referee or his countdown. But I can hear Eli. Eli. Chanting something.

I'd have to say it sounds like scripture.

And he said unto them, I beheld Satan as lightning fall from heaven. Behold, I give unto you power to tread on serpents and scorpions, and over all the power of the enemy: and nothing shall by any means hurt you. Through thee will we push down our enemies: through thy name we will tread them under that rise up against us. For I will not trust in my bow, neither shall my sword save me. But thou hast saved us from our enemies, and hast put them to shame that hated us. In God we boast all the day long, and praise thy name for ever. Selah.

Ten.

AN INTRODUCTION TO OUR AUTHORS

KIRSTEN EVE BEACHY
THE INSTITUTE OF TRANSCENDENCE
Fiction

Kirsten Beachy's fiction and creative nonfiction pieces have appeared in *Dreamseeker, eightyone, WriterAdvice,* and *The Tusculum Review.* She received her MFA from West Virginia University and is a fledgling assistant professor of English at Eastern Mennonite University. She lives with her husband, a green-eyed cat, and a flock of pensioned laying hens on the Briery Branch of the North River in Virginia's Shenandoah Valley. Her latest accomplishments include hanging drywall, butchering broiler chickens, and having every room in the house clean at the same time.

JENN BLAIR
AGREEMENT
NOTE
Poetry

Jenn Blair is a PhD candidate at the University of Georgia. She is from Yakima, Washington.

DAVID BOROFKA
THE DEATH OF NEW AURORA
Fiction

David Borofka teaches composition, literature, and creative writing at Reedley College in Reedley, California. His stories have earned such awards as the *Missouri Review's* Editors' Prize and *Carolina Quarterly's* Charles B. Wood Award for Distinguished Writing, and his collection, *Hints of His Mortality,* won the 1996 Iowa Short Fiction Award. His novel, *The Island,* was published by MacMurray & Beck, portions of which appeared in *Gettysburg Review* and *Shenandoah.* New work has recently appeared in *Image, Southern Review, Glimmer Train,* and *Manoa.*

JEFF E. BROOKS-HARRIS
THE LAST GOOD DAY
Creative Nonfiction

Jeff lives on the island of Oahu and works as a psychologist at the University of Hawaii at Manoa. He and his daughter Genevieve enjoy biking and traveling together. Jeff recently published a textbook entitled *Integrative Multitheoretical Psychotherapy.* This is his first published piece of creative nonfiction.

JEREMY BURGESS
ELI BISON BECOMES AN ANGEL
Fiction

Jeremy is still an undergraduate student, but will be a graduate student later this year. He is currently a freelance journalist for *The Birmingham News* and *Birmingham Weekly.* Social talents include bad pick-up lines, clever remarks, and the ability to grow full facial hair at a young age. He has dreams of becoming a firefighter.

AUTHOR BIOS

MARYANN CORBETT
MID EVIL
SUBVERSIVE
READING THE FIRE CODE
Poetry

Maryann Corbett's poetry has appeared or is forthcoming in *Measure, The Lyric, Alabama Literary Review, First Things, Rock and Sling*, and other journals in print and online. Her chapbook *Gardening in a Time of War* was published in 2007 by Pudding House. She lives in St. Paul, Minnesota, and works as a legal writing adviser, editor, and indexer for the Minnesota Legislature.

BARRY L. DUNLAP
EROSION
Poetry

Barry Dunlap loves ice cream, a good book, and sports (in no particular order). He has worked as a teacher and coach, a campus minister, a church planter, and (currently) in educational support services. His work has been published in *Spillway Review, Powhatan Review, Pebble Lake Review, Christianity and Literature, The Adirondack Review*, as well as other journals. Barry earned his master's in English at Southeastern Louisiana University, where he studied under Tim Gautreaux. Barry lives in Walker, Louisiana, with his wife, four children, and their Chocolate Lab Coco.

JUSTIN WHITMEL EARLEY
WHISPER NEW ORLEANS
SOMETIMES IN SHANGHAI
Poetry

Whitmel lives with his wife Lauren in Charlottesville, Virginia. He thinks Virginia a fine state and Charlottesville a charming city. He enjoys late nights and early mornings—being that they prove to be the productive times for most things. Personally, Whitmel considers a fine beverage and a blank page, or a fine beverage and a good friend, as perhaps some of the best combinations one can happen upon.

CHRIS FLOWERS
MAN NAILED TO CROSS IN PHILIPPINES
Poetry

Chris Flowers currently teaches English at the University of North Carolina at Charlotte and Central Piedmont Community College in Charlotte, North Carolina. He enjoys spending Saturday afternoons at the movies with his wife Erica and hopes to complete his first novel sometime in the next millenium. His poetry has recently appeared in *Convergence*.

HANNAH E. FRIES
SUMMER BURIAL
Poetry

Hannah grew up in New Hampshire and feels most at home when she is hiking the White Mountains, rain or shine. She graduated from Dartmouth College with a BA in English and a minor in music and is now on the editorial staff of *Orion Magazine* in western Massachusetts. Her poems have been published in the *Berkshire Review* and other journals. She loves to sing (both in and out of the shower), cross-country ski, and climb trees, and has been known to dust off her French horn when the occasion calls for it.

AUTHOR BIOS

JOHN KEATS
ARBOR
Fiction

John Keats lives in Massachusetts. He received an MA in English from Boston College. His writing has appeared in *Roux* and *Under the Sun*.

ROSS KENNERLY
LITTLE PROOFS
Creative Nonfiction

Ross Kennerly is a contributing writer for *The Real Chicago Magazine*. His creative nonfiction has also appeared in *The OffKILTer Review*. He received his BA in French from Alma College, a liberal arts school in Alma, Michigan, where he was first encouraged by a friend to seriously pursue writing. He currently lives and works in Chicago, though he will always be rooted in Michigan's Upper Peninsula. Yes, he is a Yooper.

SALLY ROSEN KINDRED
CARDINAL'S EVE
Poetry

Sally Rosen Kindred's manuscript, *Garnet Lanterns*, won the 2005 Anabiosis Press Chapbook Competition, and she received a 2007 Individual Artist Award from the Maryland State Arts Council. Her poems have appeared or are forthcoming in *Blackbird*, *Poetry Northwest*, *The Florida Review*, *Ruminate*, and *Passages North*. She lives in Columbia, Maryland, with her husband and sons.

KATHERINE NICOLE LEE
JOHN CHAPTER TWELVE
Poetry

Katherine's craziest jobs have included painting monograms on saddles, acting as interim church janitor, and researching the genetic components of fruit fly gonads at Johns Hopkins University. Having mastered these crucial life skills, she is now seeking a theological education at Fuller Theological Seminary in Pasadena, California, where she lives with her husband, Rob.

FREDERICK LORD
SLUMMING WITH LAZARUS
COMMUTING THROUGH THE RAPTURE
Poetry

Frederick (Rick) is the Assistant Dean of Liberal Arts at Southern New Hampshire University, where he also teaches English and serves as poetry editor for *Amoskeag*, SNHU's literary magazine. A finalist in 2007's Dogwood Poetry Prize and honorable mention in the Juked Poetry Prize, Lord has recently appeared in *Blueline*, *Switched-on Gutenberg*, *kaleidowhirl*, *Main Channel Voices*, *caesura*, *Bent Pin Quarterly*, and *Bayou*. He and his wife Heather, a painter, live in Bow, New Hampshire.

LINDA MACKILLOP
DOOMS OF LOVE
Editor's Choice for Creative Nonfiction

Linda MacKillop lives in the charming town of Wheaton, Illinois, with her husband Bill. On any given semi-warm evening, they can be found wandering the streets and parks of the downtown area, sipping coffee, or attending outdoor concerts. Together they have four sons. Linda's work has been published in *The MacGuffin*, *iParent*, and *The Philosophical Mother*. Recently her work also appeared in two publications by Meredith Books: *Along the Way* and *Along the Way for Teens*. At the moment the ink is drying on her first novel, *Try Again Farm*.

HELEN W. MALLON
BIOLOGY
Editor's Choice for Fiction

Helen W. Mallon grew up in a Philadelphia Quaker family. She received her MFA from Vermont College of Fine Arts in 2005. Her poetry chapbook, from Finishing Line Press, is titled *Bone China*. Her poems, essays, and fiction have appeared in various publications, including the anthology *Commonwealth: Contemporary Poets on Pennsylvania*. Her story, "Astral Projection" is included in the 2007 *Best of Philadelphia Stories* anthology. The working title of her novel is *Quaker Playboy Leaves Legacy of Confusion*.

KATIE MANNING
INTIMACY
Poetry

Katie Manning lives in Kansas City, where she works as a poet and as a youth information specialist for the Johnson County Library. She recently received the Crystal Field Scholarship for Poetry and an honorable mention prize in the Dorothy Sargent Rosenberg Poetry Competition. Her poems and book reviews have been published or are forthcoming in *New Letters*, *Driftwood*, *Number One*, and *Business Communication Quarterly*.

MICHAEL MARTIN
IT ALL COMES DOWN TO LAUNDRY
Poetry

Michael Martin lives on a small farm with his wife and seven children. His poetry and essays have appeared in many different magazines and journals, including *Journal of Pre-Raphaelite Studies*, *Eclipse*, and *Journal of Interdisciplinary Studies*, not to mention *Relief*. He teaches English at Marygrove College in Detroit, Michigan.

MAUREEN DOYLE MCQUERRY
CONVERSATION
BEYOND
Poetry

Maureen is a poet and novelist, teacher, and artist in the schools. She is the author of *Wolfproof* (Idylls 2006), first in a Young Adult fantasy trilogy. The sequel, *The Travelers' Market*, will be out in July 2008. Recent poems can be found in *The Southern Review*, *Journal of Mythic Arts*, *Goblin Fruit*, and the *Georgetown Review*.

JOYCE MAGNIN MOCCERO
OCTOBER'S ORCHID
Fiction

Joyce is writer, reader, mom, grandmom. She enjoys books, rpg video games, cross stitch, Humphrey Bogart movies, and loves to teach others about writing and reading when she can.

AUTHOR BIOS

RICK MULLIN
CATHOLIC WORKER
Poetry

Rick Mullin is a journalist and painter whose poetry has appeared in various print and online journals, including *The New Formalist*, *Contemporary Sonnet*, and the *Shit Creek Review*, which nominated his poem, *Shrine to Satan* for a Pushcart Prize. His work has been accepted for upcoming issues of *Measure*, *Blue Unicorn*, and *Light Quarterly*, and his first chapbook, *Aquinas Flinched*, is due to be published this spring by Modern Metrics, New York.

HANNAH FAITH NOTESS
PSALM 19
A WRECK
THE DISASTER TOURIST
SINGLE-POINT PERSPECTIVE
Poetry

Hannah Faith Notess is working on her MFA in Creative Writing at Indiana University. She is also editing a collection of personal essays about growing up female and evangelical. Her poems have recently appeared in *Slate*, *Crab Orchard Review*, and *Rattle* and are forthcoming in *Image* and *5AM*.

BRIAN G. PHIPPS
MISCARRIAGES
WINTER SOLSTICE
Poetry

Brian G. Phipps holds a BA in English with an emphasis in creative writing from Western Michigan University, where he also studied music composition, and he has published poetry and other writing in *Re:generation Quarterly* and poetry in *Mars Hill Review*, *Rock and Sling*, and *The Handmaiden*. He works as an editor for a book publishing company in Grand Rapids, Michigan, where he lives with his wife and five kids. In addition to writing poetry, his interests include playing ice hockey and serving as a chanter in his Greek Orthodox parish.

J. STEPHEN RHODES
LOOK UP
Creative Nonfiction

Before taking up writing full-time, J. Stephen Rhodes served as the academic dean of Memphis Theological Seminary and as a Presbyterian pastor. His poetry has appeared in *Shenandoah*, *Tar River Poetry*, *The William and Mary Review*, and *The International Poetry Review*, among others. His essays have appeared in *Gettysburg Review*, *Brevity*, *Snowy Egret*, and *The Christian Century*. He is currently working on a book dealing with the relationship between service and self-care and is seeking publication of his first book of poetry. He lives with his wife, Ann, on a farm in south central Kentucky.

MEG SEFTON
DEBORAH
Fiction

Meg Sefton is a low residency MFA student at Seattle Pacific University. She lives in Orlando, Florida, with her husband, son, and dog. When not writing, reading, or studying, she's tending the house poorly, driving her kid around in her messy car, and baking and/or burning prepared meals. Occasionally, she breaks out for a trip across the ocean. Last year she and her clan went to London. She hopes to go to New Zealand soon. Her current favorite color is blue and she has been recently enjoying fabulist stories and fairy tales. She likes coffee in any form or concentration. The same goes for chocolate.

ALLISON SMYTHE
THE SIGNIFICANCE OF PLACE
Creative Nonfiction

Allison Smythe runs a graphic design firm, Ars Graphica, in Rocheport, Missouri, where she lives and works with husband Wayne Leal, a sculptor, and their two daughters. Her work has or will appear in *The Weight of Addition*, an anthology of Texas Poetry, *Packingtown Review*, *Cranky*, *Verse Daily*, *versal V*, *The Southern Review*, *MO Writing from the River*, *The Gettysburg Review*, *Relief*, the 2007 *Texas Poetry Calendar*, *themattewshouseproject.com*, *RainTown Review*, *TimeSlice*, *Anderbo.com*, *Gulf Coast* and other journals, anthologies, record albums, and the *Voice*. Please stop by allisonsmythe.com and say hello.

MEREDITH STEWART
FORGETTING GRACE
Poetry

Meredith Stewart received her MFA from the University of Nevada, Las Vegas in 2007. She is currently exploring intentional community as a way of life in Portland, Oregon.

MARIO SUSKO
THERE AND HERE
THE OTHER SIDE
WHAT I WANT TO SAY
THE COLOR OF BLOOD
Editor's Choice for Poetry

Mario Susko, a witness and survivor of the war in Bosnia, came, in a sense, back to the U.S. at the end of 1993. He received his MA and PhD from SUNY Stony Brook in the 1970s and has taught at the University of Sarajevo and Nassau Community College, where he is currently an Associate Professor in the English Department. He is the recipient of several awards, including the 1997 and 2006 Nassau Review Poetry Award, the 1998 Premio Internazionale di Poesia e Letteratura "Nuove Lettere" (Naples, Italy), and the 2000 Tin Ujevic Award for "Versus Exsul" for the best book of poems published in Croatia in 1999. Susko is the author of 25 books of poems. His recent work includes his selected poems 1982-2002 *Reading Life and Death* (Zagreb: Meandar, 2003) and the anthology of modern Jewish-American short stories *A Declaration of Being* (Zagreb: Meandar, 2006) which he co-edited with Myron Schwartzman and translated into Croatian.

CHRISTIAN WRITING

Continue your literary journey in 2008 with Fiction, Creative Nonfiction, and Poetry from the authors of *Relief: A Quarterly Christian Expression*. Decidedly not safe for the whole family, *Relief* is Christian writing without boundaries. Come visit us at **http://www.reliefjournal.com!**

READ RUMINATE

Call for Submissions

Summer 2008 Issue 08: Submit by March 15th, 2008
Fall 2008 Issue 09: Submit by June15th, 2008

Enter Contests

Janet B. McCabe Poetry Prize
Submission deadline: May 15th, 2008. Entry fee: $15
$300 will be awarded to the winner and $150 to the runner-up. You may submit up to three poems, attached in your email as a MS Word document; submissions should also include a bio. The winner will be featured in the 2008 Fall issue of RUMINATE.

For more information go to www.ruminatemagazine.com

How do you exact revenge on a crotchety old neighbor without risking either jail time or a severe dent in your self esteem?

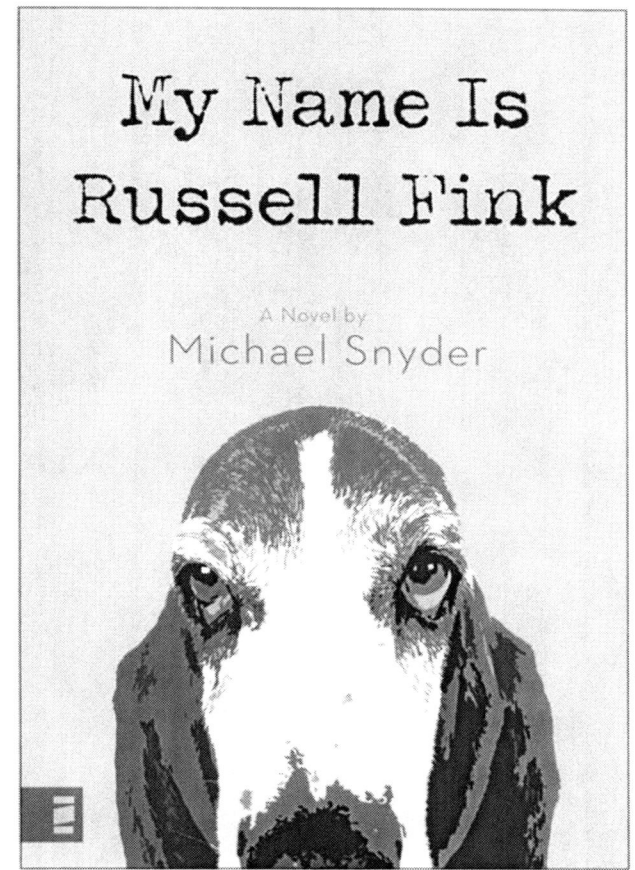

"Snyder's writing is inventive and fun"
--Publishers Weekly

"Biting humor and an offbeat, dysfunctional protagonist shape this story of reconciliation"
--Library Journal

It comes out in March. Go buy it. Seriously, you'll like it. It's written by Michael Snyder, *Relief's* Editor's Choice winner from our very first issue. We like Mike. So will you.

Available from fine book sellers everywhere March 2008.

COACH'S MIDNIGHT DINER

A HARDBOILED GENRE ANTHOLOGY OF HORROR, MYSTERY, ADVENTURE, PARANORMAL, AND WEIRD FICTION WITH A CHRISTIAN SLANT

THE JESUS VS. CTHULHU EDITION IS NOW ON SALE AT AMAZON.COM

SUBMISSIONS FOR THE SECOND EDITION ARE NOW OPEN ON THE RELIEF WRITERS NETWORK

PANSY DIDACTIC WORK SUMMARILY DISMISSED

TOUGH GUY AND TOUGH GIRL STORIES WELCOMED

THREE EDITOR'S CHOICE PRIZES OF A HUNDRED BUCKS EACH WILL BE AWARDED

EVERYBODY ELSE GETS A CONTRIBUTOR'S COPY, YOUR NAME IN LIGHTS, AND A SHOT AT BEING A DINER EDITOR

GIVE ME YOUR BEST SHOT

VISIT THE NEW WEB SITE AT
WWW.THEMIDNIGHTDINER.COM

> The following bonus story is a preview of the upcoming second edition of *Coach's Midnight Diner*, a genre anthology of horror, mystery, crime, and paranormal fiction. I sneak one in at the end of every issue of *Relief*. "Hinky Jenks" is a hard-boiled crime story that sshows us that miracles and mercy show up in the strangest places. Enjoy!
> —Coach Culbertson, Proprietor

HINKY JENKS

CHRIS MIKESELL

Hinky Jenks, Madelyn Argent and me, we could've changed the world. Now I'm here alone with the envelope from Maddy's father, and the priest with a *click-clack* heel on one of his shoes is walking the cellblock toward me.

Damn you, Jenks.

My death warrant expires in nine hours. No chance of a reprieve.

But I'm getting ahead of myself.

Argent said he won Hiram Jenkins in a poker game against Primo DeAnza, head of the upstart gang cross-town. Said he won the hand legit and Primo was worming out of his marker. My crew, we didn't care. When it came to laying into those flatheads, reasons weren't needed—like Queensberry Rules at a knife fight, they just get in the way and turn the fun into a piece of work.

So we grabbed one of Primo's boys outside a little mom-n-pop by the train station and beat him 'til he told us this guy Jenkins was a driver for one of DeAnza's heavy guns, Diego Marquez. Then we beat him some more for being a snitch.

One night while Marquez was paying a call on a skirt, we went in and removed Jenkins from behind the wheel of his Sixty Special. Left a couple sticks of TNT wired to the Caddy's ignition just to square things. When DeAnza realized we not only collected on the debt, but extracted interest too, Santa Rosa got introduced to mob warfare.

To look at the town, you'd never expect it would have its criminal element professionally run. *Hell, what criminal element?* you'd think. Then again, you'd never expect our sleepy little place an hour north of San Francisco to grab Hollywood's interest, either—but it did. The mob war and the movie biz and Jenks and Maddy and me. You wouldn't believe any of it if it wasn't true.

Hiram Jenkins—Hinky Jenks, we started calling him—came to us a driver. A good driver, maybe even as good as Benny Pullman down state. Up until we lifted him from behind the wheel of Marquez's Caddy he'd never slipped up. Never let a man get pinched. Always managed to get his boys away before the heat showed up. Of course his goof getting boosted and then DeAnza's vendetta against us meant he wasn't safe out on the street. Which meant he spent a lot of time at the Wexler Granary, playing cards in the back room and learning what ropes there were to learn.

Which meant real quick we knew half of why DeAnza kept him out in a car: the boy was just wrong.

Most troubling was his habit of eating everything with gelatin. Not as a side dish or salad, but everything he ate had to be covered in the stuff. Peas and carrots, that we didn't mind too much. Kinda looked like the stuff you might serve a kid with cut up pears inside. Vienna sausages, though—or worse, sardines. Most of us went down the road to Agostino's Bakery & Meats whenever Hinky Jenks brought out his lunch pail.

The other troubling thing was the way Jenks watched you. Always had his eyes on the door when you'd come in. Always had his hand out to take something from you, sometimes even before you'd half a mind to hand it to him. Hell, even if you were coming up from behind him he'd see you somehow and step aside.

Then one day—the day Jenks rushed us all out of the back room right before a grenade flew through a window—somebody, Fingers maybe, or his brother Shank, figured out the real reason DeAnza kept Jenks behind the wheel. Kid was clairvoyant or somnambulant or some other word that ain't even English—whatever, he could see the future. Near as we could time it, about ten seconds before of the rest of us caught up. So anytime the cops swooped in when Jenks had been driving for DeAnza, he gave the word ten seconds early and whoever could piled into his Caddy, and whoever couldn't faded out the back. When the police finally came they wouldn't find nothing but a couple stripes of rubber smoking by the curb.

Ten seconds doesn't seem like much, I know, but take your thumb and put it in a vise grip. Spin the crank a quarter turn past conversational, and you'll discover just how long ten *Allegheny*'s can be.

Jenks said DeAnza never figured it out for sure, and stupid flathead he is that makes sense. Just trusted the kid's intuition, which built into reputation, which while it never advanced him past wheelman, meant a comfortable life for a gringo in DeAnza's outfit. Said he almost drove off when we came to collect, but figured being among his own he might do better for himself. Plus, Marquez was a prick.

So we discovered this and were thinking how we could use it to our advantage—a trip to one of the Long Beach casino ships, for instance—when Jenks looked up at the door and the sappiest smile melted across his face. Eight seconds later Madelyn walked in. The boss's daughter. My girl. And Jenks was grinning at her like a kid at the bijou before the Hays Commission set up shop. Would've pasted him one right there, but by the time I turned back from gawping at the girl myself, he was out of his chair and hiding behind Pinky Magrew, big hulk of a guy.

I forgave him for not being able to help himself. Easier than walking all the way around Magrew.

Madelyn came over and whispered her dad wanted me up at their house on Park Street. I said so long to the boys who didn't hear me over the sound of them making plans to score big with Jenks's secret talent.

Salvatore Argent had always been like a father to me. In a town of izzes and ain'ts, my neighborhood was one of those with bad grammar. Argent changed things around for me, though. Like a father. Like a father-in-law, we'd hoped at one time, too. That was before he announced "the plan" and everything started going to hell, though not even Hinky Jenks could've foreseen the disaster then.

Argent's idea was to take care of DeAnza for good: frame the bastard and run him out of town, maybe even get him lynched. The West Coast premiere of Alfred Hitchcock's *Shadow of a Doubt* was a couple weeks away and would do fine. The movie was filmed locally, about the biggest thing to ever happen in quiet Santa Rosa—second only, maybe, to what we had planned. When I told Argent about Hinky Jenks and his seeing the future business, he re-evaluated the plan, added a couple touches, made it foolproof.

And so far as we could see, it was: Jenks lifts one of DeAnza's cars and takes me to the premiere before the stars arrive; then we get out—skin darkened and hair flat—and rob the looky-loos; finally, Madelyn plays her part and DeAnza gets scandalized in the process. No way the cops can turn a blind eye to that. And Santa Rosa returns to the well-managed town it used to be, with yours truly running DeAnza's operation.

While we waited for the big night, Jenks went to work with Fingers Patelli cracking safes. First night they went out Fingers showed him how to listen with a stethoscope to the tumblers falling into place. After the next job, Fingers—

pale as a celery stick in gelatin—told the story that Jenks had no sooner fitted the earpieces and the safe was open. Hearing the tumblers click ten seconds before it actually happened, Jenks had spun the dial left, around once to the right, back to the left, and *zip-zing-zoom!* five grand and a pile of Santa Rosa-Sonoma Rail stock certificates.

The Tuesday before the movie premiere Jenks accompanied Argent to his usual poker game. Stood behind the boss with me and Magrew, tapping the back legs of Argent's chair once for bluff, twice for get out while you're ahead. Magrew spent the night shoveling pistachio after pistachio into his yap, dropping the red shells on the floor. Me, I just glared across the table as if I didn't know better. DeAnza was none too happy to see his former driver, but kept his mouth shut. He wound up losing five or six hundred, though he stopped short of sinking any more of his boys in the pot. The boss walked away even, let the mayor and chief of police go home winners. "Next time," he said, clapping the mayor's shoulder as they got up from the table. DeAnza left thinking there would be a next time. Hell, we thought there'd be a next time, too.

The action that Saturday went down like clockwork. Magrew drove Jenks and me across the railroad tracks west of town. DeAnza territory. If he'd been more reasonable he'd have been welcome to it. Bars and the odd cathouse and cardroom for the migrant fruit pickers from Petaluma to Sebastopol. Business Argent didn't need, but of necessity expected a cut from. DeAnza, he had expectations of his own. Like he's equal, a rival maybe. You don't have to be no mindreader to know that push is gonna come to shove, and shove is gonna come to a shallow grave sooner or later.

Jenks knew of a fence behind a certain garage that slides open on oiled skids. Said DeAnza's boys used it when the cops were on their tails. Drive down the alley, honk as you speed past, and someone slides the fence out of the way after the cops go by. Around the block once and through the alley again, cutting your lights before you reach the gap, which disappears once you're through. Jenks figured it worked for getting a car in, it'll work for getting one out. He wasn't wrong. Axle grease on our faces, hair styled so we looked like goons out of Dick Tracy, and no one inside the garage came out to ask who we were or why we were taking the Lincoln-Zephyr.

We reached the place, the California Theatre, right on time. The chief of police gave up the schedule for the night's events during the poker game. When exactly Hitchcock and Teresa Wright and Joseph Cotten and the mayor were set to leave the train station—recreating some scene from the movie for a *Life* magazine photographer—and then driving with police escort over to the theater. With the chief and his men across town, waiting for their little parade, it was a sure thing there'd be no cops at our end. Again, things ticked along perfectly.

"Nobody panic!" I shouted, stepping out from the rear of the Lincoln. "Nobody fights and nobody gets hurt," Jenks got out from behind the wheel and made a show of his Thompson M3.

There were a hundred, maybe a hundred-fifty, fretful peacocks in their Sunday best and sparkliest, but nobody squawked. Jenks handed me the grease gun and began collecting plumage. Madelyn stood a third of the way toward the gilt-edged double doors. I don't know how good Teresa Wright looked in the picture, but she had nothing on Maddy. Low-cut black dress with ruby accents, fur coat, high heels, blah, blah, blah. Could've been in the movie, for sure, if her mother hadn't disapproved of motion pictures not being dignified. I dragged my eyes away and made another heavily accented threat.

Jenks was doing fine. Nobody talked back and the bag filled up. He had gone up one side of the crowd and was coming back the other when he reached Madelyn and she dropped her earrings and ruby choker in the bag. Behind us a car rumbled by, dragging its tailpipe. Magrew's signal that the police escort had started. Two minutes.

"Okay, everybody, we're done here. Nobody be a hero, okay?"

Jenks passed by me, toward the car. I glanced at Madelyn.

The Lincoln driving off was her cue. She stepped out of the crowd, stood in the middle of the mosaic entryway. "You cowardly bastards, how dare you—"

I brought down the muzzle of the submachine gun. Surprisingly easy. Pulled the trigger. And all the gears fell out of our little clock.

Somebody ran up from the street, jumped in front of Madelyn. Hinky Jenks. The bullets meant for her shredded his coat black and red. Jenks staggered, spun, fired a shot from his waistband revolver that clipped my leg. Then he fell backward into Madelyn's arms. She collapsed beneath him and cradled his shoulders.

I swept the nose of my gun across the crowd to keep them back. They disappeared into a gray, cotton-muffled world as I turned back to Jenks. "What the hell, Hinky?"

His eyes opened, looked at me and then up at Madelyn. The two of them—Jenks stretched across Maddy's kneeling lap, his head lolling behind the crook of her elbow—looked like a china thingummy my Aunt Olivia kept on a shelf above her fireplace.

Maddy opened her mouth, but Jenks spoke first. "Can—?" Blood bubbled over his lips from the coughed question.

Madelyn swallowed, whispered the words Jenks already knew. "The doctors say the cancer, there's no cure."

"It was this or a slow, painful . . . miserable . . ." My words dropped off as he nodded. "I'm sorry, Hinky." Jenks nodded again and smiled before his eyes rolled up white.

Madelyn and I remained frozen as Chief McHenry's far-off demand broke through the silence. Statues. Our fates sealed as certainly as Hinky Jenks's.

From that point on time sped up. While I got dragged off to the back of a police car and Jenks to a useless ambulance, the bag from our car was retrieved. After the jewelry, wallets, and watches were returned to their owners, the movie premiere—take two—went ahead as planned.

I was on my way to the gas chamber at San Quentin before the trial even started. No way the district attorney was going to let the case slip through his well-manicured fingers. Even if Argent had been inclined to overlook my failure—Primo DeAnza became even more powerful in the wake of our fiasco—the situation was beyond his control.

✦

THE PRIEST STOPS HIS CLICK-CLACKING OUTSIDE MY CELL. A guard leaves a wooden chair and retreats to his post at the end of the hall.

I sit on my bunk, arms draped over my legs, eyes fixed on the floor. From the knees down, the priest steps into my field of vision. He sits in the chair, puts a boxy black case on the floor. After crossing his legs, the priest picks at something on his right heel and flicks it through the bars.

A woman's fingernail, painted red.

I blink.

A pistachio shell.

I look at the priest's hand still resting on his shoe. The fingertips are stained pink.

"How's life treating you, Johnny?" The voice goes with the fingers. Pinky Magrew.

I look up at him. His face is faintly plum colored from the tightness of the shirt collar. There had been no anger in his voice.

"Not who I was expecting, Pinky."

"Weren't gonna squeal on your family, were ya?"

Was I? Had I been? When the letter from Argent came that morning, the morning of my execution day, the letter with Maddy's obituary and a photograph of her wasted body in a hospital gown, thin and fragile as a scattering of winter sticks, I had been—what? Angry. Afraid. Alone. I'd wanted revenge, absolution. Just someone to talk to.

"Tell me about it," Pinky says. "Your old father confessor."

I look into his eyes. Hard. Cold. Nothing like the pain and sadness of Madelyn's in the photograph. In Jenks's, lying in Maddy's arms.

I'm sorry, Hinky. He had nodded before I'd had the words out.

"I ain't got nothin' to say to nobody."

"Ahh, I'm just hassling you, Johnny. Let's do this communion thing so I can get out of here." He tugs at his collar, so whether he means out of prison or out of the disguise, I'm not sure.

Magrew opens his left hand and starts reading the words he's written there. *Agnus Dei, qui tolis peccata mundi, miserere nobis.*

He stops and unlatches the box at his feet. Something gray and wet falls from beneath the lid. After uncrossing his legs, he smears it into the concrete floor with his right toe. The lid peels away slowly from the sticky, dark maroon-stained interior.

Magrew continues reading from his cribbed notes. *Ecce Agnus Dei, ecce qui tollit peccata mundi...*

He removes a silver plate with several white wafers on it and a small red bottle. When the stopper is removed I catch a whiff of almonds. Amaretto . . . or did the wafers come from Agostino's Bakery?

"*Domine, nom sum dignus et intres sub tectum meum,*" I respond from childhood memory. "*Sed tantum dic verbo, et anabitur anima mea.*"

I receive a wafer on my tongue. Bitter. Probably not from Agostino's.

When I take the cup, it's bitter too.

The ritual that used to offer comfort, offers only sadness now. A farewell communion. Family, together—not anymore.

Magrew finishes. Assures me that a real priest will be around to do last rites later that night. That it's been good to see me one last time. That the boss don't hold no grudges any more. He makes the sign of the cross and drags the chair away.

I lay back on my bunk, thinking of Madelyn. The angel, not the blasphemy in the photograph. Did she find redemption in the end?

A stiletto of pain twists in my gut. I bend over the edge of the bed, panting, and then stumble to the steel toilet. The scent of almonds comes mixed with the stench of bile.

I fall on my knees, shuddering, as the knife turns again. Hail Maddy—Mary. Oh, hail . . . *oh, hell*. The second mouthful of vomit burns more than the first.

No more grudges, Magrew? Maybe being delivered to hell by the damned will count in my favor when the scales are balanced. The sound of my laughter comes weakly from somewhere and the cold cement floor caresses my cheek.

Me and Mary and Jesus, we were gonna change the world.

My head doesn't bother to lift itself the next time my throat heaves. My eyes sting, but they're focused in the past.

Jenks, he nodded that second time, smiled just before—less than ten seconds before . . . Is there hope?

My hands roam around my body, trying to stop the pain. My throat. My belly. They rake across my heart.

Is there anything else?

I lie on the floor gasping for air. Then I just lie there.

Madelyn smiles down on me before the world goes gray and quiet. And then silent. And finally black.

ABOUT CHRIS MIKESELL

Imagine if you will a writer whose work is so powerful that his stories have been credited with fixing broken marriages, reuniting geographically- and emotionally-distant parents and children, and in one case, causing guards and inmates at a small minimum-security facility in Boise, Idaho, to spontaneously burst into song.

Chris Mikesell is not that writer.

Chris Mikesell writes for guys, but not in the sense that some people work for food. His work has appeared in The Wittenburg Door, Ray Gun Revival, Infuze, and Dragons, Knights & Angels. A native Californian, he recently relocated from Oregon to Texas.

Printed in the United States
107096LV00004B/2/P